THE BLUE AND THE GREY

THE BLUE AND THE GREY

A Grand & Batchelor Victorian mystery

M.J. Trow

CRÈME de la CRIME

This first world edition published 2014
in Great Britain and 2015 in the USA by
Crème de la Crime, an imprint of
SEVERN HOUSE PUBLISHERS LTD of
19 Cedar Road, Sutton, Surrey, England, SM2 5DA.
Trade paperback edition first published
in Great Britain and the USA 2015 by
SEVERN HOUSE PUBLISHERS LTD.

British Library Cataloguing in Publication Data

Trow, M. J. author.
   The Blue and the Grey.
   1. Americans–England–London–Fiction. 2. Murder–
   Investigation–Fiction. 3. Undercover operations–
   Fiction. 4. Lincoln, Abraham, 1809-1865–Assassination–
   Fiction. 5. London (England)–History–1800-1950–
   Fiction. 6. Great Britain–History–Victoria, 1837-1901–
   Fiction. 7. Detective and mystery stories.
   I. Title
   823.9'2-dc23

ISBN-13: 978-1-78029-070-6 (cased)
ISBN-13: 978-1-78029-552-7 (trade paper)
ISBN-13: 978-1-78010-622-9 (e-book)

All Severn House titles are printed on acid-free paper.

Severn House Publishers support the Forest Stewardship Council™ [FSC™],
the leading international forest certification organisation. All our titles that
are printed on FSC certified paper carry the FSC logo.

MIX
Paper from
responsible sources
FSC
www.fsc.org   FSC® C013056

Typeset by Palimpsest Book Production Ltd.,
Falkirk, Stirlingshire, Scotland.
Printed and bound in Great Britain by
TJ International, Padstow, Cornwall.

ONE

'I don't believe it!' Arlette Ross McKintyre's eyes flashed fire as she looked up at the Presidential box. A handsome couple stood there, waving and smiling at the audience in the stalls as if they were the President and First Lady themselves. 'How in the name of God did she wangle her way up there?'

Captain Matthew Grand smiled at her. 'Henry Rathbone's just been made Assistant Adjutant General of Volunteers,' he said. 'I must say he looks very pleased with himself.'

And he did. Major Henry Riggs Rathbone usually had the look of a startled rabbit, but tonight, in his full-dress uniform with sash and epaulettes, his auburn hair carefully Macassared and his side whiskers flowing in the half light, he looked like a cat that had got the cream. Arlette thought that too, but she was also thinking that Clara Harris, the major's fiancée, who was also his stepsister, was looking out into the middle distance as she always did when she knew a crowd was gazing at her. A faint smile played on Clara's lips, and she instinctively ducked her head just a touch so as to present her best side – not, in Arlette's opinion, that she had one. Newspapermen were scribbling on notepads all over the auditorium, and Arlette just knew that Clara's name would be all over the Washington papers the next day. Had it not been so unladylike, she would willingly have spat.

Grand did not quite catch what his fiancée said next. It sounded like 'bitch' but that could not be right. Arlette Ross McKintyre was part of the aristocracy of Old Boston, where the Lowells and the Cabots spoke neither to each other, nor to God. Matthew Grand did not share his fiancée's petty hatreds. He had ridden under 'Fighting Joe' Hooker at Brandy Station, galloped with Custer at Gettysburg. Hell, he was just glad to be alive. The war, at last, was over. And men could start to count the cost. And he also knew the real reason why Rathbone and his lady were in the Presidential box. The papers had said that General and Mrs Grant would be at Ford's Theatre tonight, but any officer in the Union Army knew that wasn't going to happen. There had been a nasty moment at City Point a few days earlier when the General's wife had sat down on a coil of rope on a warship in the harbour. Mrs Lincoln had snapped at her, 'How dare you sit in the presence of the wife of the President of the United States?' Mary Todd Lincoln seemed to have forgotten that without Ulysses Grant, her husband might have no United States at all. No, the Grants would not be sharing a theatre box with the Lincolns, not tonight, not any night.

Arlette decided to calm down, even though she was feeling less than generous to her fellow woman this evening. She knew for a fact that even though she was sitting in the stalls, in an even fight she would always be more beautiful, better dressed and better company than Clara Harris, whose complexion was muddy, whose eyes were poppy, whose lips were cruel and unkind and whose dress already looked as though she had slept in it. Arlette loved Matthew dearly, but sadly he was still only a captain. Rathbone was a major, hobnobbing with the highest in the land; and Clara, for all her ghastliness, was the daughter of a senator. The handsome, dashing young soldier sitting beside Arlette tonight, wearing his epaulettes, sash and the red cravat of the Third Cavalry Division of the Army of the Potomac, was a graduate of West Point, second in the May 'Class of 1861'. That idiot Autie Custer had finished bottom of his class, looked like a stupid chipmunk and was a major-general. Where was the sense or the fairness in that?

It was getting late. The audience was getting fidgety, fans and papers wafting the stifling air of the packed theatre. If the President's guests were in place already, where was the President? There wasn't an empty seat in the house. Laura Keene knew why. She was the first woman in the history of the theatre to manage plays and companies. From New York to Baltimore to San Francisco, the crowds adored her, fascinated by her English accent. And here she was, in her gorgeous crinoline, about to go on as Florence Trenchard. Edward Sothern knew why as well. He stood in the wings, tweaking out his enormous side-whiskers and adjusting his monocle. He hadn't wanted to play Lord Dundreary at first and had whinged to Joe Jefferson about it; the role was too small, he had said, for an actor of his monumental talent. Jefferson had looked the arrogant buffoon in the face and told him flatly, 'There are no small roles, Eddie; only small actors.' Well, Sothern had done something about that. He had taken the role in *Our American Cousin* and, with the maximum of business and ad-libs, had practically become the star. And here they all were, the cream of the East Coast drama, and they were having to wait for the President. Did the man have no sense of occasion at all?

Harry Hawk had had enough too. He was playing Asa Trenchard tonight, and his collar – actually Joe Jefferson's – was killing him. He popped his head around the crimson velvet of the curtain and hissed at the orchestra leader, 'Strike up, for God's sake. We haven't got all night.'

William Withers leapt to attention, pulled his tailcoat into position and smoothed down his luxuriant moustache. He had written a special piece for the President, to be played in the intermission. For now, though, it would be standard fare. He rapped his baton on the rostrum to bring the musicians together. In the wings, Joe Jefferson, usurped from his role as Asa Trenchard by the fame-hungry Hawk – 'Just for tonight, Joe,' Hawk had said. 'I just fancy treading the boards again, don't know why' – stood with fingers crossed that Hawk would measure his length as he walked on stage. The orchestra struck up and the audience fell silent. At last; now they could all relax and enjoy an hour or two of nonsense after all they had been through for the last four long years . . .

It was about half an hour in and towards the end of the First Act that Withers suddenly leapt to his feet in the orchestra pit and waved his baton hysterically. His musicians struck up 'Hail to the Chief' and all eyes swivelled to the Presidential box. The cast froze in mid-sentence and bowed or curtseyed respectively as the audience rose to their feet, clapping, whistling and cheering. Mary Todd Lincoln was wreathed in smiles, and she waved and nodded in appreciation. The little woman, who barely reached her husband's shoulder, was mad, they said. Broken by the passing of her boy, Willie, she consulted spiritualists and spoke to the dead. The President was smiling too, but the man looked old and tired, as if he had fought for every inch of ground in the war himself. And he had. In the long watches of the night, Abe Lincoln had, in his mind, sadly hauled down the flag at Fort Sumter; he had bled at Chancellorsville and Little Round Top. He had starved in the prison camps of Libby and Andersonville and had seen Atlanta burn, reflected in those sad, world-weary eyes. He waved but there was suddenly no smile on his face. Edward Sothern fumed inwardly. The President would cast a gloom over the evening. The leading man had just made his entrance, Sothern thought, but he was a tragedian and this was supposed to be a comedy. Sothern shook his head. Whoever told him that the President loved the theatre was out of his mind.

Arlette McKintyre fumed too when she saw Clara Harris reach out and whisper something to Mrs Lincoln. Mary Todd nudged her husband, and he seemed to acknowledge Clara for the first time. Had Arlette been less vain and willing to wear her spectacles in public, she would have seen the expressions on the faces of the First Couple and would have gained some comfort, but as it was, she snapped her fan shut and sat back, shaking her head and tutting. Lord Dundreary was declaiming, hoping to win the limelight back from Lincoln – 'Birds of a feather gather no moss.'

In his box, Lincoln wasn't listening. His thoughts were far away, and he murmured to Mary, 'How I should like to visit Jerusalem some time.'

The world would remember, in the days and weeks and months ahead, exactly when it happened. It was halfway through Act III, Scene 2, and Harry Hawk, sweat trickling down through his greasepaint, rounded on little Mary Wells playing Mrs Mountchessington. 'Don't know the manners of good society, eh?' he drawled, in the hick Tennessee accent he had been doing all night to the surprise of the rest of the cast. 'Well, I guess I know enough to turn you inside out, old gal – you sockdologizing old mantrap!'

The audience roared their delight, and Hawk was so pleased with himself that he stepped out of character and winked at them. In the wings, Joe Jefferson covered his eyes with his hand and groaned. This may be a comedy, but that was uncalled for, unprofessional. To Hawk's horror, almost everyone in the theatre was now looking to their right, up at the Presidential box. A crash had echoed in the laughter, and grey smoke drifted in front of the flags draped there. Every soldier knew that sound. It was a pistol, its bark exaggerated by the echo and re-echo around the halls.

Grand was on his feet; so were others. Grand saw Rathbone in the Presidential box wrestling with somebody – a blurred shadow – and Mrs Lincoln cradling the head of the President, who had slumped to one side in his rocking chair. Clara Harris was screaming, stumbling back into the shadows, her hands clasped at her chest in an almost melodramatic gesture of distress. Her hysteria was taken up by everyone, the women screaming and crying although as yet they could hardly know why.

'Stop that man!' It was Major Henry Rathbone's voice. He had just lost his grip on a madman who was leaping down on to the stage, a strip of the Stars and Stripes fluttering from one of his spurs. Grand could see that the major was bleeding, the theatre lights flickering over the blood trickling down his sleeve. From his angle, he couldn't see the President at all, but he could see the man who had just shot him.

Wasn't that an actor? Grand thought to himself. Wasn't that John Wilkes Booth? He'd seen him on stage many times. And now, here he was again, eyes blazing from the handsome face, in his last starring role, the one that would surely make him famous for ever. He battered the bewildered Withers aside, hacking at the man as he ran, and raised a Bowie knife, red with Rathbone's blood, and he screamed, '*Sic semper tyrannis*,' before dashing into the wings. Harry Hawk had run backwards to get out of his way, losing his balance and falling awkwardly, at the foot of the backstage stairs. Booth jumped across him, kicking him as he went, leaving tonight's leading man flat on the ground and groaning.

In the stalls, Grand gripped Arlette's shoulders, forcing her down into her seat. 'Stay here,' he said, looking her hard in the face. 'Whatever happens. You'll be all right.'

Arlette said nothing as her man fought his way through the

shrieking, hysterical crowd. Above it all, she could hear Clara
Harris screeching for water, and she could hear the shouts of
the men: 'Hang him! Lynch the bastard!'

Matthew Grand did not know the layout of Ford's Theatre.
He only knew that Booth had run to his right and that there
was an alleyway off F Street with a door to the backstage
area. The captain shoulder-barged that door now and pitched
into blackness. He collided with a brick wall ahead of him,
his boots skittering on the cobbles. He looked right. F Street
was partially lit, and revellers, in their fifth day of forgetting
the war, were drunkenly winding their way home. There. There
was his man. Booth must have hurt himself as he landed on
that stage because now he was dragging his foot as he caught
the reins of his waiting horse. A young boy was holding it for
him, and Booth slapped the lad aside, lashing out with his
knife for good measure and vaulting into the saddle. Grand
was with him, dodging the skittish animal's flying hooves and
trying to grab the bridle. He cursed himself that he was not
armed, but he had gone to the theatre with his fiancée. That
was no place, surely, for a sabre and a brace of pistols. But
this was America, after four years of madness; when would a
man be able to walk unarmed again?

Booth rammed his spurs home, feeling the agony in his
ankle again, and he clattered out of the alleyway.

Grand stumbled over the boy and helped him up. The lad
was dazed and his face was bloody, but he would keep. At the
end of the passage, Grand could see F Street clearly. He had
just reached the corner when the light was blotted out and a
huge man stood there, in a long duster coat and wideawake
hat. His eyes burned into Grand's, and his lips parted in a
snarl. 'You didn't think it would be that easy, did you, soldier
boy? You didn't think Johnny would come alone? The Devil's
with him.' It was an English voice, like the ones Grand had
been listening to all night. Instinctively, the captain grabbed
the man's lapels, and he felt cloth tear. Then he felt a sickening
slap across the face and his head collided with brickwork. The
broken cobbles hurtled up to meet him. And the play was over.

TWO

'Hello, handsome; want some company tonight?'

The girl was perhaps eighteen, but she had done this before, many times, and was full of confidence, her shoulders swinging and her head thrown back to show her smooth throat and creamy breasts off to their best advantage. The man was not as handsome as all that, but the *demi-monde* were good at flattery. If the man was interested and they wandered together into the shadow of the stalls, she would tell him in a minute how big he was and what stamina he had. That would be after she'd helped himself to his wallet.

'Company? I thought I had some.' James Batchelor had gone to the Music Hall tonight with three colleagues. Colleagues who seemed to have vanished through the cigar smoke and the limelight. The audience was hooting and whistling as a chorus line of girls high-kicked in their frothy folderols and the orchestra belted out a polka.

The girl understood that perfectly well, because she already had her fee in her bodice, and the fee had come from the three friends James Batchelor thought he had. 'Ah, they're no company,' she trilled, sitting beside him in a rustle of petticoats. Then she paused and raised an eyebrow. 'Unless it's a bit of brown you're after. In which case—' she tapped him on the chest with her fan – 'you don't need me.'

Batchelor smiled. 'You're right,' he said, having to shout above the hullabaloo. 'What's your name?'

'Effie,' she said. 'You can call me Effie.'

'Where are you from, Effie?'

'Paradise, ducky.' She ran the closed fan down his waistcoat to his lap.

He gingerly removed it. 'Well, Effie,' he said, looking into her soft, grey eyes. 'Flattered as I am, I'm going to have to turn you down.'

She looked at him. No, he wasn't handsome, but there was something strangely vulnerable about his boyish face. She was usually good on ages, but she wasn't sure about his. Was he twenty? Thirty? Effie didn't know; but the night was young and the theatre was filling up nicely. She would have to give most of her pot to Auntie Bettie, but that still left her with a tidy sum. And tomorrow was Saturday, the best night of the week.

She leaned forward and kissed him on the cheek. 'Your loss, lover,' she said with a laugh and whirled away into the crowd.

James Batchelor took another swig of his brandy and had drained the glass. He stood up, perhaps too suddenly, and the room swayed. How many had he had? No more than two, surely? The hard stuff didn't usually affect him like this.

He had to fight his way through to the bar that ran the length of the stalls. Furtive couples were sliding back into the shadows, the raucous music covering their grunts and groans. Where the hell were they? Batchelor had to spin a couple of revellers around, mumbling his apologies, before he found a face he knew.

'You shit, Buckley!' he hissed into that face. 'When I feel in need of a girl I'll choose my own, thanks.'

'Oh, come on, Jim,' Joe Buckley said. 'You looked in need of cheering up. Effie's a good sort.'

'She certainly is.' Edwin Dyer was suddenly at his elbow. 'But if you're determined to wallow in your sorrows, at least do it in enough liquid.' He clicked his fingers and waved a waiter over. He haggled briefly over the price of the theatre's cheapest champagne while Buckley clapped an arm around Batchelor and led him to the last free table in the place.

When they had all sat down and the bubbly frothed and fizzed in the glass, Dyer looked Batchelor in the face. 'Look,' he said, 'if you're not careful, you're going to end up like old Gabriel over there.'

Old Gabriel was indeed older than the others. He had come up the hard way, from dame school to crammer to pot-boy at the Wayzegoose, that dingy little hostelry along Fleet Street where the barflies paddled in the spilled beer and lecherous old newspapermen spat in the sawdust. Gabriel Horner had been at the *Telegraph* since it started eight long years ago and he had seen dozens of young men like Jim Batchelor. They all wanted to change the world, to write their way into the heart of the nation, to leave their mark on the greatest Empire the world had ever known. All night he had avoided the lads, if only because he had heard their naive claptrap before. Now, though, it looked as if little Jimmy needed his words of wisdom.

'What's the matter, Batchelor?' He leaned across from the next table, where a couple of tarts were enjoying his liquor. 'Don't tell me you've got Crossness tomorrow!'

Batchelor looked at the old soak. 'How did you guess?' he said, straight-faced.

Gabriel Horner roared with laughter and thumped the table so that the glassware rattled. 'Sorry, old man,' he said. 'I had no idea.'

Tomorrow, the Prince of Wales would arrive by steamer from the Palace of Westminster. His party would consist of both archbishops, two extra bishops (no one quite knew why), a couple of princes, the odd duke and earl, a cartload of Members of Parliament and most of the police force of the Metropolitan Districts of London. They would all end up at the Crossness Pumping Station on the south bank of the Thames. His Royal Highness would make a speech and cut a ribbon, and everyone would come out with boring platitudes about how marvellous Mr Bazalgette's sewerage system was. And James Batchelor, the *Telegraph*'s newest reporter, would be on hand to record it all for a breathless nation.

Old Gabriel must have read James Batchelor's mind. He leaned forward again. 'It *is* newsworthy, James,' he said, as quietly as the blasting music would let him. 'Crossness may be miles of piss-pipes to you, but it's living history; believe me. It shan't be done again in our lifetime.'

Batchelor seemed unconvinced.

'It's what we journalists do.' Horner spread his arms as though there was no other explanation left.

'No.' Joe Buckley sipped his champagne. 'Young Jimmy here would rather be out with George Sala, wouldn't you,

Jimmy? Our man at the Front, reporting from Appomattox on that little war the Americans are having.'

'Yes, I would,' Batchelor said defiantly. 'I'm tired of flower shows and the price of Smithfield pigs.'

'George Sala?' Horner snorted. 'I remember him when he was scribbling drawings for Charlie Dickens.'

'If it was action you wanted,' Dyer said, chipping in, 'you should have joined the army. Gone to kill a few painted Maori down under.'

'There's a civil war going on over there,' Batchelor said, still mentally with Sala in the Wilderness, annoyed at himself because he was slurring a little. 'Can you imagine what that must be like?'

'We had a civil war once.' Horner grimaced as the cheap champagne hit his tonsils. 'If my old crammer history serves. The Man of Blood against old Noll Cromwell.'

Buckley nudged Dyer. 'Did you cover that one, Gabriel?' And they all roared with laughter. All except James Batchelor. He suddenly needed fresh air, and he stumbled out into the night, the music fading and then roaring in his ears as he went. As the door swung shut the noise ended, as though he had gone deaf, and he shook his head to clear it.

The Haymarket was bright on that April night, the gas lamps guttering in their green luminosity. The gilded carriages of the well-to-do rattled past, the glossy hacks with their high-carried tails trotting north and south. On the pavement nearest Batchelor, a little girl sat in rags, her hand out in front of her. The newspaperman ignored her at first. There were so many like her, on every street corner, in every doorway until a boot or a broom moved them on. But, three steps further on, he relented and turned back. He fumbled in his trousers' pocket and found a sixpence. He looked down into the girl's face, upturned to his and livid in the gas light. She may have been eight or nine; it was difficult to tell under the grime.

'Buy a match, guv'nor,' she said, her eyes bright when she saw his silver. There was a box of matches in her filthy hand, and the other clutched convulsively at a ragged shawl around her scrawny shoulders. Under it the thin shift was grey, crawling, like her head, with lice. In a year or two, this little waif would gravitate from selling matches to selling her body, should she live so long. If she was lucky, *very* lucky, she might end up like Effie.

There was a scream, short and sharp, and it was punctuated by a hideous gurgling sound and the scrape of hobnails on cobbles. Batchelor threw the coin at the child and doubled back the way he had come. One or two others passing by had heard the sound too, but they hurried on, looking neither left nor right. The journalist shook his head again to try to clear it. The combination of the drink, the noise and the heat of the theatre had slowed his responses, and the chill of the spring night air made him shiver. The scream had come from an alleyway that ran alongside the theatre. He could hear the music and the laughter from inside as his colleagues began to slide ever nearer to the floor.

It was pitch black in the alleyway, and he wished he had actually bought the girl's match. He even half turned to retrieve it, but the child had gone as if she had never been there, a ghost in the gaslight. He groped his way forward, keeping to one side of the passageway so that what faint light there was from the street eased the gloom. Even so, his foot hit something that was in deep shadow, and he half-stumbled. He checked his pockets, in the faint hope that he already had matches there, but there was nothing. He peered down into the darkness, willing his eyes to see something. He felt his way forward, carefully, slowly. He felt a leg first, stockinged to above the knee. The skirts and petticoats were thrown up and the thighs were smooth and bare. He used one hand to steady himself, crouching in the tight angle between the leg and the wall. With the other he fumbled for the bodice, felt naked breasts but no heartbeat. And at last he reached the neck. Its smoothness was spoilt by something jagged and tight, a ligature that bit deep into the skin. He felt his fingers wet with blood and caught his breath. He felt for a pulse, at the neck, at the wrist, smearing blood wherever he groped. He felt the face. And he pulled back. As he moved, the gaslight shone over his shoulder and his eyes had at last become acclimatized to the dark. He was staring down at a dead woman. She had been strangled, but with something that had cut as it had throttled.

It was Effie, the girl from paradise.

THREE

Matthew Grand's boots slipped in the mud of Tenth Street. A crowd surged across the road ahead of him, everybody trying to help carry the President. The man was tall, unusually tall for the times, a target waiting to catch a bullet, head and shoulders above his fellow man. Soldiers with fixed bayonets were trying to keep the crowd back as the sad little entourage made its way to the house opposite the theatre.

A sash window flew up from the rooming house's second storey, and Henry Safford popped his head out. All evening he had danced between the bonfires crackling and spitting across the city, leaping over the puddles of Pennsylvania Avenue. Strangers had shaken his hand and slapped his back. A girl he did not know had kissed him. The war was all but over, and the country that had for so long held its breath could breathe again.

'What's the matter?' Safford tried to focus on the convoy in the half-light below him.

'The President has been shot,' someone called back.

Safford looked up to where the White House carriage stood outside Ford's Theatre, the coachman like a rock on his perch, too stunned to move. 'Bring him in here!' he yelled and grabbed his candle before making for the stairs.

The knot of men carrying Lincoln adjusted their path, took the weight and lifted their precious load higher to negotiate the front steps.

Matthew Grand had no place there. There would be doctors, politicians, the devastated Mrs Lincoln and God knew who else. He would be redundant in whatever dying room they took him to. Suddenly, he remembered Arlette and doubled back to the theatre. Knots of the audience still stood there, shaking and crying. Actors and musicians were consoling each other, trying to come to terms with what had happened.

'Matthew!' The captain turned sharply at the sound of his

name, though it seemed to come from a long way away, down an empty, lonely tunnel. Arlette's uncle, Jacob McKintyre, stood there, his top hat gone, his hair awry. 'We've taken Arlette home. This place is a madhouse. The carriage is outside. Come on.'

'Later,' Grand said. 'I have things to do.'

The older man looked at him. 'You're hurt,' he said.

For the first time, Grand realized that he was bleeding and his temple was swollen and tender. 'It's nothing,' he said, fishing out his handkerchief and dabbing at the blood. 'Nothing.'

Jacob gripped his sleeve. 'Your place is with your fiancée,' he said. Arlette was never easy to deal with, and this evening he had come close to giving her a slap to calm her down. It was definitely time that Grand took a hand in her management.

'No.' Grand shook his head. 'My place is with my President.' And he pulled away.

If Captain Grand had not been there to save his President, he would do all he could for him now. He pushed his way through a crowd at the bottom of the stairs to the President's box itself. The walls and carpet were a deep crimson, the Stars and Stripes half-ripped from its housings. There was blood everywhere – Lincoln's, Rathbone's, perhaps even Booth's – who knew? Lincoln had gone now, along with Mary Todd, Major Rathbone and Clara Harris, and in their place a pale-faced actress knelt, her stage make-up running with the glycerine of real tears.

'Miss Keene?' Grand took the woman's hand and helped her to her feet. Her once-white gloves were red, and more dripped from her ringlets.

A large florid man moved as if to get between them. 'Who are you?'

'Matthew Grand, Third Cavalry,' Grand told him. 'I was in the audience earlier. You?'

'Gourlay. I'm stage manager here. Where's the President?'

'I don't know,' Grand said. 'I think they've taken him to a house across the street.'

'The Petersen rooming house?' Gourlay frowned. 'Why the Hell . . .? Oh, begging your pardon, Laura.'

Laura Keene was beyond the niceties of polite society now.

Abraham Lincoln's blood and brains had been seeping into her hands and dress and into the flag that Gourlay had placed beneath his head. A life ended. A candle blown out. She had not taken in the officer's name, but she recognized the rank badges on his shoulders. 'Captain,' she said. 'He's gone, hasn't he?'

And throughout that long April night all across the city, men came to the same realization. Honest Abe had gone to meet his maker. Lesser men would try to fill his boots.

Matthew Grand made his way down the back stairs, past soldiers who instinctively clicked to attention as the officer passed. The sulphur lights burned blue here, and Grand realized he was back in the corridor that led to the stage. The door he had crashed through half an hour before was still ajar, the cobbles of the yard glistening now in newly falling drizzle. Now that he was not chasing shadows, he could take in his surroundings. There were two stables, separated by the alleyway that ran straight and true to F Street. It was here he had caught the killer's stirrup briefly before the man had wheeled his horse and spurred through the Washington night. There was nothing here now but mushy hoof and footprints. Nothing except . . .

The captain had never wished so hard that he had his revolver with him. A figure was crouching in the darkness, the almost tangible black caused by the jut of the stable to the right.

'Who's there?' Grand called, hoping his voice would not betray the flutter in his heart.

'I was just going, sir,' a shaken voice called back. 'I didn't know whose horse that was.'

Grand straightened. The voice was young, little more than a boy's. 'Come out,' he said. 'Show yourself.'

A mousy kid half-stumbled into the half-light. Like Grand, he was bleeding from the head, a dark streak running from his hairline to his chin. He was shaking, his eyes wild and rolling, looking everywhere but at the captain's face. Grand took the boy's shoulders in both hands, forcing him to focus. He had seen this before, on too many battlefields. Boys from the farms and the hill country, covered in other men's brains. Boys whose hearts were broken. Whose minds were gone. But he had seen this particular boy before.

'What's your name, son?' Grand asked.

'Peanut, sir,' the boy said. 'Peanut John.'

'You work here, Peanut?'

'Yes, sir.' The boy was calmer now; now that he could hear the first coherent words in that night of madness. 'I keep the door, sir. And I sell peanuts. That's how come they call me Peanut John.'

'What happened tonight, Peanut?' Grand asked, wanting to know. Bringing the boy to the here and now made him shake again, and again Grand held the trembling shoulders.

'I don't rightly know, sir,' he mumbled.

'Peanut.' Grand lifted the boy's chin. 'A terrible thing has happened. You know the President's been shot?'

A single tear trickled the length of Peanut John's face, tracing a groove through the grime and blood and making him look younger still. 'Yessir,' he said, nodding solemnly. 'I've heard folks shouting it.'

'You said,' Grand replied, coaxing him gently, 'you didn't know whose horse that was.'

Peanut nodded.

'Whose horse was it?'

For a long moment Peanut John looked into Grand's eyes. He saw nothing but kindness there. And calmness of a kind that everybody needed this night. 'Mr Booth, sir. It was his horse.'

'Tell me,' the captain said, steadying the boy against the stable door. 'Tell me what happened.'

'Well . . .' Peanut John frowned, trying to focus, trying to make some sense of it all. 'Mr Spangler done found me. Asked me to hold a horse.'

'Mr Spangler?'

'Edman Spangler, sir. He's a scene-shifter here at the theatre. He said to find Johnny Debonay. He'd left the horse with him.'

'Debonay?'

'He's like me, sir. Doorman and stable hand.'

'All right. So Debonay was holding a horse.'

'Yessir. Just along the alley. He told me to hold it 'cos he had work to do.'

'How did you know it was Mr Booth's horse?'

'I seen him riding it before, sir,' Peanut John said,

remembering. 'A sorrel with a white blaze. Jumpy critter. I had trouble holding him.'

'Did you see Booth go into the theatre?'

'No, sir. I was on the front door, selling peanuts then. I didn't see him come past me.'

'Mr Booth's an actor.' Grand was thinking aloud. 'I guess he knows this theatre pretty well.'

'I guess he does, sir. He bought me a drink once.'

'He did?'

'Yes sir.' Peanut John's face creased into a smile. Little things made him happy. 'Me and Mr Spangler, we were in the Star Saloon, and Mr Booth come in and treated me.'

'What kind of man is he, Peanut?'

'Mr Booth?' The question had clearly confused the boy. But he gave the same answer he would have given if Grand had asked it the day before or a year ago. 'He's a gentleman, sir. A fine man. A gentleman of the South.'

Grand nodded. In all sorts of ways, tonight belonged to gentlemen of the South.

'Did he do it, sir?' Peanut John blurted out, his head reeling with the chaos all around him. 'Mr Booth. Did he shoot the President?'

'It looks that way,' Grand said. He looked at the boy. 'Better get yourself home, Peanut,' he said. 'Get that head seen to.'

'I found this, sir.' The boy held out his hand, and something glittered in his palm. 'I guess Mr Booth must have dropped it.'

Grand squinted in the alley's light. It was a gold cufflink inlaid with enamel. A red cross and a sword on a white background. He had never seen the design before. He slipped it into his pocket. 'Let's see if we can't give this back to Mr Booth,' he said. 'Here.' He passed the boy a shiny dollar. 'The next drink you take in the Star, Peanut John – let Mr Lincoln buy that for you.'

In the years ahead, dozens of men would claim to have been there at the end, all crammed into Henry Safford's little space in the Petersen rooming house. Four men all claimed to have been the one who placed the pennies on the closed lids of

Abraham Lincoln's eyes. The house had been ransacked and occupied, like so many in Atlanta, Richmond and anywhere else where the rebel flag had floated. Shocked soldiers had shoulder-barged locked doors, and knots of key people had taken them over as their personal headquarters. Sixteen doctors, of varying rank and expertise, had tiptoed into what was now the President's room, to watch and wait, to suggest, pontificate, argue. In the room at the front, grim with appropriately black furniture, Mary Todd Lincoln sprawled, surrounded by her ladies. She sobbed, she moaned. Occasionally, she screamed. But the guards on her door had strict orders; on no account was she to have access to the President. If, as everyone believed, these were the man's last hours, they deserved to be peaceful ones. One face the broken woman hoped for, and one that appeared before her at some hour in that night of the longest hours, was her son Robert. He was crying, his tears trickling on to his mother's hair as he held her to him.

Robert had been on his way to see his father, but someone in the hallway had told him that it was too late, that his father would not know him. So he'd gone to his mother instead. He had never seen the woman who had given birth to him in this state before, not even when his brother Willie had died. Her carefully braided hair lay loose over her shoulders, and her eyes were red with crying, mucus dribbling over her thin lips. Young Lincoln had thrown his captain's coat over his shoulders as the chaise had rattled through the chaotic Washington streets. He had jumped out and run the last half mile, jostling with revellers who had not yet heard the news, men with smiles on their lips and liquor on their breath. One or two of them cheered the man, a soldier and hero of the hour. One or two more had seen his grim-set, pale face and jeered at him. 'Cheer up, fella,' one of them called. 'The war's over. God bless old Abe!'

And it was not just grief that made the tears trickle down Robert Lincoln's face that night. It was guilt. He should have been there, with his parents in the box at Ford's. But he was too tired. He had been up for thirty-six hours without a wink of sleep and had stood on the porch of McLean's house at Appomattox when General Lee had ridden up to surrender.

Young Lincoln had never thought he would see the greatest soldier of the war, but there he was, silver-haired and, ramrod-backed, dismounting from Traveller like a man tired of life. Ulysses Grant, with nothing of the majesty of Lee, had stepped out on to that porch, a cigar glowing in his teeth, his boots thudding on the planks. Lee had stopped and swept off his campaigning hat. It was a moment of history. And the President had wanted to hear it all, over and over again at breakfast the previous day, in case his boy, the witness to that moment, had left anything out. Young Lincoln had lived on beans and hard tack for three months and had not slept in a bed since February.

'Son,' his father had said to him, 'we want for you to come to the theatre with us tonight.'

But Robert Lincoln could not keep his eyes open, and so he turned the old man down. The President smiled, patting the boy's hand. 'All right, son,' he said. 'Run along to bed.'

And he had. Now he looked across at the solemn faces of his mother's entourage, each of them trying to hold it together for her sake. *He should have been there.* If he'd been in that box, he would have stopped the madman, even if it meant taking the bullet destined for his father.

That bullet lay deep in Abraham Lincoln's brain, just behind the orbit of his right eye, which bulged alarmingly. All night long the doctors did all they knew to keep him alive. They probed the wound with a silver instrument to keep the blood flowing, keeping his heart beating and his lungs inflating in short, desperate bursts between the long agonies of silence. They replaced the blood-soaked towels around his head and prayed. All those men of science, powerless, fell to their knees as the Reverend Dr Phineas Gurley beseeched his God to do what they could not.

Matthew Grand walked out of Ford's Theatre as a grey, wet dawn replaced the shadows of the night. Tenth Street was packed with crowds, silent now after the hysteria of the last hours. None of them knew that beyond the bricks of the Petersen house, the man who freed the slaves was dying.

It was twenty-two minutes past seven by Dr Charles Leale's watch. He had been there, in the Presidential box as John Wilkes

Booth's gun-smoke was still drifting across the stalls. All night he had held Lincoln's hand to let the man know he was not alone in his darkness. Dr Charles Taft pressed the President's chest, straining to feel a heartbeat. Surgeon-General Joseph Barnes felt a last surge of blood pump through the carotid artery.

They all heard Gurley intone, 'Our Father and our God,' and Robert Lincoln sobbed on somebody's shoulder.

In the frightening, tragic silence that followed, Edwin Stanton, the Secretary of War, took off his spectacles. His beard looked greyer in that dawn than it had seemed the night before when someone had woken him with the dread news. Tears filled his eyes. 'Now,' he said softly, 'he belongs to the angels.'

In the street outside, as if somehow they all knew that the moment had come, men swept off their hats and let the rain cry its own tears on their bare heads. From somewhere a church bell tolled solemnly, the death knell of the South. The death knell of old Abe.

FOUR

James Batchelor sat back on his heels, his head spinning. Here he was, a journalist or so he had always hoped, and instead of his mind weaving a headline and a good few inches of newsprint, all he wanted to do was to be sick. He wasn't frightened at the sight of blood, or at least he had never thought that to be so; that was before he had seen this sight – of a girl who not long before had pressed her warm body against his, now lying in a pool of the stuff. That pool was spreading slowly around her head, glinting with highlights that seemed far too bright. They hurt his eyes. He put his head down in his hands and tried to stop the world from spinning.

A voice broke through the buzzing in his head.

'Wos' goin' on? Effie?'

Batchelor turned sharply, almost unbalancing and putting his hand down on the slick ground before he realized he was doing it. He snatched it up, but too late – it was sticky now with even more of Effie's blood.

'Effie?' The voice became a screech. The girl, dressed like Effie and in a crowd virtually indistinguishable from her and dozens of her kind, screamed, her mouth a black hole in her powdered face. She stumbled back from Batchelor, who reached out to stop her. Even as he did so he knew it was a mistake. She thought he had done this terrible thing. He must explain.

'No, I didn't do this. I . . .'

The girl peered forward. 'I know you. You was with Effie tonight. She come back, said you didn't want 'er. You killed 'er!' She opened her mouth to scream again, and Batchelor took another unwise step forward. The girl turned and ran for the lights of the street. 'Murder!' she screamed as she ran. 'Murder!'

The journalist was still standing there, dripping hand by his side, when the police arrived, rattles shattering the echoes in the alley. There were two of them, young constables trying to grow convincing moustaches, both failing.

'What's going on here, sir?' one of them asked, peering round Batchelor to the girl's body sprawled on the ground.

Batchelor was heartened by the 'sir'. They seemed to have realized at once that he couldn't have done this dreadful thing. 'I found her, officer,' he said. 'Her name is Effie . . .'

The other constable chimed in. 'You know the deceased, then, do you, sir?'

'Well, no, I . . . I met her for the first time this evening.'

The constables exchanged knowing looks. Batchelor could have sworn that one of them winked. The one with the marginally more luxuriant moustache spoke again, trying to keep the smirk out of his voice. 'Oh, I see, sir. You *met* her this evening.' He looked down at the pitiful heap of tawdry clothes, at the cooling puddle of congealed blood. 'Did she not give satisfaction, sir?'

Batchelor was outraged. 'What?' he roared. 'This girl is dead, and you stand there making mockery of her. What kind of man are you?'

The constable drew himself up and puffed out his chest. 'I am the kind of man, sir,' he said, 'who is going to arrest you for the murder of this unfortunate.' He flicked out some handcuffs and before Batchelor could move had deftly attached one to his wrist, clicking the other around his own. He turned his head to the other constable who was hanging back, trying not to let his eyes focus on the corpse and yet finding his eyes straying to it, almost of their own volition. He looked as though vomit would be in his immediate future. 'Brown,' the arresting officer said, 'stay with the body. Keep the crowds back. Look for clues.'

'I can't do all of those by myself, George,' the boy said. 'Can I just keep the crowds back?' That at least would give him a chance to get away from the pool of blood, with its smell of rusty death. 'At the entrance to the alley.'

'That's Morris to you, Brown,' the constable said, from the lofty height of three weeks' seniority. He looked at his friend's face and relented. 'That will do. Keep the crowds back. I'll send someone to you from the station as soon as I can.' He gave a tug on the handcuffs and nearly pulled Batchelor over. 'You come along with me,' he said, roughly. 'My sergeant will want a word with you, I have no doubt.'

'I didn't kill that poor unfortunate girl,' Batchelor said. 'She was dead when I found her.'

'Oh, yes,' Morris said, pulling him along. 'That's what they all say, sir, if you don't mind my observing.'

Batchelor dug in his heels, and they came to an ungainly halt on the pavement. The crowd was indeed gathering, and Brown was having his work cut out to keep them at bay. 'How many murderers have you arrested, do you mind my asking?'

'I don't mind at all, sir, no. I have arrested one, to date.' The policeman gave a sharp tug on the handcuffs, and they carried on walking.

Batchelor could not disguise his contempt for the man's lack of experience. 'Oh. I am a journalist, I should tell you, and when I write up this story, I will need as much detail as I can glean. May I ask who the miscreant was, the one you arrested?'

'That all depends, sir,' the constable said, slyly.

'I should also tell you,' Batchelor said, by now very much on his dignity, 'that I will not give you a bribe. It is against my principles.'

'There now, sir.' The constable perceptibly brightened up at the news. 'It is against mine too. It is good, isn't it, to meet another man who thinks as you do?'

Batchelor was puzzled. 'Then on what does it all depend, if not the amount of the bribe?'

'On your name, sir.'

'James Batchelor,' Batchelor said. 'But . . .'

'Then, sir, the murderer I have arrested is called James Batchelor. You may need that for your newspaper, sir, if you live to tell the tale.'

'If I *what*?' The journalist wasn't sure what emotion was uppermost; it was either outrage or blind fear. 'If I live to tell the tale? What does that mean?'

The policeman was imperturbable. 'Well, sir,' he said, calmly. 'The penalty for murder is hanging, as I am sure you well know.' He turned to his prisoner. 'That kills you, or so I have heard. You'd have to ask Mr Calcraft – you know, the executioner.'

Batchelor looked at the man. Was that a sardonic smile there, or not? 'I do understand all about the health problems associated with hanging,' he said, trying to adopt a jaunty outlook. 'But I didn't do it. I didn't kill that girl.'

'I think we have already agreed, sir, that's what they all say. Anyway, not to worry.' He hauled his man up some stone steps and through a forbidding door with a blue-shrouded lamp over it. Batchelor got his bearings. This was Vine Street, home of the C Division. 'Here's the station. You can explain it to my guv'nor.' He unshackled himself from his end of the handcuffs and handed the loop to another policeman, who promptly closed it over his own wrist. 'He has a bit more experience than I do of horrible, vicious, bloody murderers such as your good self.' He touched his finger to the peak of his helmet. 'Good evening, sir. It's been a pleasure.' And he turned on his heel and walked out of Batchelor's life.

Batchelor was yet again outraged. It seemed to be the pattern for the evening for him. He tugged at the handcuffs and spoke to his new captor. 'Shouldn't he stay and explain what's going on?' he asked, a little plaintively.

The policeman looked down at Batchelor's clothes, at his hands, all covered with blood. 'I think we can manage to piece together the facts,' he said. The absence of the 'sir' rang around the room. 'There's been a horrible murder, if I'm not mistaken.'

'But . . .'

'I'll just leave you in this cell for a while,' the copper said, pushing Batchelor through a thick door and disengaging the handcuffs in one movement. 'Someone will be along to see you.'

'When?'

'When they come,' the policeman muttered, but the answer was drowned by the thick slamming of the door.

Batchelor slumped on the plank of wood attached by chains along one wall. A chamber pot, swimming already with the contents of many bladders, since departed, stood in one corner. The window was high but so furred with cobwebs as to give no hint as to time of day or night, though Batchelor knew that it was gone midnight by now. He should be tired. He had already been tired when he left his colleagues, what seemed like days before. He could never sleep in this vile place, not if they kept him there for the rest of his life. Just thinking about how short that might be made goosebumps rise along his arms, and he shivered, just one convulsive movement from the crown of his head to the soles of his feet. No, he would never be able to sleep in here.

FIVE

Laura Keene had changed out of the blood-spattered dress she had worn when she cradled the President's head and was now in the gown she had had made for her star performance in *The Sea of Ice*, an eternity ago. She hadn't slept, and she had wondered throughout it all whether she would be able to face the boards again without hearing that echoing shot, without seeing that spreading blood, black in the theatre's dim light.

There was a knock on her door. Her maid scuttled to open it, and a tall, handsome captain of cavalry stood there, in full dress uniform with epaulettes and sash. He swept off his kepi. 'Would you tell Miss Keene . . .' he said and held out a calling card in a white-gloved hand.

'Miss Keene is not seeing anyone . . .' the maid began. She'd been given strict instructions. Stage-door Johnnies, star-struck adoring fans, elderly gentlemen with a certain glint in their eye – Laura Keene's maid knew all the types. The captain hardly fitted the bill for any of these, but after Friday, Laura's decision had extended to all men and most women.

'It's all right, Margareta,' the actress said. 'Please show the captain in to the drawing room.'

Truth be told, it wasn't much of a drawing room. Laura had been staying at the Pennsylvania House, but after the events of Friday, she knew she would be besieged by newspapermen and so had had her belongings transferred here. It was only temporary. She'd be off to Harrisburg in the morning.

'Captain Grand, ma'am.' The visitor clicked his heels. 'I am glad to see you looking well.'

That was no more than the truth either. When Matthew Grand had last seen Laura Keene, she was aghast, rocking backwards and forwards on the floor of the Presidential box as though the shattered head she had held there was still in her hands. Now she looked calm and serene, the grey eyes showing no hint of emotion. The long ringlets were shiny and curled again. Her cheekbones were a little wide, perhaps, and her mouth a little broad too, but she was every inch the actress and she could play any role she chose.

'May I offer you some tea, Captain?' she said.

'No, thank you, ma'am.' Grand smiled. 'I merely came to see how you were after . . . after what happened.'

'How did you find me?' She sent Margareta away with a flick of her hand.

'Your stage manager, Mr Gourlay. He was helpfulness itself.'

'Was he?' Her face twisted into an ironic smile. 'I must have words with Thomas.'

'Forgive me, Miss Keene.' Grand was inching his way in this conversation, trying to find the right words. 'How well do you know John Wilkes Booth?'

He saw her face harden, her eyes sharp and glittering. 'Not, clearly, as well as I thought. He killed his President, Captain Grand. As far as I am concerned, the man deserves to rot in Hell.'

'I see. Er . . . tell me, Miss Keene, have you seen this before?' He took the cufflink out of his pocket, the one Peanut had found in the alleyway. 'Was it perhaps one of Booth's?'

Laura straightened to her full height. For all this man wore the uniform of an officer and gentleman, for all he had shared moments of that terrible night with her, he was now being impertinent. 'How should I know what John's . . .? Oh, wait.' She frowned and took the trinket from him. 'How curious.'

'What is?'

'This crest. The cross and the sword.'

'You know it?'

'I do,' she said. 'It's the coat of arms of the City of London. What on earth is it doing here? Where did you get it?'

'Er . . . I found it,' he lied. 'Lying on the stage at Ford's. It caught my attention in the limelight, and I thought Booth might have dropped it when he landed on the boards. Is it from properties perhaps? Part of the costume department?'

'Well, I suppose . . . it could be something Lord Dundreary would wear, but why go to such lengths? You can't see cufflink designs, not even from the orchestra pit. I'm afraid I cannot help you, Captain.'

Grand pocketed the thing again and was about to take his leave when there was another knock at the door. Margareta was there in an instant but was swept aside by a rotund man with a large nose, a drooping moustache and a huge bunch of flowers.

'Miss Keene.' He bowed. 'Forgive the intrusion. As soon as I heard of the tragic events of Good Friday, I just had to offer you my most sincere condolences.'

Grand recognized the English accent at once. Was Washington crawling with these Limeys? Was it 1813 all over again?

'Thank you, Mr . . . er . . .?' Laura took the flowers and passed them at once to the maid, who stood there fuming at the newcomer's arrogance.

'Sala,' the man said. 'George Sala. My card.' And he flourished it under her nose before placing it in her hand with more smarm than was strictly necessary.

Laura's face fell. 'You write for the *Telegraph*?' she asked.

'I write for the public, madam,' he assured her, 'and the public's right to know.'

'Right to know what?' Grand asked him.

Sala looked him up and down. Grand was half a head taller, ten years younger and had a distinctly military air about him. Sala beamed up at him. 'You are . . .?'

'Standing between you and Miss Keene,' Grand said. 'Margareta, you've done more than enough door-opening for one day. I'll show the gentleman out.' He grabbed Sala by the lapels and frogmarched him to the door.

'How dare you!' the journalist spluttered. 'Miss Keene, I . . .' But the rest of his sentence was lost behind the slammed door.

Sala shook his velvet coat back into place and was about to knock again when he thought better of it. He had not cared for the captain of cavalry inside. And he cared for the steel in his eyes even less. Damn. Now he'd have to trot back to Ford's and talk to lesser fry about their reminiscences of the Night It Happened. And there was no time to be lost.

'Thank you, Captain Grand.' Laura smiled at him. 'That was very . . . gallant.'

Grand half bowed. 'I'm afraid he won't be the last,' he said.

'I am used to gentlemen of the Press,' she told him. 'But you were right to assume that I do not need them today.'

'You know he was waiting for it, don't you, Grand? The assassin's bullet, I mean.'

Major Henry Rathbone was still white as a sheet that Sunday morning. A watery sun was gilding the cannon on the parade ground below his room, and the chapel bell called the faithful to prayer. His hair looked redder than ever against the white of his pillow, and his beady little eyes never left Grand's. The captain had had to leave his pistol at the door and let himself be searched by the guards stationed there.

'He said—' Rathbone's stream of consciousness went on – 'he said he wouldn't live out his term. "When the rebellion is crushed," he said, "my work is done."'

'You can't blame yourself, Henry.' Grand was tempted to pat the man's good hand, but thought better of it. You couldn't pat a man like Henry Riggs Rathbone; it was like patting a goldfish.

'I don't,' Rathbone snapped, as though outraged by the suggestion. 'I did what I could. I wrestled with that maniac, tried to get the knife off him. I was concerned for Mrs Lincoln.'

Grand nodded. 'And Clara. You were concerned for her.'

'Why?' Rathbone frowned.

Grand fidgeted. This was an odd moment. 'Er . . . she's your fiancée, Henry,' he said. 'You know, the girl you're going to marry.'

A look of pain flashed across the major's face. He pulled his nightshirt closer around him with his good hand and shifted so that he could whisper to Grand. 'She's a fan of Wilkes Booth,' he hissed.

'Clara?'

Rathbone nodded. 'Insisted we go to Ford's.'

'Well, weren't you invited by the President?' Grand asked him.

'Were we?' Rathbone's eyes swivelled right and left. 'I don't know. I don't know anything any more.'

Grand frowned. 'Look, Henry, you're all right,' he said.

'You've had a fright, and you've got a bad cut on the arm. Of course, it must have been awful for you in the box . . .'

'Where was she?' the major asked quickly, his voice still a hoarse rasp.

'Who?'

'Clara.'

'What do you mean?'

Rathbone did his best to explain with the use of only one hand. 'The President was here. With his back to the door. Next to him, Mrs Lincoln. She couldn't see the door either. Then me, then . . . Clara.'

'Er . . .'

'Don't you see?' Rathbone hissed, astonished at Grand's stupidity. 'She *wasn't* in line with the door. She would have had a clear view of Booth as he came in. And she didn't say a word.'

Grand looked at the wrinkles in Rathbone's comforter, where he had placed the box's occupants mentally in its folds. 'She could only have seen the door if she turned round, Henry,' he said. 'But that applies to any of you.'

'No.' Rathbone shook his head, shaking his body at the same time. 'No. It was Clara. How else could Booth have got into the box? There was a guard outside.'

'What happened to him?'

'Clara bought him off. Clara and that father of hers.'

'The Senator?' Grand couldn't believe his ears. 'Henry . . .'

'I want you to go now, Grand,' Rathbone said. 'It's good of you to check on me, but as you see, I'm perfectly all right. Perfectly.' And he trembled, his eyes rolling in his head.

'Good.' Grand stood up, grateful to be away, and shook the patient's hand. 'Take care of yourself, Henry.'

Beyond the door, an army doctor waited with a small leather bag. 'I know,' he said, reading the expression on Grand's face. 'He's mad as a rattler. Wouldn't you be? With what he's seen? God help America now.'

A dim light was filtering through the thin curtains of Matthew Grand's hotel room on the corner of Sixth and Pennsylvania. There was no clock, and he could not see his watch from the

bed. It had to be morning, with a still-shocked capital creaking
into life and coming to terms with its loss. But something had
woken him. It was nothing from out in the street. It was here,
in his room.

He half sat up and was reaching out for his hunter when
he felt his hair yanked backwards and his head crunched on
the headboard. The muzzle of a .44 was cold on his temple,
and he knew better than to move.

'You're an elusive son of a bitch, Captain Grand,' a voice
said. 'I'll give you that.'

The curtains were wrenched aside, and the April dawn hurt
Grand's eyes. He felt the iron grip on his hair relax. There
were two men in his room, both in the Union uniform of
dark-blue. The one with the gun moved backwards and sat
down carefully in a soft chair. The one who had opened the
curtains crossed to the door and locked it.

'Luther.' The gunman jerked his head, and the other one
hauled the coverlet off Grand's bed, leaving him sitting, rather
ridiculously, in his nightshirt. Resisting the urge to tug down
the hem, he decided to bluff it out.

'You clearly know who I am,' he said. 'Will you return the
compliment?'

The gunman let the hammer ease forward under his thumb,
and he slid the pistol into a holster under his coat. 'I'm
Lafayette Baker,' he said. 'This is Cousin Luther.'

The younger man nodded. 'Luther Byron Baker, to be
precise,' he said. 'My ma and pa favoured men who've made
a nuisance of themselves in the past.'

Lafayette smiled. 'Luther comes from the philosophical side
of the family. Me, I'm more devoted to practical matters.'

'Really?'

Lafayette nodded. 'Like catching killers of Presidents.'
Lafayette Baker's thin lips were all but lost in his heavy black
beard, but his eyes were everywhere, darting and glowing
below the worried frown of his brow. He did not look like a
man to cross.

'What a coincidence,' Grand said.

'How so?' Lafayette asked. Cousin Luther stood against the
far wall, arms folded, watching and waiting.

'You haven't told me what you're doing here,' Grand said, pulling the coverlet back up over himself, 'disturbing an officer of the Union Army at this Godforsaken hour.'

'Officer of the Union Army,' Lafayette repeated, smiling grimly. 'Well, let's cut the bullshit, shall we? Cousin Luther here can call you "sir" because he's only a lieutenant. Me, I'm a full colonel. So, you shape up, soldier. I have some questions for you.'

'Have you?' Grand stayed on his dignity. 'On what authority . . . Colonel?'

Lafayette sighed. 'I am the head of the National Detective Police, son,' he said. 'Stanton's right-hand man. I loved my President like the next man, but there are a hell of a lot round here who didn't. I want to know which side of the picket wire you stand on.'

'I was at the theatre,' Grand told him, 'when Lincoln was shot.'

'We know that,' Luther said. 'You were seen leaving with John Wilkes Booth.'

Grand blinked. How wrong could these men be? 'I may have been seen leaving *after* Booth,' he said. 'I was chasing him.'

'How commendable.' Lafayette crossed his legs and leaned back in his chair. 'Were you armed?'

'No, I'd gone to watch a play,' Grand explained.

'So, let's get this straight. You were in the theatre when Booth jumped on to the stage?'

'That's right.'

'You'd seen him shoot the President?'

'I didn't actually see it,' Grand admitted. 'I wasn't looking that way. I heard a shot, and then Booth was on the stage, shouting.'

'Shouting what?' Luther asked.

'It sounded like, "*Sic semper tyrannis.*"'

'So it is always with tyrants,' Luther translated aloud.

Lafayette nodded. 'The motto of Virginia. Home of the good ol' boys. What did you do?'

'I gave chase.'

Luther grinned. 'D'you catch him?'

Grand looked at the man. He didn't like Lafayette Baker,

but he liked Cousin Luther less. 'All I caught was the butt of
a pistol. Or something like it.'

'From Booth?' Lafayette asked.

'An accomplice.'

Lafayette sat upright slowly, looking at the man in bed
closely. 'Why do you say that?'

'From what he said,' Grand told him. 'Something like, "You
didn't think Johnny would come alone?"'

'Johnny?'

Grand shrugged. 'I assumed he meant Wilkes Booth.'

Lafayette nodded. 'Luther and me, we've talked to a few
fellers over the last few days. Some of 'em were good friends
of Booth. Nobody calls him Johnny. He's Booth. Or John.'

'That's what he said.' Grand was sure.

'What did he look like?' Luther asked.

Grand was remembering. 'Big. Maybe six foot one, two.
Beard. Wore a wideawake and a duster.'

'You saw his face under the brim of a wideawake?' Lafayette
checked.

'Yes.'

'In the dark?' Luther butted in.

'Yes.'

Lafayette chased the idea. 'With all Hell broken loose in
that theatre?'

'Yes.' Grand was determined. He wasn't shouting, but he
was sure.

Lafayette leaned back in the chair again. He clasped his
hands and pressed his index fingers against his lips, looking
at Grand closely. 'Would you know this man again?' he asked.

Grand nodded. 'Oh, yes.'

The head of detectives turned to his cousin. 'Show him,
Luther.'

'You'll see more in the daylight,' the younger Baker said.
'Come over to the window, Captain Grand.' He fumbled in
an attaché case that came from nowhere and passed a photograph to Grand.

Grand squinted at it in the shaft of light from the window.
'What am I looking at?' he asked.

'Alexander Gardner took this at Lincoln's inauguration – the second one, I mean. Ironic, really. You can't see the President himself – he must have moved while Gardner was taking it. Luther and I are in there somewhere.'

'Lovely,' Grand murmured.

Lafayette tapped the top of the tintype with an imperious finger. 'There, up on the balcony of the White House. In the top hat. That's Booth.'

'My God.'

'But that's not I want you to look at. Down here. At the bottom, below the fence. This man?' He pointed to a figure in kepi and military jacket.

Grand shook his head. He'd never seen the man before.

'This one? The tall one next to him?'

Grand saw a man as tall as the one he had collided with in the alley, but he was younger, clean-shaven. He shook his head.

'What about this?' Lafayette's finger touched a man scowling towards the camera.

'No, I've never seen him. Who are they?' But before Lafayette could answer, Matthew Grand had snatched the photograph back from Luther's grasp. 'Wait,' he said. 'That one! That's him.' All eyes in the room fell on the indistinct features, the broad cheekbones, the thick, dark beard. 'That's the man I met in the alley.'

'You're sure?' Lafayette checked.

Grand looked at him, nodding. 'I'm positive.'

Baker slipped the photograph back into his cousin's case.

'Are you going to tell me who those men are?' Grand asked.

The head of detectives looked at him, then at Luther, then at Grand again. 'The one in uniform is John Surratt. He's a Confederate spy, passing letters between Virginia and Canada. Our sources tell us he wasn't in town last Friday, and we don't know where he is now. The big man is Lewis Powell. Also calls himself Lewis Paine. He's the one that got Seward.'

All weekend, Grand had been hearing rumours of the attack on Secretary of State Seward. A lunatic had broken into the man's home and run amok, slashing Seward's throat and lashing out at anyone, man or woman, who got in his way.

'He's known to be on the loose somewhere in the city,' Luther said. 'Only a matter of time.'

'It's our guess he'll show up at Surratt's boarding house sooner or later,' Lafayette said, nodding. 'He's a few cents short of a dollar. If he weren't, Seward would be dead by now.'

'Were they trying to kill everybody in the government?' Grand asked.

'The Vice President . . .' Lafayette checked himself. 'Tsk, where are my manners? The *President* was in the Kirkwood House Hotel. He didn't so much as stir himself as Lincoln was dying. But our information is that there was somebody sent to deal with him too and the man lost his nerve.'

'God preserve us,' Grand muttered, the enormity of the conspiracy now beginning to dawn on him.

'Oh, he has, Captain Grand,' Lafayette said, smiling. 'For all I know there was a derringer aimed at my back too on Friday.' He looked around the room. 'We're all still standing. It's the men standing next to Surratt and Powell I'm interested in.'

'He had an English accent,' Grand said. 'The man who stopped me.'

'English, huh?' Lafayette said.

'Must be lots of those,' Luther commented. 'Half the cast of *Our American Cousin* for a start. And that doctor guy . . .'

'Doctor?' Grand repeated.

'Africanus King,' the head of detectives told him. 'There were more doctors with Lincoln at the end than my dog's got fleas.'

'There's something else,' Grand said, and he crossed to his wardrobe, fumbling in his uniform pocket. He noticed that Cousin Luther's hand had slipped inside his coat, just in case. Since Friday, nobody felt safe. 'Here,' Grand said, 'either Booth dropped this, or the tall Englishman did.'

Lafayette took the trinket and weighed it in his hand. It was a cufflink, enamelled in red and white. 'Is that gold?' he asked.

'I guess. But it's the design that interests me. It's the coat of arms of the City of London.'

Both Bakers looked at him. Lafayette found his voice first. 'And you know that how?' he asked.

'Miss Keene, the actress,' Grand said. 'I showed it to her.'

'Did you now?'

'I didn't tell her where I found it. In fact I told her I'd come across it on the stage after the shooting. Wondered if it belonged to one of the cast.'

'And did it?'

'No. At least, it wasn't part of the play's costume, Miss Keene was sure of that. She just recognized the design.'

'Miss Keene is currently the guest of the US government in Harrisburg,' Lafayette said.

'What?' Grand couldn't believe it. 'You've got her under arrest?'

Lafayette Baker laughed. 'If Mr Stanton had his way, half of Washington would be in irons by now.'

'But Vice . . . er . . . President Johnson . . .'

'Ain't crawled out of a bottle for the past three days,' Lafayette said, finishing the sentence for him. 'Stanton's running the show for now. We'll play things his way.'

'And his way is to arrest everybody at the theatre that night?' Grand said, checking.

'Stands to reason.' Luther tucked the attaché case under his arm.

'But it's at my discretion.' Lafayette had reached the door. 'For now, I'm letting you walk around. But please don't think of leaving town, Captain. Luther and I have got an assassin to catch, but my eyes and ears are everywhere. Believe me.'

Luther smiled at Grand. 'You be sure and have a good day, now,' he said.

SIX

'**W**akey, wakey, sir.' Someone seemed to be shaking his shoulder, but James Batchelor was tired and wanted to sleep. Surely, it wasn't morning already? He opened one eye carefully and looked at the man looming above him.

'Who are you?' he asked. The man didn't answer. 'And where am I?'

'I am Inspector Tanner,' he said. 'You are in Vine Street Police Cells.' Tanner could be a man of few words, and he preferred to wait until the incarcerated had asked both of the inevitable questions. It saved time.

'Oh.' Batchelor remembered it all now. He glanced down at the dried blood on his trousers, on his hands, brown and cracking now, peeling off from between his fingers like tiny petals of long-dead flowers.

'And now you remember why you are here,' Tanner said. He stood upright, and Batchelor saw that he was very tall. He would have to bend to get through the cell door. 'Will you follow me? We need to get some details about you and the events of last night, sir.'

Sir? Did this mean he was no longer the Number One Suspect? He struggled to his feet and scurried after the man, who was striding off down the corridor. 'Excuse me,' Batchelor called. 'Excuse me.'

The man stopped and turned. 'Yes?'

'Am I still a suspect? In Effie's murder?' He mentally gave himself a kick. Calling her by her name like that made their relationship seem so much more than it actually was. 'The dead girl.' It was too late, but worth a try.

'That remains to be seen,' Tanner said. He turned and opened a door, stepping back. 'After you.'

Batchelor walked through into normality. Here was an office, with a small square of carpet on the floor, a desk, some chairs and, at the windows, some curtains which had seen both better days and a much larger window. There was a reassuring smell of pipe tobacco, and there, as if in proof, on a large glass ashtray on a corner of the desk, smouldered the actual pipe. Batchelor could have cried with relief; he had begun to think that the world he knew was gone for ever, but this could have been his editor's office, back at the *Telegraph*.

'Take a seat, Mr Batchelor.'

'*Mr* Batchelor?'

Tanner went round behind his desk and shuffled some paper, eventually choosing a single piece and holding it at arm's-length, squinting down his nose. He looked up. 'James Batchelor. That is you, I hope,' he said. 'I'll swing for that sergeant.'

'Yes,' Batchelor said hurriedly. 'Yes, that's me. I just wondered why I am suddenly *Mr* Batchelor, when I have been locked up in a stinking cell since last night without even a sip of water.'

'No breakfast?' Tanner asked. 'Tsk. Never mind. Hopefully we can sort this out quite quickly. Now, I have here all of your details, I think. James Batchelor . . . oh, that appears to be all I have. Oh, this is *too* bad. I really will have to have a word.' He sat down behind his desk and flicked open his inkwell. 'Now—' he dipped his pen – 'address?'

'Thirty-one, Fleet Place,' Batchelor told him.

'Oh,' the inspector said, beaming, 'nice and handy for the Hoop and Grapes.' Tanner wrote laboriously, crossing the tees with a flourish. 'Occupation?'

'Journalist.'

Tanner put the pen down. 'Journalist? How fascinating. Would I have read anything of yours?'

'Do you like flower shows?'

'Not particularly.'

'Dogs?'

'Not really.'

'Babies?'

'Only when related. I have two of my own, and they are usually pleasant enough.'

'Then you won't have read anything of mine.'

Tanner gave an appreciative chuckle. 'Still making your

way, I see,' he said. 'Never mind, you can write up this case, perhaps.'

'If I live as long,' Batchelor said, ruminatively.

Tanner looked shocked. 'My dear chap,' he said. 'Are you ill?'

Batchelor was startled. 'Er . . . no. It's just that . . . well, the constable who arrested me suggested that . . . well, that I might be hanged for killing Effie.'

'*Did* you kill Effie?' Tanner's pen was raised.

'Of course not.'

'Why would we hang you for it, then?' the inspector asked, reasonably. 'We don't just pick men off the street, you know. We like a *modicum* of evidence first. Would you like to . . .?' He gestured to Batchelor's bloody hands.

'Wash?' Batchelor was delighted. He could feel the dried and flaked blood as if it were red hot. 'I would love to.'

Tanner got up and walked to the door. Flinging it open, he shouted down the corridor, 'Hot water in here, if you please?' Turning back to Batchelor, he asked, 'Tea?'

Batchelor nodded. He was confused and tired and thought he might cry any minute, something he hadn't done since he was ten.

Tanner raised his voice again: 'And some tea.' He shut the door and slipped back behind his desk. 'Where were we?' he asked, mildly.

'That I hadn't killed Effie.' Batchelor didn't think it was possible to say it too often.

Tanner didn't pick up his pen again. Instead, he looked across his desk at Batchelor and then suddenly smiled. It transformed his face, and for the first time since he had knelt down by Effie's dead body, Batchelor felt safe. 'I didn't think you had,' he said. 'We have a number of eyewitness accounts of a man seen with the deceased unfortunate and they don't match you at all. Let me see . . .' He rummaged on his desk again and came out with a second sheet of paper, much screwed up and with stains of what looked to Batchelor very like blood on one corner. 'While the estimable Constable Morris was walking you back here and filling your head with nonsense, Brown was being a little more inventive. He asked members of the crowd whether they had seen Effie with anyone. Apart from one girl who kept saying it was you, the others were unanimous. She had spent most of the evening with a rather well-set up gentleman, tall—' Tanner broke off with another of his smiles. 'I should explain that to an eyewitness tall can mean anything over their own height, but I think in practice we can take it this time as being around five feet ten or so. You are . . . what?'

Batchelor drew himself up. He tried not to sound offended. 'Five feet six.' He paused. 'And a half.'

'And a half. Just so.' Tanner extended his arm again and read from the paper. 'The man appears to have luxuriant facial hair, Piccadilly weepers at the very outside, but some people went for the beard, so we are not too sure on that. Hmmm . . .' He appeared to be editing as he went. 'Some of the other unfortunates had some things to say that we, as gentlemen, don't need to share. And I'm not sure I could repeat them in court, either.'

There was a tap on the door.

'Ah, tea.' Tanner raised his voice. 'Come in.'

A constable came in with a tray in his hand, bearing a teapot and two cups.

'Thank you,' Tanner said, dismissively. 'I'll pour.' He looked over his shoulder at the paper again as he did so. 'Yes, facial hair . . . and that's about it, I think. A disguise, clearly. The facial hair, I mean. The height is a little harder to fake. An inch or so with built up heels, but not four inches.'

'Three and a half,' Batchelor amended.

'As you say. Three and a half. Even so, Mr Batchelor—' Tanner pushed his cup nearer – 'even so, I am convinced you did not kill the poor girl.' He leaned forward. 'I am going to share something with you, Mr Batchelor, although all my instincts say I shouldn't. The girl was strangled with a fine wire, which cut the arteries on her neck as well as severing her windpipe. She had no chance of survival; this was not anything other than a murderous attack. It didn't appear to be for gain, because her paltry earnings were still in her bodice where she had tucked them. It was done for bloodlust, Mr Batchelor, pure and simple.'

Batchelor was frozen on his side of the desk, his cup to his lip. Dreams of journalistic glory floated above his head. Headlines. His name prominently displayed. Fame. Fortune. He sighed and drank his tea.

'What is it, Mr Batchelor?' Tanner asked.

'I don't suppose I can use this information in a story,' he said, plaintively.

Tanner threw open his arms expansively. 'Of course you can, Mr Batchelor,' he said. 'That's why I have told you these gruesome details. I have, of course, held some things back. We must do that, you know. But, in essence, you have the story at your fingertips. I urge you to write it. The people of this fair city deserve to know.'

'Truly?' Batchelor's eyes were open wide. 'It will make my career.'

'Least I can do,' Tanner said, leaning back. 'After the appalling behaviour of my night patrol. Throwing you in that cell and all.'

Batchelor swigged his tea and jumped to his feet. His hot water hadn't arrived, but washing was for men who didn't have a headline to write. 'Can I go now?'

'Please,' Tanner said. 'Please do. Get some sleep. Write your story. Become famous.' He twinkled at him. 'Don't forget me when you are rich, Mr Batchelor.'

Batchelor smiled and nodded, but he was already out of the door. The headline was writing itself in letters ten feet high above his head. 'Fame!' it trumpeted. 'Fortune! Knighthood for Batchelor!' He hurried down the stairs and out into the early morning crowds of Vine Street.

Tanner, in his office, poured another cup of tea. He hadn't had a journalist in his pocket for a while now. They were of limited importance and could come expensive, but they had their uses. He smiled his beautiful smile and leaned back in his chair, content. A good morning's work, and it wasn't even nine o'clock yet.

James Batchelor skimmed along Piccadilly with his head in the clouds. The editor would have to listen to him now. He was going to go home and write the article of his life. It would be headline news. 'My Night In The Cells And What I Know About Police Brutality.' No, that wasn't really fair to Inspector Tanner, who had given him a cup of tea and some kind words. No, this was better: 'Murder In The West End; My Brush With Horror In The Haymarket.' He smiled and made several people, already eyeing his bloody hands with distaste, cross the road hurriedly.

Back at his lodgings, he washed his gory hands at last, watching the water turn to rust as he cleaned the last of the blood away. He used some soap his sister had given him for Christmas; Attar of Roses wasn't his usual perfume, but he felt that he needed something to counteract the blood, soaked into his skin. He changed his clothes and put the dirty ones in a neat pile for his landlady. He finally sat down at the small deal table he liked to think of as his desk and pulled a clean sheet of paper towards him. Dipping his pen in the ink he poised it above the virgin page. Then, a thought struck him.

'MRS BIGGS,' he wrote, in large capitals. 'Don't worry about the blood on these clothes. It isn't mine. Yrs James.'

He put it on top of the pile and pulled another sheet towards him. 'HORRIBLE HAYMARKET GAROTTING!' he began. Then, in smaller capitals, '"IT WAS DONE FOR BLOODLUST, MR BATCHELOR, PURE AND SIMPLE," INSPECTOR TANNER TELLS YOUR REPORTER.' He put down his pen and rubbed his hands together. Oh, yes, this was going to make his career.

'Yes?' The editor of the *Telegraph* didn't waste words. Thornton Leigh Hunt knew how much each one cost, to the penny.

James Batchelor stood on the square of carpet in front of the cluttered desk, on the corner of which a pipe smouldered in a large glass ashtray. 'I . . . Did you hear about the murder in the Haymarket on Friday night?' he asked.

'Not specifically.' The editor did not look up, continuing to wield his blue pencil lavishly on the pages in front of him.

'There was one,' Batchelor said, smugly. 'I was there.'

'Victim?' the editor said, clamping the pipe back between his teeth.

'An unfortunate . . .'

'No. Were you the victim?'

'Well . . . no.' Batchelor felt his crest beginning to fall.

'Perpetrator?'

'No.' This time he was more certain. He drew himself up and opened his mouth to continue.

'In that case, I don't think your little murder case can trump this, can it?' Leigh Hunt turned the paper round to face Batchelor. The headlines screamed: 'MURDER – President Lincoln Shot By An Assassin – THE ACT DONE BY A DESPERATE REBEL.' The editor raised a sardonic eyebrow as he looked at Batchelor's expression. 'I grant you, this headline is very similar to that of the *New York Times*, but I dare say they've pinched the odd idea from us from time to time. George Sala is certain of it.'

'I had no idea,' Batchelor managed to force out eventually.

'Call yourself a journalist?' the editor sneered, moving his pipe to the other side of his mouth. 'George sent the news in on Saturday by telegraph. We were beaten by the Sundays, of course, but I like to think that our coverage will be the most complete of the weeklies. Bugger off now, Batchelor, there's a good chap. They could do with some help in editorial; we're waiting for some woman who once visited Washington to come in and give us an interview.'

'Did she meet the President?' Batchelor asked.

'I don't believe so. Her late husband had his hair cut by a barber who once borrowed some scissors from the barber who once worked with the President's barber – that kind of thing. Anyway, off you go. When she gets here, have a chat with her and bring me what she says.'

'She won't say much, though, will she, sir?' Batchelor didn't see the way the wind was blowing.

'Make it up!' the editor snapped.

'But . . . that would be . . .'

'Journalism, lad.' Finally, the editor looked up at him and removed his glasses, rubbing his eyes. 'It's called journalism. Now, are you going to do this interview or not?'

'Do I have a choice?' Batchelor asked.

Leigh Hunt leaned forward, a smile playing around the corners of his mouth. 'Of course you do, Batchelor. James, isn't it?'

'Yes, sir. And in that case, I would rather not, sir.'

The editor smiled again, but there was no real warmth in it. He put his glasses back on and bent again to the pages, blue pencil at the ready. 'In that case, I'll have to let you go, Batchelor.'

'I beg your pardon, sir?'

'Go, Batchelor – I will have to let you. There's no room on this paper for a journalist who won't make up the news. Off you go. Miss Witherspoon will make up your wages till Friday.'

'Go?'

'Your grasp of English is frighteningly rudimentary, Batchelor. I'm giving you the sack, if you want the vernacular. I can't offer references, but if anyone asks me for a character, I will make you look good. As good as I can, anyway. I can't lie, of course—' and he gave a little chuckle – 'but I'll do my best.'

Batchelor felt the hairs on the back of his neck rise, as did the bile in his throat. Although never rich, he had always known where his next meal was coming from, and suddenly he stood on the brink of disaster. 'But, sir . . .'

Leigh Hunt looked up briefly. '"But, sir" never really works for me, Batchelor. I expect rhetoric, hyperbole, exaggeration.' He held up his hand to stop the man, who had drawn a big breath to begin at least one of those. 'Too little, Batchelor. Too late. Shut the door behind you as you go out. Oh, and tell Miss Witherspoon to make up your wages until tomorrow. And before you say so, Batchelor, I know I said Friday, but I am the editor and I can change my mind as I see fit. I know I can trust a truthful lad like you to do as I ask. Goodbye.'

And that was clearly that. Batchelor stood for a few more seconds and then turned on his heel and left the room, closing the door behind him with exaggerated care.

Miss Witherspoon had some bad news for him. In making up his wages until the Tuesday, she had perforce to take off monies owing for pen, paper and wear and tear on the desk, not to mention expenses which had been blue-pencilled by the editor after payment. The four shilling coins she pressed into his hand were all she could manage, she said, smiling like a basilisk. Batchelor left the office hurriedly, in case she suddenly discovered that he was behind with the coal money. With what he had hidden under the carpet at Mrs Biggs', he had just three pounds, ten shillings and fourpence three farthings in the world. He squared his shoulders and walked out past his scribbling ex-colleagues with his head high. Once he was gone, every set of shoulders slumped. *There but for the grace of God* was the single thought in everybody's head. Joe Buckley, Ed Dyer – it could have happened to either of them. It could even have happened to Gabriel Horner – in fact, more so to him since he was Methuselah's elder brother. The sword had fallen and had got Damocles, also known as James Batchelor, right between the eyes.

In the doorway he met a small woman, dressed in deepest black, with a thick veil over her face. He held the door open for her.

'I believe you are waiting for me,' she said in a voice thick with tears. 'I was once in Washington . . .'

The rest of the sentence was drowned by the sound of stampeding journalists. James Batchelor closed the door on their hyena-howling and set off in search of the rest of his life.

SEVEN

The ironclad *Montauk* rode at anchor that Tuesday along the eastern branch of the Potomac. Guards posted at the gates of the Navy Yard saluted stiffly as Captain Grand passed them. In his hand, he carried the brief message from Lafayette Baker: '*Montauk*. Nine o'clock.' Not much of a conversationalist was Lafayette Baker. The soldier who'd brought the note was a corporal in the First District of Columbia Cavalry, and he'd waited while Grand washed, shaved and put on his full dress uniform. At least Baker hadn't broken into his room this time. Even so, the note was clearly not a serving suggestion.

The hull of the *Montauk* was battered and scarred, carrying the memories of her shelling of Confederate forts along the coast of Dixie and her clash with CSS *Nashville* two years earlier. She wore her wounds with pride, as befitted a warship of the bleeding United States that had been disunited for so long. At the gangplank Grand was obliged to hand over his Navy Colt and unhook his sabre. Today, whatever her past, the *Montauk* was a floating prison, and there were dangerous men on board.

One of them was watching Grand as he disappeared into the darkness of the hull. Luther Baker was lolling on the top rail, a pipe in his mouth and a coldness in his eyes. The investigation into Lincoln's assassination was going well, but he didn't like Matthew Grand. And he didn't trust him.

The blackness of the *Montauk*'s hold hit Grand like a wall, and he had to check himself against the planking of the hull. The steps took him down into more darkness, a sailor with a candle leading the way. 'Watch your step, sir,' was about all the man could offer by way of advice. They turned a corner at the end of a narrow passageway. The smell down here was revolting; tar and rope and gunpowder and the river all mingling to make Grand's gorge rise. He held on to himself, especially as candlelight was now helping to make sense of the scene. Between Grand and the flame, a huge black shape loomed – one of the *Montauk*'s massive twenty-four-pounders, the gun port closed and locked, the screw in position.

There was a rattle of chains, and Grand nearly fell over a pair of shackled feet. In the half light, he could make out a hooded figure slumped against the wooden wall with its iron ribs. Next to him was a second, shackled and hooded too, but bigger. His shoulders were huge, and even in his chained position he was a head taller than the other man.

'Good morning, Captain Grand.'

The voice made him turn. Lafayette Baker was sitting on a low stool, in his shirt sleeves, a bottle of rye and a half empty glass glinting in the candlelight. 'It's good of you to come.'

'I didn't feel I had a choice,' Grand said.

Baker ignored him and got to his feet. He reached down and hauled the canvas hood off the first man. 'Allow me to introduce,' he said, 'Lewis Thornton Powell, also known as Payne. He likes cutting throats, especially if they belong to Secretaries of State.'

Lewis Powell was Grand's age or a little younger. Unusually for those days, he was clean shaven, although his face was bruised and bloody. It took the man a while to acclimatize his eyes to the light, and he squinted up at Grand. *Another Federal uniform. Another officer. Was he supposed to be impressed? Or was this a specialist torturer Lafayette Baker had brought in to get the information he wanted?*

Baker wanted to know: 'Have you seen him before?'

Grand shook his head. 'Never,' he said.

Baker took another swig of rye. 'Mr Powell and I have been having a long chat,' he said, nursing his knuckles. 'He assures me he's a handyman who was hired to dig a drain at a house right here in Washington. The house of Mrs Mary Surratt. Know that name?'

Grand shook his head again.

'You're not much help this morning, Captain,' the detective said with a sigh.

'If you're asking did I see this man at Ford's, no, I didn't.'

'Oh, we know he wasn't there,' Baker said, putting his glass down and leaning back against a beam. 'Four days ago, while you were in the theatre, no doubt enjoying the play, Mr Powell here was knocking on the door of Secretary of State William Seward in Lafayette Square. He claimed to have medicine from Seward's doctor – you may or may not know the clumsy old bastard fell out of a gig earlier in the week. Then he forced his way in and fired his gun at Seward's boy, Fred.'

Baker leaned down to the prisoner. 'But that darned gun just wouldn't fire, would it? If I were you, Lewis, I'd send me a letter to Colonel Colt. Man's got a right to expect his weapon of choice to work, huh?' He slapped Powell across the face, and the big man winced, straining against his chains. Baker chuckled. 'The thing about old Sam Colt's guns is they've got a weight, haven't they? So Lewis here, he brains young Fred with the butt. He was all set to do the same to Fanny, Seward's daughter. She's a sweet kid; I've met her several times. Anyway, having been let down by Colonel Colt, friend Powell here takes refuge in Colonel Bowie, whips out his knife and stabs Seward himself.'

Baker leaned back again. He continued: 'Now, the rumour is that Mr Powell is slow-witted. Easily led. Poor boy, that wicked John Wilkes Booth worked on the lad and persuaded him that what he did was for his country's good.' The detective looked at Grand, the chill smile gone from his face. 'Well, I can tell you, Captain, that Lewis Powell is about as slow-witted as a rattler. But he did make one mistake – he assumed he'd done the job on Seward. Which is a shame for him, 'cos the old bastard's still alive, if not exactly well. And you still say you've never seen this man before?'

Grand nodded.

Baker threw the hood back over Powell's head and whipped the canvas away from the other one. 'What about this one?' he asked.

Grand looked at the second prisoner. He was older than Powell, with short brown hair and a straggly beard. Again the captain shook his head.

'You're sure?' Baker asked.

'I am,' Grand said and heard the detective laugh. It was not a sound many people heard.

'You know, you're like Peter the disciple,' the detective said. 'If I had a third conspirator here, no doubt you'd say you don't know him either. Denying three times before the rooster crows kinda makes me suspicious, Captain. Say hello to Edman Spangler.'

'Spangler?' Grand echoed.

'You know the name?' Baker watched the man intently.

'I've heard it,' Grand said. 'When I went back to Ford's after the shooting, I talked to a peanut seller . . .'

Baker nodded. 'John Burroughs.'

'Peanut John, yes,' Grand said. 'He mentioned Spangler. Said he was a stagehand who told Peanut to hold Booth's horse.'

'If only it was that simple,' Baker said. 'You see, Spangler here knows John Wilkes Booth pretty well. In fact, he's known him for the best part of five years. Mr Spangler has the habit of telling people around the theatre not to say which way Booth rode. Ain't that right, Edman?' He delivered a kick to the man's ribs, and the stagehand groaned. He had clearly received several of those in the last few hours.

Baker put the hood back over Spangler's head and motioned to a guard, half hidden in the shadows. 'Any conversation between these two,' he said, 'I want to know about it.' He beckoned Grand to him, and they made for the upper deck.

'You remember Cousin Luther.' Lafayette Baker had hauled on his tunic by the time they reached the deck, and the lanky detective nodded at Grand.

'Captain Grand.' Luther showed no inclination to shake the man's hand or to salute him.

All three men looked across the Navy Yard, with its cluster of masts and spars like a forest at the edge of the water. 'Yonder.' Lafayette pointed to the wooden bridge that crossed the Potomac. 'That's the way Booth went when he left you.'

'We didn't exactly part as friends,' Grand reminded him. He felt his temple, tender and puffy under the bruise. 'And I've still got a score to settle.'

'Settle it, then,' said Baker flatly.

'How?' Grand frowned.

'You see, what worries me a tad—' Lafayette motioned

Luther closer – 'is that you claimed a minute ago you didn't know our friends downstairs.'

'That's right,' Grand maintained.

'Now, that's odd.' Cousin Luther had opened his ubiquitous attaché case and produced the same inauguration photograph that he had shown Grand at the hotel. Lafayette tapped two faces at the bottom. 'That's Lewis Thornton Powell,' he said, 'and that's Edman Spangler. And you saw this photograph . . . what . . . thirty hours ago? You've got a short memory there, son.'

The detective was right, at least about the photograph. That was definitely Powell under the brim of the wideawake and that could well be Spangler in the derby standing next to him.

'I'd know this man again,' Grand insisted, pointing to the tall bearded individual standing to Powell's right.

'Well, I'm glad,' Lafayette said, handing the photograph back to his cousin, 'because I want you to find him.'

'Me?'

The chief of detectives nodded. 'We're burying the President tomorrow, Captain Grand. I assume you'll want to be there, pay your last respects?'

'Of course,' the captain said.

'Good. After that, you're going to England. There's a ship leaving New York on Friday.'

'England?' Grand repeated.

'You said the man you met in Baptist Alley had an English accent.'

'That's right.'

'And the chances are he wears English – specifically London – cufflinks. Kinda narrows down the options, don't you think?'

'London's the biggest city in the world, and, anyway, he could still be here in Washington,' Grand reasoned.

'He could,' Lafayette said, 'but the word's on the streets now. You've already met two of the conspirators, and we're catching more every day. If he's a Britisher, he'll be on his way home by now.'

'Canada?' Grand said, looking at all the options. 'Isn't that a possibility?'

'We've got Canada covered,' Luther said. 'If he turns up there, we'll know it.'

'I've got a fiancée,' Grand said. 'I'm in this man's army.'

'For the greater good.' Lafayette smiled. 'I'm sure your fiancée – Miss McKintyre, isn't it?'

Grand nodded; this man knew *everything*.

'She'll wait for you. And as for the army, well, there's two ways of looking at it. Catch the conspirator and they'll make you a general. Don't catch him and the war's over anyway. Hell, there are a lot of men who'll need a career change in the next few days.'

'What about expenses?' Grand asked.

'You'll be on my payroll,' Lafayette said. 'A National Detective in all but name. Money's no object – within reason. Besides, you've got kin in . . . where is it, Luther?'

'Hampstead,' his cousin said, 'a little village, they tell us, north of London.'

'I've never met them,' Grand said. It was no more than the truth.

'They might provide a bolt-hole for you. Or at least a cover. Tell them – tell anybody who asks – you've had a bad time in the war. You need to get away for the good of your health, let's say.'

There was a mysterious light in the man's eyes. Was this some sort of test, Grand wondered. Was Baker giving a potential suspect a chance to exonerate himself? It seemed an extraordinary risk, yet everything about these April days was extraordinary.

'Can I think about it?' the captain asked.

'I'll find you tomorrow,' Baker said, nodding. 'At the funeral. Let me know by then.'

And Grand took his leave.

The Bakers watched him go, collecting his weapons at the gangplank before crossing the yard. 'We've got him, Luther,' Lafayette said. 'Better make the arrangements. Oh . . . and let our friend know.'

James Batchelor was not a natural sleeper-in, and his three pounds, ten shillings and fourpence three farthings nest egg had not encouraged him to go out and drown his sorrows in drink. He had returned to his room at Mrs Biggs' and done some serious financial planning, costing food, rent and other expenses to see how long he could survive with what he had to hand. The final reckoning had made his mouth go dry and a strange high-pitched buzzing fill his ears. It appeared that he could either stay in his room at Mrs Biggs' house for another three weeks or eat. He had to think quickly and decide whether he wanted a roof over his head or something in his stomach. He hadn't led an easy life, he had never been rich or even well off, but he had never had to make that choice before. He got up as dawn was breaking and washed hurriedly, dressed and was about to clatter down the stairs when he saw Mrs Biggs appearing at the bottom and politely stood aside as she came up, carrying a pile of linen and puffing and blowing as usual.

'Mr B,' she gasped.

'Mrs B.' It was their little joke, and Batchelor's heart sank a little at the thought of leaving, as he feared he must.

'Your laundry,' she said, handing it over. 'I hope you don't mind—' she dropped her voice – 'I've had to charge a bit extra. The . . . stains . . . took some shifting.' She managed to leave an unspoken question dangling at the end of the sentence, which Batchelor studiously ignored.

He picked up a corner of the shirt and examined it. 'Lovely,' he said. 'White as snow. Could you put it in my room for me? I'm just off out.'

'Not at work, Mr B?'

Batchelor's heart jumped in his chest. Did he have some mark of Cain on his forehead? 'Late start today. Flower show.'

'That's early.'

'Um . . . spring cabbage, that kind of thing.'

She wrinkled her forehead. 'That will be hard to write about,' she offered. 'Quite boring, cabbages are.'

'They are, Mrs B, and that's why I must be away. There's a book all about them in the library at the paper, and I will have to do a bit of looking up.'

She patted him with her free hand, wrinkled with washing. 'You're so clever,' she murmured. She liked professional gents as a rule but you had to be careful with journalists because, say what you liked about them, they loved a drink. But young

Mr Batchelor was going places, that was plain, and a bit of blood on his shirt now and again she could overlook. And that reminded her – the pat turned to a finger in the buttonhole. 'As I said, Mr B—' she smiled up at him, her face like a kindly currant bun – 'it was extra.'

'Can you put it on my rent, Mrs B?' he asked. 'Only, I really must run if I'm to do my reading about cabbages.'

'I think I'll have to have it now, Mr B, if that's quite all right with you. I need to pay the girl; you know how it is with these rough girls, they won't wait.'

'No, I did not know that. How much would you like?' His heart was in his boots, but he couldn't see a way out.

'An extra shillun if you've got it, Mr B? I never worry about you owing me, you know that, but the girl . . .'

'I do understand.' Batchelor rummaged in his pocket and handed over a coin which, to him, represented a dinner he now couldn't have.

The woman pocketed it and squeezed past him to the door of his room. 'I'll just put this washing away for you, shall I?' she said, smiling.

'Thank you,' he said and watched her open the door. Every move struck him like a sting of hail; it might be the last time anyone ever did his laundry and put it away for him. He felt his mouth go dry again and swallowed hard. 'Those cabbages won't wait,' he said and clattered down the stairs and out into the street.

James Batchelor made his way home that evening dispirited and just a little poorer. He had eaten no breakfast and had known by twelve that that was a false economy – he had gone into an alehouse and bought a pie and a pint which he had devoured so fast that he had indigestion all afternoon and had spent more than he would have on two sensible meals. Live and learn, he told himself, live and learn; if he didn't die of starvation first. He had started along Fleet Street, presenting himself to editors of the newspapers whose offices lined the road on either side. He had started high – no harm in selling himself short – and ended up speaking to a rather odd gentleman who was doing preliminary work on a publication,

Boys of England, which he was hoping to launch shortly. After some time speaking at cross-purposes, he had declined to engage Batchelor, on the grounds that he was low on funds. If Batchelor would like to work for nothing, of course, or, better still, should he be of independent means . . . But the young man had turned him down and gone home wearily, having charmed a costerwoman to sell him a cabbage for a farthing, a trophy to take home to Mrs Biggs. Every little helped when worming a way to a landlady's heart, and at this rate, he would need a little goodwill before long.

The canal had never looked more dismal. It was grey, like the sky in the early morning, and it was the open sewer of Washington, the graveyard of 20,000 cats.

All night had come the sound of hammering from the East Room of the White House where an army of carpenters had been erecting the wooden steps and tiered seats that would give everyone a clear view of old Abe as he lay at rest. As the first weak rays of the sun gilded the Capitol, the Washington Monument and the cold columns of the Lee mansion, the cannon roared in the forts that circled the city as the gunners in their black armbands went through their paces in a land at peace. Then the bells rang out: all of the churches, with their solemn, sober peals, and the more hysterical clanging of the firehouses.

Answering a silent and invisible signal, the grey of the dawn became the bright sun of spring, without a single cloud to frown on the occasion. The magnolias, blooming early in Lafayette Square, fluttered with life, and the crowds now gathering picked the blossoms to strew on the coffin lid or to thread into their buttonholes. Everywhere was black – the crêpe and the ostrich feathers of mourning. Only the little children wore white, squinting up to the sun and not under-standing why their parents were crying. Some joined in, distressed and confused, and were hushed, pressed to shoulders shaking with grief. Not a shop was open, not a market stall.

The great and the good went in to the White House by numbered ticket; and the crowds along the route whispered to each other – 'there's Grant', 'that's Farragut' – and a few hats came off in respect as President Johnson entered ahead of his cabinet. William Seward was not there. The old man was still lying in his bed, his throat and chest bandaged, his family terrified, his heart broken. Nobody noticed Lafayette Baker and his cousin, with plainclothesmen from the District of Columbia Cavalry, mingling with the crowd. No one knew their hands never left the butts of their pistols all day. Or that their eyes were everywhere. No president would be left unguarded again.

Matthew Grand stood with a knot of other unattached officers along Pennsylvania Avenue. A much-needed leave had brought them all to the capital but their units were still in the field. Lee may have surrendered, but there were rednecks out there still, Johnny Rebs for whom the war would never be over. Across the broad street, on a raised platform, Grand could see the McKintyres, all in black, waiting with their friends.

The great guns boomed, each one taking up the echo until they stuttered into silence and the grim procession moved forward. Ahead of the tall hearse with its black drapes and huge, spindle-spoked wheels, a platoon of coloured soldiers marched proudly, the Stars and Stripes floating wide in the sun. Behind the hearse, Lincoln's horse caracoled and strutted, held fast by a White House groom. The flags and the strange silence of the crowd clearly unnerved the animal, as it tossed its head and snorted. The President's goatskin boots were reversed in the stirrups, and men wept as they remembered old Abe in the saddle, riding in that curious lanky way of his, with his top hat tilted back.

Then came Robert Lincoln and Tad, his little brother, trying not to cry, in an open carriage. Men's hats came off as they passed, and women felt their own motherhood and sobbed into their handkerchiefs, for the sorrow of all fatherless children everywhere. They were otherwise silent, like the forty-abreast Negroes, stretching from curb to curb across the Avenue. Old men who had been born slaves and had lived to see the year of Jubilee. Old women, bowed down with toil in the fields. Children, large-eyed and white toothed. And free. All were dressed in their Sunday best, although it was Wednesday.

The muffled drums of the infantry kept the pace, agonizingly slow, achingly final as they saw Abe Lincoln home. As the hearse reached Grand's position, he drew his sword, saluted the six white horses and their sad load with a flourish. The others around him followed suit, and there was the flash of the sun on their blades. Later, they would all swear that a new star, never before seen, rose above the gleaming white of the newly finished Senate building. And they would all say that no thrushes sang for a full year after they buried Lincoln.

After he had passed, the crowd stayed, silent and still. They had seen it, they had heard it, but they didn't want to believe it. That he was dead and laid in the grave and had left them alone to face a future that didn't seem so rosy any more. Then slowly, one by one, heads low, tears still drying on their cheeks, they made their way from that sad place, until all that was left was a flurry of fallen magnolia and the echo of a distant drum.

EIGHT

Matthew Grand stood on the top step of the McKintyre house in Eighth Street, automatically polishing each boot on the calf of the opposite leg, flattening his hair into place and tugging his jacket into line. He hitched his shoulders and placed the bouquet of flowers front and central. This wasn't going to be the easiest conversation he had ever had with Arlette, but whatever else she would have to complain about, it wasn't going to be his appearance. He rang the bell and took a step back. The McKintyre household did sport some staff who knew how to open the door, but if it was Bella, Arlette's old nurse, who got there first, he knew he would be dragged in, hugged and generally mussed about before he ever got within a spit of his fiancée so he took precautions.

'Sir?'

Grand expelled a breath. It was the butler. Still prone to the odd cuss when he dripped soup on the cloth, he nevertheless didn't go in for too much hugging. The man stepped aside and let Grand in, closing the door silently behind him.

'Miss Arlette,' Grand said, when no one seemed to be going anywhere fast.

'I will see if Miss Arlette is at home, sir,' the butler intoned. 'The household is in mourning.'

'Aren't we all,' Grand muttered, but raised his head with a stoic half smile and looked at the man. Louder, he said, 'I do understand. But this is important; if you could ask her to see me, please?'

The butler walked away without a backward glance. He did like Captain Grand – so polite always. Not like that spoiled little madam he was planning to marry. On soft feet he paced along the hallway and opened a door. 'Captain Grand, madam. Are you at home?'

He was answered by a flurry of female voices, some seemingly at odds with the others, but eventually, getting the gist of the comments, he withdrew, closing the door behind him; but the oak, stout as it was, was no match for the shrillness reaching fever pitch beyond it.

Grand watched the flannel-footed butler step carefully back down the hall. He wondered idly if the man ever hurried, if his expression ever changed.

'Miss Arlette is not at home, Captain Grand,' he said, bowing slightly from the hips. 'If you would like to leave your card . . .?' He held out his hand and waited.

Grand was a little disconcerted. He had not expected this response, and there was no time to plan another visit before he would have to be away. But before he could answer or give the butler a note, the door down the hall swung open and then slammed shut, with Arlette on Grand's side of it. The twitters from the room reached a crescendo and then died away. Arlette turned and, with a wriggle to rearrange herself and a toss of her curls, she launched herself at Grand, nearly bowling the butler over. He turned away, deadpan. 'Call me a liar,' he muttered as he went through the green baize door to where sanity ruled.

Grand staggered a little as Arlette clasped him round the waist and buried her head against his chest. 'Matthew,' she whispered. 'Where have you been? I was so worried.'

'No need to worry,' he said, grasping her shoulders and pulling her away from his best uniform jacket. 'I wasn't sure whether you'd see me.'

'We're in mourning,' she said, sulkily.

'Well, of course,' Grand agreed. 'But . . . I wasn't sure how things were between us, after . . .'

'I was upset.' She stamped her foot and shook her curls. Grand couldn't help thinking that perhaps she was getting a little old for that. He pushed the unworthy thought to the back of his mind. 'Then . . . well, Aunt and Mama have been fretting. They weren't sure what was happening, you running off like that, anything could have happened.' She clasped her hands under her chin and looked up at him. 'Matt, I do love you. Let's get married now, this week. There's no need to wait.'

Grand cleared his throat. 'I've got to go away, Arlette,' he said. He couldn't wrap it up, it wouldn't be fair.

She stepped back and put her hands to her hips. Her voice dropped low and threatening. 'You've got to do *what*?' she snarled. You could criticize Arlette McKintyre for a lot of things, but you could never say she was boring. The girl was as changeable as a pennant in a hurricane.

'I have to go away,' he repeated. 'It's on urgent business, and I'm not sure where I'm going or when I'll be back. If I *get* back,' he said, hoping to raise some sympathy. 'It might be dangerous work.'

'Dangerous?' she said, tossing her head. 'You've just been in a war, Matthew. You never made too much of that being *dangerous*. What can be so *dangerous* now?'

'I can't say,' Grand said, miserably. He had hoped things would go smoother than this, that he could get away without a scene, that he could sail away to do God knew what and write a few letters to the girl back home and then come back and marry her or not, as the cards fell. But it looked as if Arlette had other plans.

'So,' she said, closing her mouth with a snap. 'You can't say what you're doing, or where? Can you tell me when?'

'Later today,' he said, quietly.

'Oh, later today. Well,' she said, tugging at the ring, which didn't seem to want to leave her finger. 'In that case, Mr Grand, you must excuse me. With all the shops shut, I only have one thing on hand to give you as a present to wish you bon voyage.' Her ring came free, and she threw it at him. It missed by a mile and pinged off a piece of her grandmother's silver, displayed on the hall table to collect visiting cards. 'It went over there.' She pointed to a dark corner. 'You'd better fish for it; you'll need it for the next poor gullible fool who you manage to convince you want to marry. Now—' and she spun on her heel – 'good day to you, Mr Grand.' And she stamped along the hall and slammed back in through the drawing room door, to be greeted with cries and wails from the women inside.

Grand stood there, perplexed. He had expected a few tears, perhaps the exchange of a little memento to remind them of each other. This storm had come as a bit of a surprise, though he knew Arlette to be possessed of a temper worthy of the worst shrew in the state. He was still standing there when the butler reappeared and walked past him to open the front door. The butler stood there silently, holding it open, and Grand eventually got the message and left the house. As the butler closed the door, he muttered something to Grand.

'I'm sorry,' Grand said, shaking his head. 'I don't think I quite . . .'

'I said,' the butler repeated, slightly louder, 'congratulations, sir.' He smiled his wintry smile.

'Oh, no . . .' Then Grand saw the butler's eyelid close in a slow and conspiratorial wink. 'Oh, I see. Yes.' He smiled a beaming smile to thaw the butler's own. 'Thank you. Congratulations indeed.' And with a lighter heart, Matthew Grand turned and almost trotted down the street, giving his by now somewhat battered bouquet to a puzzled lady waiting to cross the road.

The *City of Manchester* was the pride of Inman's Line. An iron-hulled steamer with four masts and a single smoke stack, her monstrous boilers powered engines of 400 horsepower that shuddered and growled as the ship left harbour on the Friday.

Matthew Grand looked up at the spars overhead and the scudding clouds above them. The sails were furled, and hopefully, if the engines behaved, there would be no need of canvas on this journey. The tug *Fury* had signalled its farewell, and the *Manchester* cut through the water past Castle Clinton, the little stone fort that was the immigrant station for Manhattan Island. God alone knew how many huddled masses had passed through those gates in the past four years; Irishmen fleeing the poverty of their wretched country, Germans looking for a brave new world, everybody in search of El Dorado. Many of the men had ended up in Yankee blue uniforms, lured by the promise of the $1,000 reward. Others had drifted South, to put on Confederate Grey. Some of them had not lived out their first week.

Manhattan grew small until it was a grey ghost floating on the edge of an April ocean. There was no hint of spring in the wind, much less of the first summer of peace. The slaves were free and the war was over. But could anyone just start again, as if the whole thing had never happened? Grand watched his native land fade to nothing on the horizon.

'I know you.'

The voice made him turn. On the deck ahead stood a plump man with a large nose and heavy moustache. 'Do you?' Grand asked. He knew the man too but had no wish to renew their acquaintanceship.

'I'm George Sala.' The man held out a hand. '*Telegraph*.'

Grand looked at him.

'It's a London newspaper,' Sala explained. 'I've been covering the war.'

Grand shook the still-extended hand. 'So have I,' he said, straight faced.

'You're Miss Keene's . . . friend,' Sala said. 'When we last met you were in uniform.'

'Third Cavalry of the Potomac,' Grand said.

'Ah, the Red Tie Boys,' Sala said, beaming. 'It is an honour, sir. May I know your name?'

'Grand,' he told him. 'Matthew Grand.'

'Ah, a captain, if memory serves?'

'That was then,' Grand said. 'I've resigned my commission. It's just plain Mr now.'

'Hm.' Sala fished out an expensive cigar case from his pocket. 'Havana? They were giving them away like confetti at Delmonico's last night – I couldn't resist.'

Grand knew he had fourteen days in this man's company whether he liked it or not. They'd be sharing meal tables, walking the same deck. He might as well make the best of it, so he took a cigar.

'Capital ship, this, isn't it?' Sala struck a lucifer for them both. 'I came out on some clipper full of Irish. My editor said I needed to rough it, find the real America.'

'And did you?' Grand blew smoke to the rigging.

'Shiloh. Antietam. Vicksburg.' Sala reeled off the battles he had seen. Battles where men advanced shoulder to shoulder in open country, ripped down by the staccato rhythm of the Gatlings and the roar of the twelve pounders. 'You tell me.'

Grand nodded solemnly. 'Oh, yes,' he said. 'That's the real America all right.'

'Do you know England?' Sala asked. 'Been before?'

'No,' Grand said, glad that the subject had changed. 'No,

I'm looking forward to it.' He caught an odd look on George Sala's face. 'Can it be that different from the States?'

For a moment, Sala looked at him. Then he burst out laughing. 'My dear boy,' he said with a chuckle. 'You have absolutely no idea.'

In the nights, Matthew Grand saw him again, the tall man in the wideawake and the duster coat, the skulker in the alley, the smiler with the knife. As the *City of Manchester* lurched and rolled in the Atlantic breakers and the engines thudded their monotonous rhythm, John Wilkes Booth held up his knife, the blade dripping with Henry Rathbone's blood. '*Sic semper tyrannis*' boomed around the cabin, glancing off the hatches and the creaking lifeboats before dying away over the darkening waves. Over it all, Grand heard his elusive quarry laughing, although he had never heard him laugh, and repeat, over and over again, 'The Devil is with him. The Devil. The Devil.'

And when he woke, it took him several minutes to prove to himself that he was alone.

The offices of Messrs Inman stood in a square near the docks that seemed to stretch for miles, and as soon as Matthew Grand had booked into the American Hotel and had his luggage stashed there, he was standing at a counter looking at a jovial clerk who was only too happy to help his American cousin. Jovial clerks, however, had learned to be circumspect over the last four years. Who knew what colours a visitor might wear? Was he blue or was he grey? Lancashire itself had declared for the blue long ago, but cotton, its lifeblood, came from the grey, from the blockaded ports of the South, and times were hard. A third of Liverpool's trade was with America, and people were starving in Manchester.

'Welcome to Liverpool, sir,' the clerk said, beaming. Keep it light. Keep it general.

'I'd like to see the manifest,' Grand said, barely acknowledging the greeting, 'of the *Orient*.'

'The *Orient*, sir?' The clerk frowned.

'Your ship,' Grand said. 'The one that arrived two days ago. It's in the harbour now.'

'Indeed it is, sir,' the clerk agreed, taking off his pince-nez and wiping the lenses. He didn't need to look out of the grimy windows to recognize the ship's double smoke-stack beyond the cotton warehouses. 'But I'm afraid the manifest is confidential.'

Grand took a different tack. Perhaps he'd been too brusque, too determined to find the man he was looking for. 'A friend of mine,' he said, 'may have been travelling on the *Orient*. I promised to look him up when I got to Liverpool.'

'I'd like to help, sir,' the clerk said, his voice trailing away, 'but . . .'

Grand rummaged in his pocket and pulled out a roll of notes. 'I only have dollars,' he said.

The clerk's face broadened into a grin. 'That's perfectly all right, sir. Four of those, I understand, make up an English pound. And—' he became confidential, leaning forward over the counter – 'if I may say so, I'm glad they're not those confounded Confederate dollars. Worthless as of last week.'

'So.' Grand smiled, humouring the idiot. 'The manifest?'

'Oh, I can't give you that, sir.' The clerk frowned, suddenly a model of rectitude. 'It's against company policy.'

'But, I . . .' Grand spluttered, watching his dollars disappear into the man's inside pocket.

'I can't give you the passenger list,' the clerk said, 'but I can tell you where to find it. Inman and Co's headquarters, Leadenhall Street, in the City of London.'

Grand took a brief breath, fighting down the urge to knock this man through the wall. 'And will I have to go through this ritual all over again?' he asked. 'Parting with yet more money?'

'As I said, sir.' The clerk beamed again. 'Welcome to Liverpool.'

One of them swayed in the shadows, drunk. She was . . . what? Eighteen? Nineteen? The age was right. And the colour of the hair. Almost the colour of corn. But suddenly, there was a clatter of boots on the cobbles and a flash of scarlet. He vaguely knew the uniform – the fusiliers from the Tower. Three stripes on his arm. *Perhaps* the interloper could afford her. Anyway, the moment had gone.

He turned the corner into the Haymarket, watching. Always watching. It was the small hours now, and the theatre crowds had gone home. He ducked into the darkness. A peeler, in that ridiculous Roman helmet they all had to wear nowadays. He checked his half-hunter. Quarter past one. He knew their routines, Peel's raw lobsters, the clueless boys in blue. The copper would saunter down this side of the street, relying on the gaslight to see by. He would check the locks and the window sashes, rattle the gates on the railings, move on the sleeping drunks. Then he would cross the road, walking north at that steady two and a half miles an hour. How bloody predictable. You could set your watch by them. And how lucky for him.

There was another girl, younger, prettier than the first. He felt his heart pounding in his chest, his lips brick dry. And he was still watching her when a face filled his vision.

''Ello, ducks,' the face said. 'Looking for company?'

He took this one in immediately. She was probably only in her mid-twenties but could have been any age. Her lips were bright crimson in the gaslight, and her cheeks were rouge-red. She was a park woman, at the bottom of the heap of ladies of her calling, the most unfortunate of unfortunates. This was not her usual stamping ground, he knew that.

'No,' he growled at her. 'Go away.'

The woman was not used to that kind of response, not at the dead of night. Not from a well-set-up young man. It was a Music Hall joke that men only wanted one thing, but in her line of work, she knew it was true.

'You can have a feel right here,' she said, hauling up her tattered dress with a waft of something unspeakable mixed with the cheapest of cheap perfumes. 'Won't cost you nothing.'

His instinct was to hit her, send her sprawling in the gutter where she belonged. But she might scream, and then the copper on the far side of the street would come running, shaking his rattle to summon assistance. And he didn't need assistance for what he was going to do. He closed his face to hers. 'I told you, no,' he said, and he brushed past her.

The theatre stood in darkness now the night's show was over. Her torrent of abuse was still ringing in his ears as he walked briskly past its classical columns, plastered with the current bill of fare. The Great Maskelyne was on his way to stun the gasping crowd with his magic at the Alhambra next week. But *he* had magic of his own, the tight coil of wire in his pocket, and he cradled it again in the palm of his hand as he walked north.

There she was again – the one he had seen a moment ago. The one with the golden hair. Was this fate? That she had not gone, vanished into the blackness of the London night? Or was it her destiny to wait for him, inviting the caress of the coil of wire, biting like fire and ice into the flesh of her neck? He checked the copper behind him, too far away to come to her aid. He had to be careful, of course; take her into some dark alley, move quickly. There'd be no sound. He'd fumbled it once before, and the girl had screamed. But he'd heard no more about that. There was nothing in the papers. No knock at his door. Girls like these put up with a bit of rough – it was all in a night's work.

He walked up to her, confident, alert, ready. They both knew how this worked.

'Hello, dearie,' she purred. 'Lonesome tonight?'

'How much?' he asked her, his voice a hoarse whisper now the moment was here.

'Depends on what you want.'

'I want to tail you,' he told her.

'What, just like that?' she trilled. 'Ain't you the gentleman! No supper? No hotel?'

He looked her up and down. The girl was far above the park harlot he had just escaped from. Her dress was velvet with a tight bodice and lace-trimmed sleeves. Her golden hair was piled high under a jaunty cap with feathers, and cheap jewellery flashed from her fingers and at her throat, the throat he was about to cut with his wire.

'I don't have time,' he said.

'Oh dear.' She closed to him, resting her hand on his arm, making, as was expected, the first move. 'Disappointed earlier, were you? Caught in the act? I know,' she soothed. 'Annoying, ain't it? Well—' for a moment she pouted – 'I wouldn't normally let you do me out here. Auntie Bettie would *not* approve.' She ran a hand over his crotch. 'But I can see you're an impatient sort. So . . .'

She let him slide her round the corner of the theatre into an alleyway that led to a backyard. He took her hand and drew her further into the shadows, away from the Haymarket and the patrolling constable and whatever life she had known. He took her away from all that she held dear.

'That'll be half a crown,' she said, her voice hard now that she was talking business. He flipped her the coin and let her unbutton his flies. She moved her hand quickly up and down, smiling, looking up into his face, 'There, now,' she said. 'That's better, isn't it?'

'I haven't paid half a crown for this,' he said.

She spun round, legs splayed and hauled her skirts up over her back. There were no drawers, nothing in the way. But it wasn't her arse he was interested in. She felt his fingers, iron hard in her hair as he jerked her upright. Then there was something cold and sharp around her neck. Her hands came up, fluttering, helpless and her eyes bulged in the blackness. He twisted the loop as tight as he could, using both hands now to help him, and he felt her warm blood spurt over his knuckles as she sank forwards. He kept her upright, bending his back and supporting her weight on his. He heard her boots scrabble on the cobbles, once, twice. Then stillness. Silence. And a dead weight in the Haymarket night.

He looked up the alleyway. Across the street, the copper was checking locks, blissfully unaware as yet that another girl had died on his patch. In the alleyway, he wiped the wire on the girl's dress and slipped it away. He fished in her pocket for his half crown and took it back. No more. No less. He wasn't a thief, after all. He stood up and remembered just in time to do up his flies; this was Victoria's England, when all was said and done, and he had a certain reputation. People might talk.

NINE

Thornton Leigh Hunt was not having the best of mornings. George Sala was back at the *Telegraph*, behaving like royalty as usual, swanning into the paper's offices and carrying out a progress. Yes, he was telling everybody, a knighthood was definitely on the cards. If only someone could persuade the queen out of her self-imposed reclusion, the old trout would be tapping his shoulder with her blade any moment. *Sir* George Sala – yes, he liked the way that rolled out.

His editor did not like it. And it was brought home forcefully just how peaceful it had all been while Sala had been in the theatre of war. Stories were coming in thick and fast but all Leigh Hunt had time to do now was to prepare for the wretched homecoming banquet which, in a weak moment, he had promised to throw for the returning hero. And if he was not careful, other papers would grab the headlines.

'Another murder,' he said to the outer office in general, 'in the Haymarket. Who was on that? The first one, I mean?'

'Er . . .' Edwin Dyer's old man had once told him never to volunteer, but he was perilously close to it now.

'No, it wasn't you.' Leigh Hunt was sure about that. 'Buckley? You were there, weren't you? When this Effie Thing died?'

'We both were, sir.' Joe Buckley stood up like a sacrificial lamb. Everybody knew that when Thornton Leigh Hunt snapped his fingers, everybody jumped.

'But it was Jim Batchelor who found her, sir,' Dyer said, trying to get his friend off the hook.

'Who?' For a moment, the cub reporters could not be entirely sure whether their lord and master was being ironic or whether he had already consigned James Batchelor to the wastepaper basket of newspaper history.

'I wasn't *too* far away, TLH.' Gabriel Horner peered over his pince-nez at the man, willing his old eyes to focus.

'No,' said Leigh Hunt on a sigh. 'You never are. I want you on the International Exhibition. And what about the Richard Cobden obituary? The man's been dead for a month.'

The old man beamed. 'Working on it, TLH.'

'You two,' the editor snapped. 'My office.'

They stood on Leigh Hunt's carpet like naughty boys in front of the headmaster. 'TLH indeed,' the great man muttered. 'Learn nothing from old Gabriel, gentlemen; he is a dinosaur. Now, to business. What do we know about the second murder?'

Dyer and Buckley looked at each other. 'Not a lot, sir,' Buckley ventured. 'It only happened last night.'

'The girl may still be stiff and stark,' Leigh Hunt agreed. 'All the more reason to move swiftly. This is C division again, so our friend Inspector Tanner is bound to be called in. Either of you know him?'

'No, sir,' they chorused.

'Right. Buckley. Get yourself over to the Yard. Find out what Tanner knows. I don't want *The Times* stealing this one from us. Or, God forbid, the *Ebullient*. Dyer – scene of crime.'

'Er . . . where is that, sir?'

'Well, I don't know, man. I didn't kill the wretched girl. Find out. You're supposed to be a journalist. Ask some questions. Knock on a few doors. And gentlemen . . . keep your hands in your pockets. The *Telegraph* isn't made of money, and some of those coppers don't get out of bed for less than a fiver.'

Buckley and Dyer found themselves out in the bustle of Fleet Street before they could so much as sharpen a pencil. They adjusted their hats to a more rakish, journalistic angle and checked in their pockets for notepads – to take down the golden prose of Inspector Tanner in the case of Buckley, and to make lightning sketches of the mise en scène in the case of Dyer.

Dyer broke the impasse. 'Right, then. I'll be off to the Haymarket, shall I?' He turned away.

'Is that strictly the right direction?' Buckley asked, tossing his head. 'Isn't the Haymarket more over there?'

'Possibly, possibly,' Dyer hedged. He had been born within yards of Fleet Street and knew the city like the back of his hand. He had hoped to fool Buckley, a country boy come up to make his fortune, but no luck this time. 'I was thinking of finding something to eat first. Oh . . .' He patted his pockets dramatically. 'I don't have a pencil with me. There's one on my desk. I'll just go back and get it. See you later.' And he dived back through the double doors of the *Telegraph* offices and disappeared from view.

'Pencil!' snorted Buckley as he turned his steps towards Scotland Yard. 'Pencil, indeed!' He wasn't looking forward to this assignment. He was essentially a desk journalist by inclination, rewriting the execrable prose of lesser men. When a multi-syllabic word was required, Buckley was your man, the whole office were agreed on that. When you wanted something pithy, attention grabbing and mostly inaccurate, it was Dyer. For something to be delivered six weeks after the deadline, Gabriel Horner was definitely the man to seek out. James Batchelor had been a good all-rounder, but James Batchelor was on the scrap heap; no one mentioned him these days, and his seat was hardly cold. Buckley squared his shoulders and set off for Scotland Yard. Half an hour should do it, straight down Fleet Street and then the Strand, but his feet weren't in it any more than his heart and so it was anyone's guess when he would get there. Perhaps the famous Inspector Tanner wouldn't be available; that would be the best outcome. Buckley looked moodily at his feet as he ambled away, out of his circle of comfort, heading west.

James Batchelor was counting his increasingly meagre store of money when there was a tap on the door, swiftly followed by the dragging noise of that same door over the thin rug he had spread in front of it to try and stop draughts. He turned, scooping the coins and one screwed-up note into his pocket as he did so.

'Mrs B,' he said, beaming. 'Hello.'

'I wasn't expecting you to be here, Mr Batchelor,' she said, and the unwonted formality made the hairs prickle on the ex-journalist's neck.

He sniffed extravagantly. 'I have rather a bad cold, Mrs Biggs,' he said, matching surname for surname. 'I thought

I had better stay at home for a while until it has passed. I sent a note with some urchin; I hope they received it at the office.'

She narrowed her eyes at him. 'I was wondering if perhaps you had lost your position, Mr Batchelor,' she said and folded her arms under her substantial frontage.

'No, no, Mrs Biggs.' He managed a hollow laugh. 'I'm one of the *Telegraph*'s star reporters. They would never let me go.'

She didn't speak for a moment, but when she did it was to utter words to make his blood run cold. 'I was wondering when you might be able to let me have some rent, Mr Batchelor,' she said.

He rummaged in his pocket, showing willing as best he could. 'How much is owing, Mrs Biggs?' he asked, trying to sound casual. 'This cold—' with another wet sniff – 'has rather addled my brain.'

'Ten shillings,' she said, and he rummaged some more. That wasn't as bad as it might have been. 'That's the arrears. With this week's on top – and you know I don't usually ask for rent in advance from my better gentlemen, Mr Batchelor, but you *have* let things slide – that makes fifteen shillings. It would oblige me if you could pay in full. These rooms are very sought after, as you know.'

He pushed coins around in his hand, trying to make the right money. Finally, it came to fifteen shillings, and he handed it over. With the pound note and few remaining coins in his pocket, his total worth had now shrunk to around just less than twice the amount he had handed over. His money was trickling away even faster than he had forecast.

His landlady secreted the money so quickly that Batchelor had no idea where it went. A thought rushed through his mind that he had once heard that Edwin Dyer never paid rent, simply seducing landlady after landlady for free lodgings before moving on when his charms grew stale or they wanted to come to a more permanent arrangement. He asked himself if he could ever do that and came up with a resounding: 'No!' But Mrs Biggs was asking him something.

'Pardon me, Mrs Biggs?'

'I was asking, will you be able to manage the rent next

week, Mr Batchelor? With your having been off from your
office, and all. I do have a waiting list, you know. This is a
very respectable house and—'

'Mr Leigh Hunt thinks the world of me, Mrs Biggs.'
Batchelor was on his dignity now. 'He will pay me in absentia.'

'I don't really care where he pays you,' his landlady said,
turning to the door. 'As long as I get my rent.'

She swept out, and Batchelor could have kicked himself.
He could see himself being given the keys to the street at any
moment, and he hadn't even had the wit to leave with arrears
owing. He was an idiot, and more than that, he was a destitute
idiot. Or, in twenty-six shillings' time he would be. There
were more feet on the stairs and another tap on the door.
Dyer's head poked round.

'Anyone at home? I gather from your landlady you have a
cold in the head.'

'Dyer?' Batchelor jumped up off the bed and went forward,
grabbing the man's hand. 'Are you here from the office?'

'Yes and no,' Dyer said, sitting on the room's only chair.

Batchelor looked at the man and didn't speak. Dyer was not
his favourite person, and he was sure the feeling was mutual.
He decided that he could wait until Dyer chose to say why he
was there.

'I'm after a favour, James,' Dyer eventually said.

'I'm not in a position to lend you any money,' Batchelor
said, shortly. How typical of Dyer to ask for a loan when he
had nothing to his name.

'I am in a position to give you some, though,' Dyer said,
shoving a hand into a trouser pocket and coming up with a
tightly folded five-pound note. Batchelor had to restrain himself
from grabbing it. 'All I need is a little work from you, off the
record, we might say. There was a murder in the Haymarket
last night . . .'

'Another one?' Batchelor was aghast.

'Yes, another one.' Dyer could tell this might be hard work
after all. 'Hunt has sent me and Buckley off to look into it
but . . . I won't beat about the bush, James, it doesn't suit me,
this kind of work. I thought you could do my bit. Look around
the scene of crime, talk to people. You're good at that. The

common touch, you might say. Then you could write it up and give the copy to me to file. What do you say?'

Batchelor wanted to pace the room awhile, pulling his lip thoughtfully before turning the lazy bastard down. But this was not the time for niceties. 'I'll do it,' he said.

Dyer pocketed the banknote. 'Wonderful.' He jumped to his feet. 'Well, I must be going. If you could send the copy round this afternoon that would—'

'Money up front,' Batchelor said quietly. He knew Dyer of old.

'Oh, I don't think so, old chap. Money on delivery.'

'No delivery, then,' Batchelor said. 'I must have the money up front. There will be expenses, you know.'

Dyer stood, irresolute. He really didn't want to do this job. On the other hand, he really didn't want to part with the fiver. With the couple of hours this bought him, he could nip back to his lodgings and give his landlady a treat – that should buy him a few more weeks; the woman was old and ugly but she was getting restive. A little spontaneity would stand him in good stead. He took out the note again. 'All right,' he said. 'Don't let me down, now.'

'I won't,' Batchelor promised, pocketing the cash. 'I'll have five hundred words with you this afternoon.'

Dyer opened the door and turned. 'By the way, your landlady . . .?' He raised an eyebrow.

'No!' Batchelor was quick to disabuse him. 'I just pay my rent.'

Dyer shook his head and clicked his teeth. 'What a waste,' he said. 'You should use the equipment God gave you and then you wouldn't be desperate for money. Must go. Make sure you don't let me down.'

Batchelor heard him slam the street door and sat down on the bed, in shock and relief. Some time. He had bought some time. And all for doing a job of work that would have earned him a few shillings when he worked for the *Telegraph*. If Dyer wanted to throw his money away, who was he to stop him? He pulled out his penknife and sharpened his pencil. On the hunt for a story; it was what he did best.

TEN

Batchelor was hunched over on the bed, drafting his story. He hadn't been to the scene of the crime yet. In his experience, it never paid to go out without planning what you wanted to hear from eye witnesses – they were all just as likely as he was to make it up anyway. So the bare bones were there – the sad unfortunate, separated from life so cheaply; the eye witnesses, shy and frightened, being persuaded by the journalist to part with their scraps of information. The City of Eternal Night. The Modern Gomorrah. Oh, yes; he hadn't lost his touch.

Again, he heard footfalls on the stairs. Again, there was a tap on the door.

'It's not done yet,' he called, folding the paper over.

'What's not done?' Buckley's voice came from the doorway.

'Oh, it's you, Buckley. Nothing. Nothing. Just a little something I was writing for one of my fellow lodgers.' Batchelor sat firmly on the paper. 'Can I help you somehow?'

Buckley sat down on the only chair. 'I wonder if you could do me a favour, Batchelor?' he said. He held up a hand. 'Not money. No, not a loan, more of a job. Subcontracted, as it were.'

'A job?'

'Yes. I don't expect you will have heard, but there was a murder in the Haymarket last night. Hunt has sent me and Dyer off to cover it, but to be quite frank with you, it isn't really my cup of tea. I went to Scotland Yard but the man who seems to be dealing with the murders . . .'

'Inspector Tanner.'

'That's the chap. Well, he didn't seem to be there and . . . well, I wondered . . . after your little bit of trouble, you probably met him, that kind of thing. So, I thought that you might like to pursue the story, so to speak.'

Batchelor's expression hadn't changed, and Buckley rushed on with his explanation. 'For money, of course.'

'Up front,' Batchelor said. Best not to have any complications later.

'Oh? Oh. Well, yes, of course. I thought three pounds.'

'Five.'

'Five?'

'It's the going rate. For freelance work.'

'Is it? Freelance work seems exceedingly well paid if you don't mind my saying so. Well, five pounds it is.' He searched in his pocket. 'Do you mind coins?'

'Not at all.' Batchelor wouldn't have minded farthings at this juncture. 'So, you want me to go and interview Tanner. Do you want me to write the article for you or just make notes?'

'Oh, write it up.' Buckley suddenly remembered their differing styles. 'Leave it a bit short, so I can put in some long words.'

'I certainly will,' Batchelor said with a smile. 'It wouldn't be a Buckley piece without some nice long words, now, would it?'

Buckley smiled back, unsure whether mock was being made or not. He got up and dusted his jacket down with his pocket handkerchief. 'Nice place you have here,' he said, politely.

'I like it,' Batchelor said, seeing him to the door.

'I don't need to tell you,' Buckley said, out of the corner of his mouth, 'that this is strictly confidential.'

'Naturally. I will send the copy round with a lad later today.'

'I look forward to it.' Buckley took the stairs circumspectly, skirting Mrs Biggs looming at the bottom. 'I'm sure I will be seeing you around, Batchelor. Goodbye.' And with a slam of the door, he was gone.

George Sala was right – Matthew Grand had never seen a city like London. And he had never seen so many people in one place before, except perhaps on a battlefield. But battlefields were different, surreal, other-worldly places where skylarks still sang over the thunder of the guns. Here, the crescendo of noise came from the rattle and clatter of the drays, the coal wagons, the haywains; from the roar and whistle of the locomotives on their viaducts and the laughter and chatter of the

crowds, punctuated by the cries and squawks of the street
vendors.

There were no muddy streets here, no roads called by
numbers or letters; just an interminable rabbit warren that
went on and on. Flower sellers pressed their lucky heather
on Matthew Grand. Grubby men offered to polish his boots.
Ragged urchins cadged his coppers. He was everybody's
friend in this city of strangers—

''Ello, mate!'

'Buy a flower, darlin'!'

—and he didn't even want to think what delicacies they
were offering him. The roasting chestnuts looked just about
edible, but eels and mash he would leave alone.

A growler took him to the foot of Ludgate Hill, and he saw
the great dome of St Paul's rise ahead like a sunlit good deed
in the naughty dark world below it.

The cabbie leaned down to tell him, 'It's solid up ahead,
guv'nor. Best walk from here. Straight on. About half a mile.'

It was solid indeed. A cab horse had died in its traces,
blocking the road, and the traffic had come to a standstill.
Cabbies snarled and bellowed at each other, horses whinnied
and shied. If Grand heard it once, he heard it a dozen times
– 'Why ain't there a copper about when you need one?'

The corpses of cattle and pigs hung from the pigeon-haunted
rafters of Leadenhall Market, and live chickens clucked and
fretted in their baskets until a cook or serving maid selected
one and it was silenced and stilled by the poulterer's cleaver.
Blood trickled in the runs built into the sloping floor and ended
in the gutter. Children played there, dabbling their fingers in it
and darkening their faces like the drunk and defeated Seminole
Indians Grand remembered in the county fairs of his childhood.
They took no notice of the tall American in the wideawake
striding through the offal on his way to destiny. Somewhere in
these streets, Grand hoped . . . Grand *knew*, a conspirator was
lurking; the man he had come three thousand miles to find.

'The manifest?' Inman and Company's clerk was a weaselly
little man, his skin a parchment yellow like the pages of his
ledgers. 'I'm sorry, sir, but I'm not at liberty to give out information of that nature.'

The note was in Grand's fist before the clerk had finished his sentence.

'On the other hand—' Inman's man took the money and hauled open the ledger in one almost seamless movement – 'what did you say your friend's name was?'

'I didn't,' Grand said, a second note in his hand.

The clerk smiled, took the captain's offering and spun the ledger to him. There they were, the thirty-eight passengers who had sailed from New York on the *SS Orient*. Twelve of them were women and Grand could discount them. The men were a different matter, and even a man and his wife travelling together would not automatically rule out the husband as a friend of John Wilkes Booth.

Matthew Grand nearly dropped the ledger when he saw it. The list was not alphabetical but clearly written up in order of boarding. And there, twenty-first in the list, was Charles Dundreary. The character that Edward Sothern had been playing in *Our American Cousin* on the night they killed Lincoln. That could not be a coincidence, surely.

'This man.' Grand tapped the name with his finger. 'What can you tell me about him?'

'Nothing, sir.' The clerk frowned. 'We do not ask to see our passengers' credentials.'

'You must have an address, surely?'

The clerk sighed and waited. Grand recognized the hiatus and produced his third note. This was becoming expensive. A second ledger appeared, smaller than the first, and the clerk riffled through its pages. 'Ah, here we are,' he said, squinting at his own writing. 'Charles Dundreary. The Alhambra. Oh, that's odd.'

'Why?' Grand asked. 'Where's the Alhambra?'

'Well, it's on the east side of Leicester Square, sir, but it's not where it is; it's what it is. The Alhambra is a Music Hall. Leotard the Magnificent, the trapeze artiste, tops the bill. The Great Maskelyne after that. And then—' the clerk closed to Grand and dropped his voice – 'dances forbidden in Paris.'

'I see,' Grand said.

The clerk snapped shut both ledgers. 'No, no one *lives* at

the Alhambra, sir. I fear your . . . friend . . . has chosen to deceive. And it's not a place for young gentlemen like yourself, either. It's quite disgusting what goes on there.'

'I'm sure.' Grand nodded. 'And thank you.'

'I don't know what the world's coming to,' the clerk muttered as the captain strode to the door. 'What with filthy dancing and murders . . .'

'Murders?' Grand paused with his hand on the brassware.

'Why, yes, sir. On the *SS Orient*. I assumed you knew. I thought that was why . . .' His voice trailed away.

Grand was back in front of him in a second, looking the man grimly in the face. 'You'd better tell me all about it,' he said.

'Oh, I couldn't do that, sir,' the clerk assured him. 'I'm not at liberty to—'

But he never finished his sentence, because Matthew Grand had hauled him halfway across his counter, paper and inkwells going everywhere. 'I've paid Messrs Inman and Company more than enough, one way or another, over the last few days,' Grand said, twisting the man's lapels so that his eyes bulged. 'Now why don't you do your bit for Anglo-American relations and tell me *exactly* what you know?' He relaxed a little and flicked the errant lock of hair on the clerk's forehead back into place. 'There's a good chap.' All in all, his English accent wasn't too bad.

He let the clerk go so that his throat could work properly. The man licked his lips, and his eyes swivelled left and right. There was no one within shouting distance. Only old Mr McAvoy in the inner office, and he would never hear a cry for help anyway. All the clerk could do was to come clean with what he knew.

'It was three days out from Ireland, sir,' he whispered, as though the ledgers themselves had ears. 'A Mr Winthrop was found dead in his cabin.'

'Not of natural causes, I assume?'

'No, indeed, sir.' The clerk closed to Grand, carried away with his own narrative. 'There was a large wound in his chest which had pierced a lung and a valve of the heart – or so the ship's doctor said. He was not wholly sure – this was the first such incident he had ever known on board a ship – but he thought the weapon was a Bowie knife.'

'Was it found?'

'Apparently not, sir. All the passengers were questioned, of course, by the captain and his first officer, but to no avail.'

'Who would handle this case,' Grand asked, 'when the *Orient* got to Liverpool?'

'Well, normally the Liverpool police, sir. But in view of the fact that the late Mr Winthrop was a Londoner and that the detective branch at Scotland Yard have a reputation for these things, I understand it is being handled by them.'

'Scotland Yard?' Grand had never heard of it.

'The Metropolitan Police Headquarters, sir.' The clerk could not keep the patronizing tone out of his voice. 'It's in Whitehall Place, sir. You can't miss it.'

By the time the clerk had finished his story – told with a little too much glee for Grand's liking – the American was uneasy. He had thought that he was trailing a conspirator, a man who had sought, however wrongly, to assassinate a man for higher political reasons than sheer bloodlust. Now, he wasn't so sure. The thought of two murderers – or would-be murderers – being on one ship with a passenger manifest of less than forty seemed unlikely in the extreme. And yet . . . He became aware that the clerk was speaking to someone else, behind him at the desk.

'Can I help you, sir?' he was saying, in simpering tones. 'I believe this gentleman is just leaving.'

'Yes,' a pleasant voice said, from over Grand's shoulder. 'I am Inspector Tanner, of Scotland Yard. I wonder if I might have a word with you. I am investigating the murder of William Winthrop on the *SS Orient*, and I believe you are the man I need to speak to.'

The clerk flicked Grand a warning glance and slid the ledger along the desk, motioning Tanner to step that way. Grand took the hint and left, pausing in the doorway to try and catch a glimpse of London's finest. But Tanner had his head down in the ledger already, and so Grand just got an impression of a pair of shoulders, a trim back and some highly polished heels.

He opened the door, stepped out on to Leadenhall Street and realized he had London at his feet and its nearly three million people to hunt through to find his man. The thought that the streets within five minutes' walk of where he stood held the same number of people as the whole of his home city made his head spin, but he was young, rich and handsome; what could possibly go wrong?

James Batchelor's head was fizzing with the thrill of the chase. He had dithered on the doorstep of his lodgings, undecided as to whether the scene of the crime or Inspector Tanner would provide him with the most information, and had finally decided on Tanner. He could build on what he learned at Vine Street when he went to the Haymarket later. He had a lot of words to write before the presses started rolling, and anything that could save time would be of the greatest help. With his head down and his thoughts elsewhere, he would have overshot the police station had he not cannoned into someone walking the other way.

'I beg your pardon.' Batchelor and Inspector Tanner spoke in unison and raised their hats as if they were a Music Hall turn.

Tanner stepped back. 'Mr Batchelor,' he said with a smile. 'Just the man I was hoping to bump into. I've been doing some work on this latest murder atrocity, and I thought you might like to have some details for one of your articles.'

'That's exactly why I'm here,' Batchelor said.

'Really?' Tanner was impressed. 'Fleet Street works quicker than I realized. I haven't really worked out the details yet, but you are very welcome to listen as I think aloud.'

Batchelor was delighted. This was journalistic gold. It was well known that Commissioner Mayne disapproved of the gentlemen of the Press, just as he disapproved of little boys throwing snowballs in the parks, but he was wise enough to let his detective inspectors use their discretion. And nobody, surely, could be more discreet than Dick Tanner. Batchelor opened the door for the inspector and waved him through, blushing as he realized that he was inviting the man to enter his own place of work.

Tanner, always the gentleman, gave him his smile and walked in and made for the stairs. 'I worry that the weapon was never found,' he said, half to himself and half over his shoulder to Batchelor, following him up the stairs.

'Was it found in the last incident?' Batchelor asked. This was news to him.

Tanner cast his mind back. The last incident had been some years before but . . . yes, now he came to think of it, the weapon had not been found on that occasion either. The Yard man was impressed with the Fleet Street man's thoroughness. 'No, you're quite right, Mr Batchelor,' he said. 'It was not. But, of course, the wound was very different.'

'Not the throat?' Batchelor had hauled a pad out of his pocket and was hastily making notes. He had tried to come to terms with Isaac Pitman's squiggles but had always been totally unable to read it back. Instead, he relied on a few pithy remarks which hopefully would mean something to him in an hour or so.

'Indeed not,' Tanner assured him. 'One thrust to the chest, deflating the lung and collapsing the left ventricle of the heart. We are looking for a tall man—' he turned and gestured at Batchelor, a knife striking at his chest – 'from the angle of the wound, and also a right-handed man. We have looked at the available suspects and have managed to come up with about two dozen. Alas, Mr Batchelor, many of those are halfway to Western Australia by now. We are tracking the others down as we speak.'

'You have suspects? And why Western Australia? Are they already convicted felons then?'

'No, just able seamen doing their jobs, as I understand it.'

'What were they doing in the Haymarket last night?'

Tanner had reached the landing and, turning, looked down at Batchelor, poised on the stair. 'Haymarket? Last night? I'm talking about the stabbing on the *Orient* six days ago.'

'I'm talking about the Haymarket last night.'

'So I understand. I believe that crime will be on my desk for me to look at later today, but for now it is the *Orient* that commands my attention, Mr Batchelor.'

Batchelor wilted where he stood. 'I need a story by this

afternoon,' he said into his hat, which he clasped on his chest with both hands. It was a posture which had served him well over the years. 'I . . . I just must have the story, Inspector Tanner.'

Tanner was not an unreasonable man, and he had decided to keep an eye on this up and coming young man. A journalist in the pocket was worth three on the street any day. He blew down his nose and set his mouth for a moment, then turned for his office. 'Come along, then, Mr Batchelor,' he said. 'Let's see what my desk has to tell us about the latest Haymarket atrocity.'

Suddenly not dejected any more, Batchelor took the last stairs two at a time and followed Tanner with a hop and a skip, closing the door firmly behind him.

Dick Tanner may have had a soft spot for Batchelor, but he had work to do. As soon as he had given him the very barest of bones – essentially, all he had – on the latest Haymarket killing, he was back on the street and hotfooting it to the undertakers' premises where the mortal remains of one William Winthrop awaited him. Tanner was not really a blood and guts man. He was never keen on even fresh bodies, but William Winthrop was now almost a week dead and not getting any fresher. The undertakers were getting testy, and he had finally had notice from above that if he didn't go and view the victim in the next few hours, heads would roll. And 'above' meant Chief Inspector 'Dolly' Williamson. The head rolling would be real. Tanner squared his shoulders and decided that it couldn't really be that bad.

It was bad. Bad didn't begin to describe the smell in the shed of Messrs Warren and Warren, Undertakers to the Gentry, at the bottom of their yard. This was where they put all the corpses described by the elder Mr Warren as 'unfortunate' – in other words, those too pungent to be any nearer their actual place of business. Tanner, happily, didn't have to stay long. The cause of death, a clean cut where a knife had been slid in between the top two ribs, almost in the centre of the chest, was obvious, and so was one other thing: the face was all too familiar. Blinking and coughing from the smell, Tanner retreated gratefully back to the fresh air of the yard, heavy with the clean scent of pine wood-shavings.

'Has the family come forward?' he asked Warren, who stood beside him in his habitual pose of abject attention, his hands placed just *so* against his watch chain.

'We have been unable to locate any next of kin.' Warren's voice was sonorous and deep, as though it came from the bottom of a well. Or a crypt, Tanner couldn't help thinking.

The undertaker looked at Tanner, wondering if he always looked that colour. He delved into his pocket and brought out a small tin, which he proffered.

'No, thank you kindly,' Tanner said, raising a hand. 'I don't take snuff.'

'Oh, this isn't snuff,' the undertaker said. 'It is a concoction of my own devising; a mix of thymol in a new product from America called petroleum jelly. You just pop a little under the nose, like so—' he dabbed a small glob of the stuff on his moustache – 'and it kills the smell, at least to a degree. I also find it makes the moustache glossy, but that is a side effect. Try some.'

Tanner dabbed his finger into the goo in the small tin and gingerly applied it to his nostrils. He inhaled and smiled. The man was right – the smell had almost gone, though he knew it would revisit him in his dreams. He got back to the point. 'So, no next of kin. Do you mind me asking where you have been looking?'

'The shipping line gave us an address, but there must have been a clerical error. No one lives there; it is simply a gap between two houses in Pimlico. The trail goes rather cold when you have no address.'

Tanner reached into his pocket and brought out a piece of paper and a stub of pencil. He thought for a moment, tapping his teeth with the pencil lead, then wrote a few lines and gave the note to Warren. 'Try there,' he said. 'I'm not absolutely sure of the number . . . No, wait, don't worry. I'll go and give the sad news. I will need to interview his next of kin, anyway.'

'Could you let us know as soon as you can, Inspector Tanner?' Warren asked. 'Mr Winthrop is beginning to . . . give offence.'

'I do understand,' Tanner said. 'I think, in the circumstances, that you can go ahead with any arrangements and be ready to get him underground whenever you have an opportunity.'

'But . . . the family . . .' Warren was confused. Winthrop had been on a transatlantic voyage, nice clothes, apparently wealthy. He didn't like to annoy the well-to-do – customers didn't grow on trees, and with the nice weather coming business always tailed off for a month or two, until the drains problem picked up again in August.

'I believe that Mr Winthrop's family situation is quite complicated,' Tanner said.

Warren was amazed. 'You can tell that just from ten seconds in my shed with he who has passed over?' he asked, not failing to use his usual euphemisms even in his amazement.

Tanner leaned forward, and their glossy moustaches almost met in the middle. 'Sir,' he said, solemnly. 'I *am* a detective at Scotland Yard.' And with that, he made his way back out to the street, humming quietly under his breath.

Richard Tanner made his way through the back streets of Piccadilly as to the manner born. He turned into Cork Street and then into the Mews behind it, looking around him for clues; it was a long time since he had been here, and he didn't want to miss the door. A rather mangy lurcher sprawled across an entry was all he needed, and he stepped over it carefully, hoping it was the gentle-natured creature he remembered, rather than a more savage descendant. He walked down the dark passage and tapped on a peeling door.

'Yes?' a woman's voice cried out in genteel tones. 'Who is it?'

'It's me,' Tanner said. 'Bill.'

The door was flung open, and it was only with uncharacteristic adroitness that Tanner avoided the large and mouldy cabbage that hurtled out. The vegetable was followed by a head, a pretty head with rather wayward mousy curls, but wearing an expression that it didn't take a genius to interpret. The fury was replaced by surprise.

'Mr Tanner!' the woman said. 'Whatever are you . . .? Oh!' Her eyes filled with tears, and her mouth turned down. Peggy had always worn her heart on her sleeve; that was mainly the reason why her husband didn't take her with him when he was out on the con game.

'I'm sorry, Peg,' Tanner said. 'Can I come in?'

The kitchen he entered was dimly lit but clean and pleasant. Peggy and Bill Whicker lived as snug as bugs in a rug, with no servants to clutter the place up and make things difficult. Peggy kept things nice, and the children – three of them, all hearty boys – were in very minor public schools on the strength of their father's dubious earnings. All their headmasters assumed that Bill was a missionary, a role he played particularly well.

Peggy sat down suddenly on an overstuffed armchair by the range and looked up at Tanner, pleading hope dying in her eyes. 'He's not coming home this time, Mr Tanner, is he?'

'No, Peg.' The inspector shook his head. 'Not this time.'

For a moment, Peg Whicker's lip trembled and her bosom heaved. Her husband and Dick Tanner went back a few years, since the plainclothesman had pounded the Whitehall beat with A Division, and he still wore a stove-pipe hat and swallowtail. But he was still the law, one of Peel's Raw Lobsters, and she would not do her crying in front of him. 'What happened?' she asked.

'He was stabbed to death,' Tanner told her, 'on board the *SS Orient* on his way back from America. Do you know what he was doing there?'

Peg Whicker found something to do with her hands, working on a sampler she came back to from time to time. 'I wouldn't know anything about it,' she said.

'Come on, Peg.' Tanner smiled. 'You can do better than that. Whatever Bill was up to, he's past caring now, and I can't touch him for it.'

'Who did for him?' she asked, revenge suddenly replacing grief in the turmoil of her heart.

'That's what I'm trying to find out,' Tanner told her, 'and perhaps the reason for him going to America might give us a clue.'

Peg Whicker thought for a moment. 'Gold,' she said. 'Confederate gold. Ever since Atlanta everybody knew the

South was going to lose. Bill said there'd be rich pickings. Perhaps he could smuggle people out or at any rate get them to part with their money. I got a letter . . .' She rummaged in her sideboard drawer and passed the paper over to the Yard man.

He noted the date – five weeks ago; two weeks before he sailed on the *Orient*. It was postmarked Washington. 'May I borrow this, Peg?' Tanner asked. 'Who knows, it might give us a hint as to why he was murdered.'

She nodded, and he turned to go. In the doorway he stopped. 'Are you going to be all right, Peg?' he asked.

'Don't you worry about me, Mr Tanner,' she said with a sniff. 'Bill and me had a few bob put by, if you catch my drift.'

Tanner smiled. 'Oh, I do, Peg,' he said. 'I do.' And the sound of his boots on the bricks of the entry almost hid the sound of her crying.

'Can I help you?'

James Batchelor had been asked that before and always in that tone. What it really meant was: 'Who the hell are you and what are you doing here?'

'I hope so.' He smiled at the old man with the slop bucket. 'Batchelor, *Telegraph*.'

'Show starts at half past two.' The old man brushed past the young one and threw the contents of his pail into the gutter. The young man didn't *look* like a theatre critic, but what did he know? '*The Tempest*, by whatshisname.'

'I'm here about a different kind of show,' Batchelor said. 'The one that happened here last night.'

The old man stopped and looked the journalist up and down. He wasn't a swell, that much was certain. Copper, maybe. *Telegraph*, my arse, the old man thought. 'I wouldn't know anything about it,' he muttered.

'Who would?' Batchelor called after the retreating figure.

The old man stopped. 'Have a word with his mightiness, the impresario. He owns the bloody place. That's where the buck stops, don't it?'

It do, thought Batchelor to himself, but he had noticed, even in his brief newspaper career, that the men at the top hardly ever stopped the buck or carried the can or whatever piece of journalese he cared to name. 'Where will I find him?'

The old man was moving planking aside so that he could get past. 'Well, usually, any-bloody-where, but today, your luck's in. Try the first floor.'

The old man had not been vague in his description. The entire first floor of the Haymarket theatre was given over to its owner. The opulent drawing room was heavy with velvet and brocade, and oils of great actors, past and present, loured down at Batchelor as he knocked and entered. David Garrick looked sourly at him, as did Colley Cibber and Edmund Kean. Only Sarah Siddons had a kind smile.

'Would I have seen you in anything?' a voice boomed from behind a screen.

'Er . . . hello?' Batchelor could not see anybody at all.

'I said . . .' A swell emerged from the velvet drapery, a quill in one hand, an inkwell in the other. He was in his shirtsleeves and a vest of exquisite brocade. 'Oh, no. If you're here about the Caliban understudy, I'm afraid you're . . . well, can I be blunt? Too short. Too short by half.'

'No,' the newsman said. 'I'm James Batchelor.' He fumbled for his card. '*Telegraph*. I'm investigating the murder here last night.'

'Oh, I see.' The man frowned. 'Yes, that was dreadful. Quite shocking. I have a Press man somewhere who can answer all your questions.'

'If you are the theatre's owner, sir, I was told to see you.'

'Indeed?' The swell arched an eyebrow and put down his writing implements. 'By whom?'

'An old gent in the alleyway.'

'Old Lavenham?' The swell laughed. 'You mustn't mind him, Mr Batchelor. Salt of the earth. Worked for my father when he ran this place.'

'So you are . . .?'

'Oh, forgive me.' The swell extended a hand. 'Roderick Argyll, impresario, at your service.'

Batchelor shook his hand. 'And can you help me?'

'With this wretched girl's murder? No, I'm afraid not.'

Argyll reached into the pocket of an astrakhan coat hanging on the back of the door. He pulled out a meerschaum of exquisite quality.

'I almost witnessed the first one, you know.'

'Did you really?' Argyll gestured to a chair, and Batchelor sat in it. 'I wasn't in London then. But there was a hell of a stink about it, apparently. It's bad for business.'

'That depends on the business,' Batchelor said.

Argyll looked at him for a moment, then burst out laughing. 'I like the cut of your jib, laddie,' he said. 'Look out here.'

Batchelor joined the man at the window, which gave an unrivalled view of the Haymarket itself. The bright sun of early May glanced off the gleaming harness of the barouches and gigs that purred past. 'There.' Argyll pointed to a cluster of parasols moving as one on the far side of the street. 'The Haymarket march past.'

'March past?' Batchelor didn't follow.

'I thought you said you were a journalist.' Argyll gave him an old-fashioned look.

'Flower shows, I fear,' Batchelor said. 'The opening of a new sewer is an intellectual challenge for me.'

'Oh dear.' Argyll tutted, trying to contain his smirk. 'Well, allow me to enlighten you. The girls under the parasols work for a Madame – probably Auntie Bettie or Lady Eleanor. The thug with them—'

'Thug?' Batchelor interrupted.

'Bully. Protector. Pimp. Call him what you will. His job is to make sure that the girls make suitable assignations. If a gentleman is so minded, he can avail himself of Auntie Bettie's Tea Rooms or Lady Eleanor's Snug. In which case the gent in question will choose the girl and off they go. The deal is struck, and Auntie Bettie collects the proceeds. The girl gets ten per cent – fifteen if she's lucky.'

'You are very well informed, Mr Argyll,' Batchelor said.

'My dear fellow, I was born in this theatre. Well, two floors up, to be precise. I was toddling past ladies of the night before I had more than four teeth in my head. And yes, before you ask, it goes on under this very roof. Respectable theatre by day, Music Hall and bordello by night. The peelers and I have an understanding. Inspector Tanner is very accommodating.'

'Is he now?'

Argyll leaned towards his man. 'Oh, I'm sure the Society for the Rescue of Young Women would be horrified to hear me say it, but give me a doxy over an actor any day. So arrogant, all of them. Take Harry Hawk, for instance. Laura Keene was telling me—' He broke off, sensing that he had lost his audience of one, 'Look, it's not my place to teach you the facts of life, sonny, and I would say it's a little late for all that. But a gentleman on the town seeks, shall we say . . . diversion. Hence the Haymarket march past and the Haymarket theatre. You'll find it's much the same in Rotten Row and the stock exchange. Quite a high ranking clientele for some of these doxies. Heavy swells with plenty of time and plenty of cash. I don't judge. I just help them spend their money.'

'And the murders?' Batchelor said. 'Two girls dead in three weeks.'

Argyll's smile vanished. 'Well, that's what I mean about being bad for business. I've noticed the house takings are down over the last few days. As of today, they'll probably fall again. Some lunatic is ruining trade.'

'You were here last night?'

'I was.'

'Did you see anything? Hear anything?'

'My dear boy, the girl died in the early morning. I was in my private apartments next door.'

'Alone?'

Argyll looked horrified. 'No,' he said after a moment.

'Mrs Argyll?' Batchelor had the natural tenacity of the news hound; that much was certain.

'Mrs Argyll disappeared with a cotton planter several years ago,' the impresario said. 'The lady I was with on the night in question has, as far as you are concerned, no name at all. Suffice it to say that she is a married lady whose husband believes she is visiting a sick relative. I'm sure I don't need to elaborate.'

'Er . . . no,' Batchelor said. 'And the scene of the crime?'

'The alleyway, I believe, alongside the theatre – the way, I

presume, you came in. You'll have to talk to old Lavenham
about the details. There's not much that passes him by.'

It was Lavenham who had washed the girl's blood away after
somebody found her. The old man pointed to the Very Spot.
He didn't like talking about any of this, of course. The dead
girl was no better than she should be, but she was somebody's
daughter and old Lavenham had granddaughters of his own.
No, he assured Batchelor, who was scribbling away furiously
with his pencil on Edwin Dyer's behalf, he wouldn't dwell on
the horrors of the body itself. Her dress and petticoats had
been thrown up, ready for business, so to speak, and her eyes
were bulging, the pupils crossed. Her tongue was purple,
sticking right out of her mouth through gritted teeth, and her
throat above her lace collar was a bloody mess of torn flesh.
No, old Lavenham couldn't talk about things like that.

James Batchelor sketched the alleyway when the old man
had gone, still smacking his lips over the salacious details he
couldn't talk about. The wall of the theatre rose to its four
storeys to his right, and there were gutters and drains along
the alley at regular intervals. To the left was stabling for
carriages, but the double doors were locked and the padlock
rusted. It looked as though no one had used these premises in
a long time. The alley was a cul-de-sac of death, ending in a
locked door into the backstage area of the theatre. The door
that Batchelor had entered by was off to the right, and
Lavenham had told him that this was Mr Argyll's private
entrance. Everybody else went in to the theatre via the front
doors, which were opening, as Batchelor left, for the afternoon's performance. The journalist measured out the alleyway.
It was the same width as that on the other side, a mirror image
of the place where he had stood not long ago, stumbling over
the still-warm corpse of Effie, the girl from paradise. For a
moment, the poet lost somewhere in James Batchelor's soul
looked up at the Haymarket Theatre, like some great and grim
altar on which two girls had been sacrificed.

ELEVEN

Willis's Supper Rooms had never been so crowded, not even when they'd founded the Liberal Party there. The great and the good of the world of Fleet Street squeezed themselves into their tail coats and white ties, and the champagne flowed with the good talk, and the music swelled with the collected egos.

It was George Sala's night, paid for by the *Telegraph*, and the speeches were long and gushing. Thornton Leigh Hunt did not stay long after the entrées; Willis's had just had the decorators in, and the man was allergic to paint. Rather than pant and sneeze his way through the turbot, he made an excuse and left. Which was just as well because had he caught sight of the uninvited guest, there may have been a scene.

George Sala himself had invited James Batchelor, but he was on nobody's guest list and the major-domo had squeezed the ex-journalist in between Buckley and Dyer, each of whom had cause to be eternally grateful to their former colleague, so they tolerated the proliferation of elbows at the lower table.

Matthew Grand was also there – and he did not want to be there at all. He had realized during his first few days in London what an experience it was *not* to be known. In Washington, the uniform had a cachet of its own – the famous red tie of the Third Cavalry of the Potomac even more so. Here, in the largest city in the world, he was Mister Nobody. Until tonight, that is. Sala had asked the band at Willis's to strike up something American when he called upon Grand to say a few words, and Sala died a thousand deaths when 'Hail to the Chief' blasted through the assembly rooms. Diehard journalist that he was, he scribbled a hasty note on a menu to the bandleader – '"Hail to the Chief" is only played in the presence of the President of the United States. Rather bad taste considering Lincoln. Play something lively.'

The band leader was mortified that he may have given

offence, and his baton switched pace, whirling furiously in the air as he mouthed, 'Dixie!' at his startled orchestra.

They were not so startled as Matthew Grand, however, who smiled wanly at Sala. 'Cheer up, Mr Sala,' he said, hearing his host groan. 'Song of the South it may be, but it *was* written by a Northerner.'

When the speeches were over and Willis's Rooms were thick with cigar smoke, Batchelor inevitably turned to murder. 'So, gentlemen,' he said. 'Where are we on the Haymarket horrors?'

Both his ex-colleagues shot glances at each other, neither prepared to declare their shortcomings openly. 'It's a maniac,' Dyer said at last, cutting the end of his cigar. 'Pure and simple.'

Since no words of wisdom came from Buckley at all, Batchelor took the man to task. 'There's nothing pure about murder, Edwin, and in my experience it's hardly ever simple.'

'What are your thoughts, then?' Buckley asked.

'Someone down on whores,' Batchelor said, thinking aloud. 'He likes them young. He's personable . . .'

'How do you know that?' Buckley asked.

'Because two of them have willingly gone into alleyways with him. He must appear to be a regular punter. Flashes the gold, I shouldn't wonder.'

'Yes, but it's the method.' Dyer blew smoke rings to the ceiling. 'Wire around the throat. Garrotting.'

'Thuggee,' a voice croaked from across the table. Gabriel Horner would go to the opening of an envelope, and a chance of supper at Willis's was far too good an opportunity to pass up. Especially with port of this vintage. Next to snipes' kidneys at the Cock in Fleet Street, this was seventh heaven.

'Come again?' Dyer frowned. It wasn't always possible to follow the old man's train of thought.

'The Thuggee—' Horner leaned back, happy, as always, to be the centre of attention – 'were a Hindu sect of killers. Our brave boys came upon them in central India. What was that now . . .? Oh, must be thirty years ago.'

'Before we were born,' Dyer reminded him.

'Yes,' Horner said, sighing. 'Obviously. Anyway, they preyed on travellers – won their friendship, rode with them on their caravans through the mountain passes. Then they'd strike, the Phansigars, the noose-operators. Of course, they didn't use wire; they used a yellow band of cloth – rather like the American's red tie, I fancy.'

All four of them looked at Grand, still talking with Sala at the top table. The prize-winning journalist had prevailed upon the ex-captain to sport his red tie on this special occasion, even if he technically no longer had a right to wear it.

'But wasn't there a bit of a rage for it, Gabriel?' Batchelor asked. 'A few years ago. Here in London, I mean?'

'Oh, yes. But you must remember that, all three of you. You were already in the business by then.'

'I was tea boy on the *Graphic*,' Dyer said. 'They didn't let me anywhere near a story.'

'Don't look at me, Gabriel.' Buckley raised his hands. 'I was destined for a career in the church, remember. Didn't have my famous screaming row with my mother until late 'sixty-three.'

'Jim?' Horner couldn't believe how quickly people forgot. Ah, the journalists of today!

'Flower shows,' Batchelor said. 'And I know more about Mr Bazalgette's Embankment improvement scheme, I'll wager, than Mr Bazalgette. Crime? That, I was told, was for *real* reporters.'

'Quite right.' Horner nodded, pouring himself an outsize port. 'Well, take it from *this* real reporter, it was nasty while it lasted. Oh, flash in the pan stuff, really, but it woke the boys in blue up a little, so it served its purpose. Two men would work it. A tall one would strike from behind, loop a rope, or scarf or something similar around a victim's neck. The second one, his partner in crime, so to speak, would then rifle said victim's pockets while said victim's hands were at his throat trying to remove the noose. No real harm done, as it happened – a few rope burns and, of course, the loss of one's wallet, but nothing like this.'

Batchelor nodded. 'No, this is different.'

'Not *that* different, though,' Horner persisted. 'Dark alleyways, attack from behind.'

'But nothing stolen, Gabriel,' Dyer said, chipping in. 'Ladies of the Night. That adds a new dimension, don't you think?'

'I do.' Horner nodded. 'Who's on the case?'

'I am,' Dyer and Buckley chorused.

Batchelor had to bite his tongue.

'You know they caught John Wilkes Booth?' George Sala turned to Matthew Grand on the top table.

Grand nodded. 'I heard. Though I'll wager your telegraphic services have told you more than I know.'

'The Sixteenth New York Cavalry found him in a tobacco barn at the Garrett farm near Bowling Green. There was a fire. Somebody shot Booth in the neck. He died soon after.'

'When was this?' Grand asked.

'The twenty-fifth, as I understand it.'

'Eleven days after he killed Lincoln,' Grand said, thinking aloud.

'That's Lafayette Baker for you.' Sala refilled the ex-Captain's glass. 'Say what you like about him, the man gets results.'

'Who?' Grand looked suitably blank.

'Lafayette C. Baker, head of the National Detective Police. I met him once in Washington. I understand he was in command of the Sixteenth. I'm surprised you didn't come across him, what with you being at Ford's Theatre that night.'

'I may have done.' Grand sipped his port. 'You meet a lot of people in a war.'

'Yes,' Sala said. 'I'm sure you do. Still, you must be delighted. There's a trial under way, you know, for the others – Atzerodt, Powell, Mrs Surratt, the rest.'

'Is it likely a woman could be involved in this?' Grand asked.

Sala shrugged. 'Look around you, Matthew,' he said. 'Good men. Good company. Good – if I may say so – speeches. All washed over with excellent port. The war and that madness at Ford's seems eternity ago, doesn't it? Are you finding it as restful as you'd hoped? As good an escape as you'd planned?'

'Escape?' Grand frowned. 'Oh, from the war. Yes. Yes.'

'Good.' Sala's smile was like a basilisk's, cold and deadly. 'Because what you see here is a facade, old man, a passing show. Out there, in the mean streets tonight, people are dying.

Some will perish of disease, the hacking cough, the tortured lung. Others will fall, drunk as the dead, into Old Father Thames, and his coldness will lap them. Some wife will cross her husband and he will kick her to a jelly with his hobnailed boots. Some tart . . . some tart in the Haymarket may meet her last customer.' And he grinned and cackled like a harlot. *''Ello, ducks, lookin' for some company?'*

Grand looked at the man. This was a side to George Sala he had never seen before. He felt the hairs crawl on the back of his neck.

'Could a woman be involved in the assassination of the President of the United States? Perhaps not. But put the question another way. Could a woman be involved in the murder of a man in a theatre? And the answer is yes. Emphatically yes. Now—' he leaned back and patted Grand's arm – 'you flag down a waiter for more port. I must answer a call of nature.'

'Capital speech, GS.' Gabriel Horner staggered to his feet as George Sala approached, and he shook the man's hand.

'Gabriel Horner!' Sala beamed. 'I thought you were dead.'

'Oh, I am, old boy,' the old newspaperman said, chuckling. 'It's just that I've forgotten how to lie down.'

'Batchelor, a word.' Sala beckoned the lad over.

'Mr Sala—' Batchelor extended a hand – 'may I say what an honour . . .'

'Yes, yes.' Sala tugged him away from his cronies. 'That's more than enough smarm for one evening. I understand you are out of a job.'

'Well, I . . . How did you know that?'

'I am a journalist, dear boy.' Sala led him to a relatively secluded corner of the room. 'I didn't invite you here tonight, dismissed and discarded individual that you are, for your pretty face.'

'Oh, I—'

'Shut up and listen. Do you want your job back? On the *Telegraph*, I mean.'

'Of course,' Batchelor said.

'Right. I want to introduce you to someone. And I want

you to watch him. Use whatever powers of persuasion you have. If he so much as farts, I want to know about it.'

'Who is it?'

'Grand.'

Batchelor stepped back. 'Your guest of honour?'

'There's only one guest of honour here tonight, Jim, my boy. And that's me. Captain Grand has come to London to forget. The war. The blood. Bla, bla, bla. But I'm not sure it's that simple.'

'I don't follow.'

Sala spun him round so that his back was to Grand, who was making small talk with a sub-editor on the top table. 'Look, I can't say too much. But I can tell you that Captain Grand was at Ford's Theatre the night Lincoln was shot.'

'My God!'

'And he may be involved.'

'Involved? You mean . . .?'

'Come, come, lad,' Sala hissed through gritted teeth. 'I'd expected rather more from a man like you. I *had* heard great things . . .'

'What do you want me to do?' If Batchelor had been a trifle warm with the port, he was stone cold sober now.

'Get to know the man. You're doing an article on him for the *Telegraph*. An American's view of the Civil War, what he thinks of London, that sort of thing. Human interest piece. And you'll report to me every day. Clear?'

'Er . . . what if he doesn't go along with it?' Batchelor asked.

'Tell him you're working on the Haymarket murders.'

'Why?'

'Because I've got to know our brave captain reasonably well over the last few weeks. He has a morbid fascination with sudden departure, believe me, probably because of Lincoln. He'll be hooked. I can't stay with him; he'll smell a rat. But he doesn't know you and won't suspect. Come on, I'll do the honours. Oh—' Sala pressed a hand against Batchelor's jacket. 'And I should warn you, he carries a gun. It's a point thirty-two calibre Colt, and he wears it in a shoulder-holster. Here.' He patted Batchelor's chest.

Then Sala whirled back to the smoke-filled room. 'Matthew

Grand, I'd like you to meet James Batchelor. You two will get on like houses on fire.'

The next day, James Batchelor walked carefully down Fleet Street, heading for the Cavendish on Jermyn Street, where Matthew Grand had taken a room. He was remembering all over again why he didn't like drinking port; there was nothing wrong with the drink at the time, of course, but afterwards it seemed to lie heavily in his stomach, his head and his feet in equal measure, and making due progress down the street seemed much more difficult than it should have been. He surveyed the city through slitted eyes; the spring sunshine seemed to have added glitter this morning, dazzling off brass nameplates and wrought-iron railings.

'Jim!'

His name rang through the fog in Batchelor's head. Turning it very slowly, he saw Dyer and Buckley standing outside the *Telegraph* offices, looking not a little bleary themselves. He nodded to each man carefully.

'You look as if you may be a man with a mission, Mr Batchelor,' Dyer said, his voice croaky with too many of George Sala's cigars the night before.

'I am, Dyer, thank you for noticing.' Batchelor was relieved that he perhaps didn't look as dreadful as he felt. 'I have a job. Just a freelance one, you know. It may lead to more. But I am just off to see Matthew Grand at his hotel.'

'Grand? Sala's guest from last night?' Buckley was amazed, and anyone within earshot would have known that at once, just from his tone. The big American was a bit of a mystery, and Buckley was piqued that Batchelor might be the one to crack it. 'You're a lucky man.'

Batchelor shrugged his shoulder. 'Well, right man at the right place at the right time, Buckley,' he said. 'It could have been any of us, I suppose.' The 'suppose' put across his message loud and clear. 'I can't stop, though. I don't want to be late.' And he spun on his heel, waited for his head to catch up, and was on his way before either journalist could think of a witty riposte.

*   *   *

John Herold was terrified. His legs had no feeling in them below the knees, strapped as they were to his stirrups, and for hours, it seemed, that damned old Negro whose transport they had commandeered had been wailing about how he had a murderer's blood on his hands, in his wagon. It would never come off. They had bundled Herold, stumbling and cursing in the darkness, into the rat-scurrying hold of the *John S. Ide* on its way to the Navy Yard. Even in the darkness of night, he knew this place. It was within blocks of his home on Eighth Street, and his dad had been a clerk here. For hours he'd been trying to explain to the men of the Sixteenth New York Cavalry that he didn't know what was happening, that the man they'd just killed in the blazing barn at Garrett's Farm was a madman he'd met on the road, a madman who had forced him to go along with him at gunpoint.

Riding with the Sixteenth that night was Colonel Lafayette Baker. With his slow drawl and shambling gait, Herold appeared stupid enough, but *nobody* put one over on Lafayette Baker. He would work on Herold later. For now he was shackled with the other conspirators, the sparks ringing off the shackles in the darkness of the *Montauk*'s hold and Herold mumbling incoherently under the canvas hood.

It was well and truly light by the time John Wilkes Booth lay on a carpenter's table on the ship's lower deck. No one knew how long the autopsy would take, least of all the surgeon-general himself, so a canvas awning was slung overhead to shield the grisly work from prying eyes at the other end of telescopes and even from the sun itself. Joseph Barnes began his work at a little after ten, surrounded by the officers detailed to be there by Secretary of War Stanton himself.

Lafayette Baker strutted backwards and forwards. His once-handsome face was gaunt and bearded, the carefully Macassared hair greasy and unkempt. He hadn't slept, and his back was in agony after days in the saddle. He wanted all this to be over, and not even the satisfaction of having caught Lincoln's killer sat well with him.

'The cause of death,' Surgeon-General Barnes was muttering to his assistant, 'was a gunshot to the neck. The ball entered just behind the sternocleido muscle . . . er . . .' He placed his tape against the probe. 'Two and one half inches above the clavicle, passing through the bony bridge of the fourth and fifth cervical vertebrae . . . Am I boring you, Colonel?'

Baker stopped pacing. All eyes under that canvas were fixed on him and Barnes. 'Just tell me,' the colonel said, 'is this son of a bitch John Wilkes Booth or not?'

Barnes sighed and put his tape down. He tilted the dead man's head, pointing to the neck. 'Here,' he said, 'a scar shows the presence of a fibroid tumour. I understand from my colleague Dr John May of this fair city that he removed that for Booth a couple of years back. And here—' he held up the corpse's left hand – 'the initials JWB. I understand from the son of a bitch's sister that he carved that tattoo on himself when he was a boy. Funny how Indian ink lies on paper, but never on skin.'

Baker grunted something and marched off, Cousin Luther in his wake. 'One more thing,' he growled as he reached the *Montauk*'s gangplank. 'Did the bastard suffer?'

Barnes looked down at the body and resumed his work, talking in the same quiet tone as his assistant wrote down every word. 'Paralysis of the entire body was immediate, and all the horrors of consciousness of suffering and death must have been present to the assassin during the two hours he lingered.' The surgeon-general looked up at Baker. 'In layman's terms, Colonel, yes, the bastard suffered.'

The Cavendish was quietly imposing, one of the oldest hotels in London, and when Batchelor pushed open the ornate glass door he found himself in opulence which was many steps above his usual station. Staff in livery scurried to and fro with silent concentration on their faces, every one with a mission to please. Luggage was efficiently whipped up stairs, was brought downstairs to be disposed into waiting cabs. Maids in frilly caps bustled up the stairs with freshly laundered sheets, wafting past the journalist on a lavender scented breeze. He realized he was staring, but didn't seem able to close his mouth, which was hanging slightly open. He shut it with a snap when a voice murmured in his ear.

'Can I help, sir? Or is sir looking for the tradesman's entrance?' Insolence was only just overlaid by subservience.

The next sentence, it warned, could go either way and could end up with sir on the pavement with a flea, as opposed to hot breath, in his ear.

Batchelor pulled himself together. 'I'm here to see Captain Grand,' he said.

The owner of the voice, a slightly built man in a suit so perfectly fitting that he could have been born in it, moved behind the desk, as though on castors, and ran a perfect, pale and elegant finger down the page of the ledger.

'No Captain Grand here,' he said, with a barely concealed sneer. He raised a hand to call over a beefy youth who was stacking luggage in a corner. He raised an eyebrow at Batchelor, waiting for the next move.

'*Mr* Grand?'

The elegant young man closed the ledger and folded his hands on top of it. 'Tell me, sir,' he said, with the slightest hesitation before the last word, 'do you intend to go through the whole range of names until we find one with which I can agree?'

'I have an appointment with Captain, or *Mr*, Matthew Grand this morning in this hotel. If you are intent on making things difficult for me, I'm afraid that I will have to make sure that he knows of the difficulty, who is to blame and why I did not keep the appointment. I will also have to tell the newspapers, specifically Mr Thornton Leigh Hunt, editor of the *Telegraph*.'

The young man looked slightly less self-satisfied, but otherwise held his ground. 'We do have a Mr Grand here,' he said, distantly. 'I will see if he is in.' He went out through a door behind the desk and was gone a few minutes. He returned with a smirk. 'Mr Grand is Out,' he said. Again, he folded his hands on the ledger, and now the smile was edged with ice.

'Out?' Batchelor said. This was marvellous. Not only had he traipsed halfway across London, he had made a fool of himself at this hotel and had also made a fool of himself in front of Buckley and Dyer. Of all the pompous, self-satisfied . . .

'Mr Batchelor?' The voice behind him made him jump. He turned round and found it was Grand, immaculate in a suit of rather foreign cut, a perfectly tied cravat at his throat, a perfectly groomed felt hat in his hand. 'Am I late? I just went out for a walk while I was waiting for you and rather lost my way. I'm sure Theodore here has made you comfortable?' He smiled, looking from one man to the other, willing them to like each other.

'He has been . . .' Batchelor, wordsmith by trade, couldn't think of a single thing to say.

'Mr Grand,' Theodore said, apropos of nothing, and then lapsed into a confused silence.

Grand looked again and saw more accurately what had been happening. He took Batchelor by the elbow and led him to the door and then out on to the pavement. 'Sorry about that,' he said. 'Theodore will be sorry, too, that he was rude when it comes to the time to tip. However, you're here now; can I tempt you to some coffee? Is there a coffee house around here?'

'Any number, I'm sure,' Batchelor said. He thought it was time he said something in case Grand started to suspect that he was a little mentally challenged.

'Then let's find a good one,' Grand said, slapping him on the back. He had had this man foisted on him, when the last thing he wanted was company. What he had to do needed solitude and a free hand. Still, the little journalist could perhaps be useful when it came to finding his way around. And perhaps even for finding a tall man who lurked in shadows, a man with cufflinks of red and white enamel. When he had his bearings – and it wouldn't take him long – he could ditch him and strike out alone. 'My treat.'

Batchelor fell into step as best he could. The man was tall, certainly, but there was an added something about his stride which made him hard to keep up with. He seemed to cover more ground with each pace than other people, and every now and again the Englishman had to do a hop and a skip to stay abreast.

Grand noticed and immediately slowed his progress. 'Sorry to make you run,' he said, good-humouredly. 'I do walk fast. Tell me if I do it again; all my friends complain. Used to moving at the speed of the cavalry, I guess.'

'Not at all,' Batchelor said, trying to catch his breath. 'It's probably good for me. A sedentary life, journalism.'

Grand looked up at the name above a window they were passing. 'A coffee shop,' he said. 'Is it any good?'

Batchelor had no idea. This was Jermyn Street. He didn't

M.J. Trow

have the kind of money, or the kind of leisure, to enjoy random cans of coffee in the day. But it looked clean enough and he had never heard anything bad about it, so he nodded and shrugged. Grand pushed open the door, and they went in.

Both men were surprised. Grand was expecting something similar to his hotel; in Washington, the coffee houses were usually rooming houses as well, if not full blown grand hotels. Batchelor had no idea what to expect, but this slightly cleaner alehouse look was probably not it.

A waiter, wearing a long, wraparound apron and an ingratiating expression, approached. 'Table for two, gentlemen?' he asked. 'Coffee? Tea? Crumpets? Muffins?'

The two looked at him, undecided.

'Toast?' The waiter was running out of options. 'We don't start meals until twelve, I'm afraid.'

Grand was first to come to. 'We'll have coffee and muffins,' he said and led the way to a table at the rear of the room, dark and private.

Batchelor followed and hoped that Grand was serious about the treat being his. His recent brush with total destitution had made him careful. They sat down and looked around, two strangers thrown together and with little to say. Batchelor drummed his fingers on the table, in time to some tune in his head. He realized it was one of the jingles from his last visit to the Music Hall, the night he had found Effie, and he stopped himself, putting his hands on his thighs under the table. They sat like this until the coffee and food arrived.

Grand picked up the plate and looked at it quizzically. He had definitely ordered muffins, but these were not they. He opened his mouth to call the waiter back, but was forestalled by Batchelor, who grabbed a hot muffin, dripping with butter and crispy toasted at the edges.

'I haven't had a muffin for years,' he said. 'They were a special treat at home when mother was baking.' Some butter ran down his chin, and he wiped it off with the back of his hand, smiling at the memory.

Grand stood corrected. There was a lot to learn about this country, that was for sure. He picked up one of the doughy circles and bit into it dubiously. It was good! Not a muffin, perhaps, but good all the same. He managed to eat it without the butter drool and sipped his coffee. Also good; he had not heard good things about English coffee – the country, he had heard, was obsessed with tea – but this was well up to Washington standards. Better than much of it; certainly better than that at Arlette's house. He waited to see if his heart would do a little flip at the memory of her, but no, not a thing.

'So, Mr Batchelor,' the American began. 'How can I help you?'

'I beg your pardon?' Batchelor asked, round a mouthful of muffin.

'I gather you are preparing an article on an American in London.' He spread his arms. 'Well, here I sit. An American in London if ever there was one. What would you like to know?'

Batchelor hurriedly wiped his fingers down his trousers and fished in his pocket for notebook and pencil. 'I wonder if we could begin in Washington,' he said, mindful that Sala wanted as much detail of the night at Ford's as was forthcoming.

'Well, I hadn't been in Washington long before . . .' Grand glanced down for a moment, composing himself. 'Before the President was shot. I had gone to the theatre with my intended, Miss Arlette McKintyre.'

Batchelor scribbled. This was easy.

'The President was shot. Arlette and I agreed to go our separate ways. I came to London.'

Not so easy, perhaps. This man could precis like no one Batchelor had ever met. He was a man of very few words indeed. Perhaps he could get him a job in the advertisements department.

'So, you . . . you didn't have any involvement in the shooting, at all?'

Grand's hand was inside his jacket and his face set in a snarl in less time than it would take to tell. He leaned forward and hissed at a startled Batchelor, 'What do you mean by that, exactly, Mr Batchelor?'

Mr Batchelor was damned if he knew, exactly. In his nervousness, he had blurted out the very question that George Sala had wanted raised. But it was too much to the point. It sounded as though Grand had fired the Derringer himself.

'Er . . . what I meant was . . . what happened . . . er . . . at Ford's?'

Grand subsided a little, and Batchelor was relieved to see that both the man's hands were back on the table. 'One minute we were watching the play, the next . . . well, it's a cliché, I know, but it all happened so fast. Booth appeared on the stage in front of me, maybe as close as I am to the aspidistra over there. He yelled something and ran. I followed.'

'My God!' Batchelor was impressed. While he had been attending flower shows and the opening of sewers, this man had witnessed the murder of a president and had chased his killer. 'You didn't catch him, I suppose?'

'No.' Grand's face fell. 'No. Let's just say I bumped into a co-worker of his.'

'Co-worker?' This was not a term Batchelor knew.

'Fellow conspirator,' Grand explained.

Batchelor had been following the American despatches avidly on this over the last week. 'Who was that? Atzerodt? Surratt? Herold?'

'None of these,' Grand told him. 'The man I bumped into has no name. Not, at least, that I know.'

'You must be pleased, at least, that they've caught most of them. You've followed the trial?'

Grand nodded. 'As far as I can. The Limey take on it.'

'The Limey . . .?' Batchelor frowned. 'Ah, yes, I see. Well, there you are. Here is a golden opportunity, Mr Grand, to put across the *American* side of things. You see, we've never had a president over here, and our civil war was a long time ago. Of course, madmen take potshots at the queen from time to time, but mercifully, no harm done.'

'I thought you wanted my opinion of London,' Grand said.

'Oh, I do, I do, but I think our readers would like to know more about Ford's Theatre and from a Man Who Was Actually There.' He was writing the banner headlines in his mind now. Leigh Hunt would *have* to reinstate him once this was public news.

'That's off limits,' Grand told him and watched the journalist's crest fall. 'But if you can help me, I can give you the story of a lifetime.'

TWELVE

The Great Vance strolled across the stage, twirling his gold-topped cane with one hand and his magnificent mustachios with the other. The topper was tilted at a rakish angle over one eye and the other sparkled in the limelight. He was centre stage, and the crowd roared their delight. Even those with their backs to him swivelled their chairs and applauded as his dulcet tenor threatened to shatter the chandeliers.

'Do you have the Music Hall back home, Captain Grand?' Gabriel Horner leaned across the table.

'I guess we do,' Grand said, nodding. 'Except we call it vaudeville. And that's just plain Mr Grand, by the way.'

James Batchelor had promised to show the American the sights, and after a turgid day at the Tower (entrance to the Armoury 6d; to the Regalia, which everyone else called the Crown Jewels, another 6d) and the Zoological Gardens (admission one shilling – Grand was paying), the Haymarket with its razzle and dazzle seemed ideal. It also gave Batchelor a chance to relive the night that still haunted him, the night that Effie had offered him her services, the night she was dead at his feet. He suddenly remembered the match girl, the one he had felt sorry for and who had vanished like a will-o'-the-wisp. What had she seen? What did she know? Why did she leave so fast, at that very hour? He made an excuse and wandered into the Haymarket night.

'See her riding in the Row,' Vance sang. 'Such a joy from head to toe. She's the one that I adore, I will love her ever more.'

'Brings tears to your eyes, don't it?' Dyer chuckled, raising his champagne glass to the singer.

Gabriel Horner shook his head. 'Such cynicism in one so young,' he said.

'We'll get on to the naughty stuff later, Mr Grand.' Dyer

nudged the man. 'There's No Shove Like the First Shove, if you catch my drift.'

Horner chuckled. 'The point is, Mr Grand, that in the Music Hall, nothing is quite real. Nothing is quite what it seems. Take the Great Vance up there. What do you see? A heavy swell in finely-tailored kecks with boots that would cost me a year's pay working for the *Telegraph*? His name is actually Alfred Peek Stevens, and when I first met him he was a solicitor's clerk, earning a pittance and shivering in a garret somewhere.'

'Didn't he do blackface?' Dyer asked. 'At the South London Palace?'

'He did,' Horner said. 'I suppose you have plenty of those for real at home, Mr Grand?'

Grand smiled. 'Our blackface minstrels are as white as yours, Mr Horner,' he said. 'Coloureds aren't allowed on stage, even in my particular neck of the woods.'

'No, of course not.'

'You're quiet tonight, Joe.' Dyer half turned to Buckley, sitting beside him. 'The Great Vance not to your liking?'

'Sorry,' Buckley muttered. 'I was thinking about those murders.'

'Ah, yes, dreadful. Did you know, Mr Grand, that an unfortunate – nay, *two* unfortunates – were murdered not a stone's throw from where we are sitting?'

'The last time Mr Grand was in a theatre,' Horner murmured, 'a president was murdered not a stone's throw from where he was sitting.'

'You seem remarkably well informed, sir.' Grand shot him a glance that would have unnerved a more sober man.

'I am a newspaperman, sir.' Horner sat more upright. 'It is my job to be well informed.'

The orchestra reached a crescendo, and the Great Vance bowed and preened to his adoring audience.

'Now's the interval,' Dyer told Grand. 'This is where the show really starts.' He caught the expression on Buckley's face. 'Oh, for God's sake, Joe, cheer up, man. Look, here's Lily. You can have her tonight.'

Lily was lovely. Her dark tresses tumbled over her bare shoulders, and her gown was bold even by Haymarket standards. She led a throng of similarly dressed girls through the theatre's auditorium, and they swayed seductively past the tables. Grand noticed that they ignored any table at which a lady sat and they circled the waiters who arrived carrying trays of champagne and pails of ice.

'Evening, Lily.' Edwin Dyer leered, half-standing in a mock bow.

She looked briefly at him, then fixed her smouldering gaze on Grand. 'Why, Edwin, who is your handsome friend?'

'Er . . . allow me to introduce . . . Matthew Grand, this is Lily.'

The ex-Union officer rose to his feet. 'Lily . . . er?'

'Just Lily.' She smiled, extending her hand for him to kiss. 'I haven't seen you here before,' she said.

'He's from over the water,' Buckley said. 'The land of the free.'

'Really?' Lily insinuated herself next to Grand, her breasts all but tumbling out of her bodice.

'Mine, I think.' Another female voice made them all look up. 'Hello, boys.'

An auburn beauty stood there, a long feather boa circling her neck. Her left hip was thrust out at a provocative angle, and she too had her gaze fixed on Grand.

'Piss off, Jeannie, I saw him first.' Lily's tones were less than velvet.

The auburn girl looked up and down the room with its chatter, its smoke and its noise. 'He's *my* side of the fence,' she said.

'You was always boss-eyed,' Lily said.

'Well.' Jeannie smiled at Grand. 'Let's let the gentleman decide for himself, shall we?' she said, and she hauled up her elegant dress to allow Grand to assess her wares.

'Good God!' The cry came from any or all of the half dozen men around the table.

'I thought she was really a redhead,' Dyer said with a smirk, but it was the last comment he was able to make because a well-aimed kick from Jeannie saw him reeling backwards off his chair, crashing into a flunkey whose tray and glasses went everywhere.

'Bitch!' Lily snarled, and she grabbed the other girl's hair and swung her round. The rest was shrieks and bared teeth and flying nails as the girls went at each other.

Grand tried to separate them, but all he got for his pains was Lily's boot in his groin. There was chaos everywhere, and the band played faster and louder to drown out the furore.

'They don't pay me enough to get my nose broken,' Buckley shouted at Dyer, and he fought his way to the door.

'That makes two of us,' Dyer said, but his progress was slower because he had to get upright first with boots stamping all around him and furniture splintering as he rolled on the floor.

'Two bob on the redhead,' Gabriel Horner crowed, loving every minute of this but despairing of the feeble showing by the young reporters of today. Some people were keen to take his money, but the theatre's heavies were already at work, cracking heads together and restoring order. It was all in a night's work for them. And Matthew Grand learned a whole new vocabulary from Lily and Jeannie before they were flung out into the night.

When all had calmed down and the furniture was righted and the champagne flowed again, the orchestra's pace and volume lessened. Gabriel Horner waved over a waiter and ordered more champagne on the strength of his winnings. 'You must be a little bewildered by all this, Mr Grand,' he said.

'I don't recall it happening much in Washington,' the man had to agree.

'Oh, don't let it go to your head . . . er . . . well-set-up sort of chap though you are. Any new face is likely to be a magnet to the Juliets of a night. No, the problem is strictly one of geography. You are sitting, technically, in Lady Eleanor's patch. Imagine, if you will, a line between us that runs from the stage to the auditorium's doors – a sort of Mason-Dixon line if I may so describe it. I am in the South, Auntie Bettie's domain. You are in the North, Lady Eleanor's. Lily is one of Bettie's girls, so she was in the wrong to fix her colours to your mast, if I'm not mixing my metaphors there. It's an agreement those ladies have – Eleanor and Bettie, that is. Ironically, it's designed to avoid the kind of fun . . . er . . . unpleasantness we've just experienced. There will, I fear, be hell to pay for it all later. Eleanor and Bettie are not the forgiving kind.'

'Did you see where Jim Batchelor went?' Grand asked.

'No, I didn't, I'm afraid.' Horner sipped his champagne. 'But, like all these young whippersnappers today, no stomach for a fight.'

Grand stood up. 'I'll take my leave, Mr Horner,' he said. 'I've had plenty of excitement for one day.'

The little match girl was not there that night. Neither were the patrolling coppers who had laid hands on James Batchelor and taken him in for questioning the night Effie died. The usual march past marched past the journalist, and gentlemen in theatre capes and collapsible hats scurried by, avoiding his gaze. There were, after all, plain-clothes policemen about these days and private enquiry agents in the pay of suspicious wives. Batchelor went north towards Piccadilly Circus, wondering how he could tackle Auntie Bettie, whose girl Effie had been. That would have to wait for another night.

Matthew Grand realized as soon as he was outside the theatre that he was all but lost. He had never been here before, not in this part of London, and he didn't care for the clientele walking past him. There were roughs in threadbare bum-freezers, flat caps and scarves; heavy swells dressed like the Great Vance inside; and ladies of the night like the two who had fought over him. Not once did he see a policeman or a man of the cloth.

A lad, perhaps sixteen, accosted him: 'Bit o' brown, guv'nor?' The boy was wearing lipstick despite the rough clothes. Matthew Grand had no idea what that was and turned him down.

'Get lost, Maryanne!' a hard-faced trollop yelled at the boy. 'Can't you see the gentleman needs a bit of red?' She turned her sweetest smile on him. 'What's your fancy, handsome?'

After the events of the last weeks, Matthew Grand had no idea what his fancy was. Was that weeks? Or was it years? Since that flag came down at Fort Sumter, his life had been one of turmoil, march and countermarch, reveille and recall.

In the watchfires of a hundred circling camps he had seen his future written in blood. And now, here he was, in an alien land that had not known war on its own soil for generations. It was a land of wealth and bustle, and this, the greatest city in the world, had no heart. It had not lost its President, had not had the soul ripped out of it.

'I said,' the girl said, 'what's your fancy?'

Before Grand could answer, there was a scream, shrill and stark, one that would chill anyone's blood. The girl backed into the shadows and disappeared as surely as Batchelor's match girl had. No one else seemed to notice. Cries like that and screams of murder punctuated the Haymarket any night of the week. The crowds kept surging, and the carriage wheels turning. Only the ex-captain of cavalry had noticed. Only the man from Ford's Theatre knew instinctively that something was very wrong. The sound had come out of the blackness, the alleyway next to the theatre. An alleyway that reminded him of that bad Good Friday. He half expected to see Peanut John steadying a skittish horse halfway along its length and to come face to face with a man with the devil's face, one who said to him, 'You didn't think it would be that easy, did you, soldier boy? You didn't think Johnny would come alone?'

The hairs crawled on the back of his neck, and Matthew Grand snatched the Colt from under his frock coat. There was no room for a horse in this theatre alleyway. Only for a dying harlot. He half-stumbled over her boot, where she had kicked it off in her death agony, and had not yet reached her body when a bullseye lantern flashed directly in his face. 'You. Keep back. This is police business.'

Grand could see nothing beyond the lantern's beam. A copper had come out of nowhere. 'Get back,' the constable barked. 'There's a woman butchered.'

The man's voice was still ricocheting around Matthew Grand's head as he slid the revolver away and made for the light.

The crowd on the Navy Yard shore had grown thick as the sun began to set on the capital. Most of them were Southerners, women with red eyes and blurred make-up, gentlemen taking off their hats as their dead hero floated by. He was not Booth the murderer who had shot his President, defenceless, in the back of the head; he was John Wilkes Booth, the Avenger who had gone to a martyr's grave in a whirlwind of fire.

Now he was being carried to his last resting place along the Anacostia River. They watched the little rowboat turn with the current to the jut of land, dark against the evening, called Giesboro Point where the slaughtered horses of the Confederacy were already being boiled down for glue and bones – the end of Jeb Stuart's cavalry. The watcher with the telescope was keeping a running commentary on what he saw. The two bearded officers in Yankee blue were lowering John Wilkes Booth over the side. They heard the rattle of the chain and the splash of the water and saw both men and the sailors who had rowed them into midstream take off their hats. The Southerners nodded. It was the least those Goddamn Yankees could do.

The Goddamn Yankees let the lead weights go and replaced their hats.

'Do you think they'll fall for that?' Luther Baker asked his cousin.

Lafayette Baker looked across to the crowd on the shore. It was difficult to see in the gathering dusk, but it seemed they were breaking up, going home. 'I sure hope so,' he said. 'Boys. Row for Greenleaf. Mr Booth here—' he kicked the corpse in its tarpaulin – 'has a meeting with a cellar in the Old Penitentiary. You boys seen nothing, heard nothing; got it?'

'Loud and clear, Colonel,' one of the sailors said and grinned as Lafayette Baker threw coins at them.

'Luther, we've got work to do. This bastard's going to Hell, and we're sending him part way there ourselves.'

Luther Baker had never considered himself much of a master-builder. And he wasn't much of a gravedigger, either. Even so, he took pride in the job he and his cousin Lafayette had done, especially in a hurry, especially by candlelight. This part of the Old Penitentiary was off the beaten track, a storeroom for the war years, and now the man who had killed Lincoln would rot under the flagstones, themselves covered with ammunition chests and gun limbers. The Bakers had done the job themselves, away from prying eyes and the gossiping tongues of prison guards.

Lafayette rested his back, glad the work was finished. It was unseasonably warm for a May evening, and his shirt was clinging to his back. 'News from our friend, Lu,' he said, swigging from his hip flask and pulling a crumpled telegram from his trouser pocket. 'Captain Grand is taking in the sights of London, apparently. Hasn't tipped his hand yet.'

'Why'd you let him go, Laff?' Luther asked. 'If you think he's involved?'

'Why did we just bury John Wilkes Booth in the middle of the Anacostia?' Lafayette chuckled. 'Smoke and mirrors. Grand is a soldier and by all accounts a damned good one. If he ran wild in these United States of ours, we'd never find him. Over there, in a strange country, he'll be off his guard. He won't think we're still watching.'

'So it's all down to our friend.' Luther nodded, reaching for his coat.

'And in this business,' Lafayette said, 'a man never knows who his friends are, does he?'

Grand knew he had to think fast, and so he let his military training take over. He put his head down and charged for the man behind the light. He knew deep down that he should really walk forward rationally, slowly, with his hands in the air, speaking clearly and explaining just what had happened. He knew that he should remain calm and not antagonize the Limey policeman; he became aware of another gap in his knowledge of England, and right at this moment it was a very important one. *Are English policemen armed?* Somehow, it had just never cropped up in any conversation he could remember having. He hoped that his hunch – that they carried nightsticks, no more – was right. To his surprise, the policeman at the top of the alleyway stepped aside and, taking advantage of the speed he had built up, Grand leaned hard to the left, swinging around the end of the alleyway and heading back the way he had come. He was aware that rattles were ahead of him, and he prepared to slip past them, using the element of surprise if he could. Not many people liked to stand in the way of over 200 pounds of Matthew Grand at a dead run.

In the end, it didn't take a head-on collision to stop him, just an elegant boot extended by one of Auntie Bettie's girls who had seen the way the wind was blowing. Although she hoped the handsome American was innocent of murdering anyone, she couldn't be too careful. She and her sisters had become the prey on the prairie of the Haymarket and, with the instincts of her kind, she had acted to try and improve the odds. Grand went down like a poleaxed steer and lay at the feet of Constable Morris groaning faintly.

The girl stepped forward. 'Any reward?' she asked, knowing the answer before she heard it.

'No,' Morris said shortly. 'If this gentleman turns out to have been running for a cab, you may be subject to proceedings. So if you'd like to come along of Constable Brown, here, we'll take your details at the station.'

''Ere,' the girl said, shaking herself free of Brown's hand on her sleeve. 'I didn't do nothing. He was running away from where that copper was flashing his bullseye. I just done what any law-abiding citizen would do.'

'Law-abiding?' Morris said. 'Don't make me laugh. What copper, anyway?' He was feeling a little puzzled himself. He had definitely heard a commotion – that was why he had come running. But there were only two men on duty in the Haymarket that night, both of them looking at each other.

The girl pointed towards the head of the alleyway and looked surprised. 'There was definitely a copper there,' she said. 'I saw his bullseye. He called out. Something about a woman murdered. Butchered. Something like that.'

Morris looked at her. She seemed to be telling the truth, and he was still smarting from the reprimand he had had from Tanner when the last girl had died. 'Stay here,' he said to her. To Brown, he said, 'Stay with this bloke. Don't let him get away.'

Brown looked down at Grand, who had decided, in the small piece of his mind still functioning, that he was actually really tired and could do with a sleep. Accordingly, he had curled his arm around his head and was snoring gently. But still, Brown thought, better this menial task than the gore which awaited Morris in the alley. The crowd had started to thin. With any luck, all this would be a false alarm and he could carry on his beat as though none of it had ever happened. But one look at Morris's face as he appeared from the darkness put paid to that. It was another one, there was no doubt. The Haymarket murderer had claimed another soul.

'I'll mind her,' a voice croaked at Brown's elbow. 'You've got places to be.'

'Who are you?' the constable asked.

'My name's Lavenham,' the man said. 'Hall keeper at this theatre. Know it like the back of my hand.'

'What do you mean, you'll mind her?' Brown wanted to know.

'It's another one, ain't it?' The old man squinted up at him. 'Same as the other two. My granddaughters are their age. What if it was one of them, eh? Not that they'd be selling their bodies in the Haymarket nights, but you never know.'

Constable Brown knew that leaving a civilian in charge of a corpse and a murder scene was contrary to every regulation in the book, but he didn't like corpses or murder scenes. 'All right,' he said. 'We're taking this bloke in. You don't touch anything. And above all, you don't let anybody down that alley. Understood?'

Lavenham nodded, and the constables and their dead weight were gone.

The Haymarket murderer slipped away as the crowd began to go its separate ways. Lavenham's invective against the morbidly curious was surprisingly effective. The killer had not come out looking for a victim this particular evening, but after his first time, when he had gone home with blood on his hands, his face and his shirt and had been lucky to get away with it, he had come prepared. His clothes were dark, his cuffs tucked into the sleeves, unfashionably short, but he had never aspired to sartorial splendour. He carried, in an oiled silk bag in his pocket, a damp cloth, which he used to wipe his hands and face, just in case any spray from the last pump of the woman's heart should land on him with the mark of Cain. This time, as he examined the cloth covertly in the light of a window, he had not needed these preparations. He was as clean as his conscience. Humming quietly to himself one of the Music Hall's most catchy tunes, he swung into step with a group of swells, out on the town and getting more excitement than they had bargained for, and surged through the door of the nearest pub and raised his voice with theirs, calling for ale, for gin, for whisky, and so he disappeared, one among millions, until he stepped out again, hunting.

Grand was presenting rather a problem for Morris and Brown. He was stirring, but far from conscious, and he was too heavy to be carried, even if any of the small crowd remaining looked keen to help. Auntie Bettie's girl had taken the opportunity to leave the scene, so at least they only had one miscreant to deal with – if he proved to be a miscreant and not simply a well-meaning bystander. Morris took off his helmet to scratch his head.

'How are we going to get this big bugger down to the station?' he asked Brown.

'Drag him?' Brown was beginning to wish he had followed his old dad into the mud-larking trade. It wasn't clean and the hours could be shocking but at least no one ever asked you your opinion.

'In that suit?' Morris was shocked. 'It would ruin it.'

'But . . .' Brown was confused. 'If he's the Haymarket Murderer . . .?'

'I see your point,' Morris conceded. 'But if he *isn't* the Haymarket Murderer, it could take you and me years to pay off that suit.'

Brown saw his chance and took it. 'Not me,' he said, hurriedly. 'You're the senior man, as you always remind me. It would be your fault if his suit gets ruined.'

'Not if you're doing the dragging,' Morris chipped in quickly.

A voice from the pavement stopped them before the argument became too heated.

'What say one or both of you help me up?' Grand said, each word seeming to be dredged up from a huge depth. 'Then I can walk to the station, though I don't think I was planning

to catch a train, was I? Everything seems a little . . .' He
searched for a while for the right word. 'Murky.'

The policemen were galvanized into action and helped
Grand struggle to his feet. They managed to steer a middle
ground between helping a stricken gentleman get up and
restraining a potentially violent criminal, and eventually the
American was upright, but leaning heavily on Brown.

'What time is my train?' he asked, trying to focus his
eyes.

'Come and have a sit down first, sir,' Morris suggested,
impressing himself with his ingenuity. 'We'll make you a cup
of tea. Just till you feel better.'

Grand looked at him solemnly. 'You're a policeman,' he
told him. Morris saw remembrance dawn behind his eyes and
held on to his arm a little harder. 'A policeman was shouting.'
He stood up straighter and shook off Morris's hand. 'He shone
a light in my eyes. Say! There's a dead girl in that alley!' He
tried to stumble back to where he had found the body. Morris
caught hold of his coat, and as Grand swung round, still
unsteady on his feet, his Colt gleamed from under his armpit.

Morris jumped back. 'Watch him, Brown,' he yelled. 'He's
got a gun!'

Brown let go of Grand, who fell again, this time on to his
hands and knees, where he stayed, shaking his head to clear
it.

Brown and Morris, for once moving in a concerted effort,
pulled him up, one on either arm, and securely handcuffed
him, with his hands behind his back.

'I think I will have to ask you to come with us to the police
station,' Morris said, firmly.

'What for?'

It was a reasonable question, the policemen both thought.
He may have murdered the dead woman in the alleyway,
although that seemed unlikely owing to the complete lack of
blood about his person. Other than that, apart from knocking
himself out on the pavement, he had done nothing. Carrying
a gun wasn't against the law, it was just . . . not very British.
And as far as any of the men knew, that was not as yet a
crime.

'Er . . . we need to check your papers,' Morris offered eventually. 'As a foreigner, we need to check that you are who you say you are.'

'Why?'

Again, not unreasonable. It wasn't as though anyone out on the streets that night could prove who they were with total certainty.

'New legislation,' Brown said, off the cuff, and Morris gave him an admiring nod.

'Is it in your Constitution?' Grand demanded.

Brown had enjoyed history at school and dredged up a piece of information. 'England doesn't have a written constitution,' he announced proudly. 'We leave that to the new countries.'

Somehow, there didn't seem to be much of an answer to that, and Grand, against the grain, decided to go quietly.

The pavements that evening weren't really empty enough for a young journalist out for a walk to clear his head. Every other step there seemed to be someone after Batchelor's money, whether for food, drink or other less salubrious products. When he had been accosted twice by rather dubious gentlemen offering to pay him for his services, he decided to turn back. He still had his ticket and would no doubt be able to inveigle his way back in to the Music Hall and rejoin what some people might describe as his friends. He made his way back to the Haymarket and was about to go up the steps into the foyer when something caught his eye.

The something was Grand's rather distinctive hat, pale and wide-brimmed, kicked into the gutter and with a footprint squarely in the middle of its dented crown. Batchelor stood there looking down at it and then bent to pick it up, trying to push it back into shape, without notable success. He looked this way and that, knowing as he did so that it was pointless. Grand was nowhere in sight or earshot; the journalist hadn't known him long, but he was sure that Grand would not go quietly, no matter what had happened to him; he also knew that it was now his job to look for him and rescue him if he could. He felt a responsibility for the big American as well as the feeling that his disappearance might give him a story others of his erstwhile colleagues would kill for. Not to mention the story the man had already hinted at.

Like a bloodhound, he quartered the scene, looking for clues. There was no blood on the pavement, so that was a good thing. There were some scuffs in the grime, but that meant little. He discounted checking inside the theatre; wherever Grand was, he had not calmly gone back inside, leaving his battered headgear behind. Batchelor looked up the street. What lay in that direction? There was only one answer – Vine Street Police Station. If that was where he was, it could mean one of two things. Either Grand had been arrested for causing some sort of affray, which was not that unlikely, or he had been set upon and then taken there for safety. Whichever the case, Batchelor knew that he would be confused by the strange ways of the London police force; it wasn't too long since that he had been in its clutches, and he had been rather confused himself – and he had lived in the city all his life. Trying not to run and therefore arrive hot and dishevelled, the journalist headed off for the police station as quickly as he could.

THIRTEEN

I t took Batchelor a while to establish with the desk man who he was, but as soon as he mentioned an American, the tone changed and the sergeant was sweetness and light. This kind constable would take the gentleman down to see him because, indeed, there was an American in Interview Room Number One.

By the time the euphemism dawned on Batchelor he found himself in the same cell he had spent the night in before, devoid of anything but a solitary candle to lighten his gloom. Before he had a chance to protest, the door had slammed shut and the grille scraped to. After that, the only noises were footfalls and the rattle of keys. His brain whirled. What was going on? He had only popped out, it seemed to him, for a moment's air, and now here he was again, in one of the most stinking cells in London. Last time he had been accused of murder. What would it be now?

After nearly an hour he heard the footfalls coming back and the rattle of keys again, this time in his lock. The door swung wide and Inspector Tanner stood there. 'Well, well, well . . .'

The man looked as though he had not slept for a week, and his tie dangled around his neck, his waistcoat undone.

'This is becoming something of a habit,' Batchelor chided him.

'It certainly is. Are you looking for Mr Grand?'

'I am.' Batchelor was on his feet.

Tanner beckoned him forward. 'Mr Grand is helping us with our enquiries,' he said.

'Ah, the *Orient*. Yes, yes, of course.'

'The *Orient*?' Tanner frowned, his arm still across the door and blocking Batchelor's way out into the murky, tile-clad corridor.

'Er . . .'

'We seem to make a habit of talking at cross purposes, Mr Batchelor. The help that Mr Grand was giving us relates to a murder in the Haymarket.'

'The Haymarket?' Batchelor repeated. 'But he knows nothing about the murders in the Haymarket.'

'Oh, but he does,' Tanner said. 'He was there.'

'What?' None of this was making sense to the former Fleet Street man.

'Mr Grand tells us he saw the murderer. Further, he believes the murderer to be a policeman. Now, what's this about the *Orient*?'

James Batchelor took stock of his situation and came to a decision. 'One murder at a time,' he said. 'You tell me how Grand is involved in the Haymarket, and I'll tell you about the *Orient*.'

Tanner looked at him. 'I've got a better idea,' he said. 'Why don't we cut out the middle man, so to speak, and all of us talk about this together?' And he dropped his arm and led the way down the corridor.

They walked up a flight of stairs and turned left at the top, through a door marked 'Private'. Inside the room they entered, a gas light fizzed and flickered, flashing green shadows on the face of Matthew Grand.

'I believe you gentlemen know each other,' Tanner said.

Like the inspector, Grand had discarded his suit jacket and loosened his tie. There was a cup of coffee on the table in front of him, along with his papers and a .32 calibre Colt pistol, with a short barrel suitable for a shoulder holster. That holster was still under his left armpit.

'Matthew.' Batchelor grabbed a chair and sat down next to him. The man's forehead was swollen and bruised. 'I hope this is not the work of the Metropolitan Police, Inspector.'

'No, no,' Grand said. 'It's the work, I understand, of a fast-thinking lady of the night. One of your scarlet sisters tripped me up on the sidewalk. It's my own damn fool fault.'

'Quite so,' said Tanner, sliding back his own chair. 'Just to make all things clear, Mr Batchelor, where were you tonight? Before you came looking for Mr Grand, that is.'

'At the Haymarket,' Batchelor said.

'You missed all the fun.' Grand winced, feeling his head throb anew.

'Fun, Mr Grand?' Tanner's face assumed an aspect that Batchelor hadn't seen before. 'You call the murder of a young woman *fun*?'

'Murder?' Batchelor repeated, looking desperately from one face to another.

'I was referring to the fisticuffs of earlier,' Grand explained. 'Oh, but of course, you missed that too.'

'Will somebody *please* tell me what's going on?' Batchelor shouted, way past the end of his tether by now.

'Certainly,' said Tanner. 'I understand there was the usual rowdyism at the Haymarket, involving a number of unfortunates with Mr Grand in the middle of it. No one called us, so we must put that down to part of Mr Argyll's idea of entertainment. So far, so humdrum. But this is where it gets interesting. Version one is that Mr Grand, here, inflamed perhaps by the proximity of so much pulchritude, goes out into the street, accosts a girl and strangles her with wire.'

'I told you—' Grand began.

'Version two—' Tanner cut him short – 'is that somebody else did that and Mr Grand merely arrived on the scene moments later. Does any of this sound familiar to you, Mr Batchelor?'

The journalist nodded, open-mouthed. 'It does,' he said at last. 'My exact experience with Effie.'

'Now—' Tanner leaned back – 'I ask myself: what are the odds of two gentlemen who know each other both stumbling on similar murders in the same part of London, only a few nights apart? Strains credulity, don't you think?'

'It has to be coincidence,' Batchelor said.

Tanner chuckled, but it was mirthless. 'Search the detectives' handbook from cover to cover, Mr Batchelor,' he said, 'and you will find no such word. In short, the Metropolitan Police do not believe in coincidences.'

A silence followed in which each man tried to guess what was going on in the minds of the other two.

'Tell me about the *Orient*,' Tanner said, looking hard at

Grand. Grand, in turn, looked hard at Batchelor. Nothing.
'You see, as soon as the incomparable constables Morris
and Brown brought you in here, I knew I'd seen your face
before,' the inspector went on. 'It was at the offices of Messrs
Inman, the shipping line, in Leadenhall Street. Technically,
of course, I was out of my patch, treading on the toes of
my colleagues in the City Force, but needs must when the
devil drives.'

Grand looked up. 'The devil?'

'I never forget a face, Mr Grand,' Tanner went on.

'Neither do I,' the American assured him.

Another silence.

'Oh, for God's sake, Matthew, tell him,' Batchelor blurted
out. 'You're looking for a needle in a haystack, and this is the
man with a magnet.'

For a long moment, Grand said nothing, then he leaned
back in his chair. 'Very well,' he said. 'I'm looking for a man
named Charles Dundreary.'

'Why?' Tanner asked.

'He owes me money,' Grand said, ignoring the look that
Batchelor gave him. 'Swindled me in a card game back in
Washington. The bastard ran to New York and caught the
Orient. I followed.'

'On the *City of Manchester*, yes,' Tanner said, nodding.
'How much does this Mr Dundreary owe you?'

'Five hundred dollars.'

Tanner whistled through his teeth. 'I can see why you want
to find him,' he said. 'But of course, what intrigues me is that
there was a murder on the *Orient*.'

'There was?' Grand appeared the innocent.

'You know very well there was,' Tanner said. 'I overheard
the clerk at Inman's, telling you all about it.'

'I was merely curious,' Grand lied. 'It has nothing to do
with me.'

'Oh, but I think it does,' the inspector said. 'Either Mr
Dundreary was the victim of that murder – which we both
know he was not – or he was the murderer.'

'Again,' Grand said, shrugging, 'that may be the case.

Dundreary may be a murderer, but I want him for another reason altogether.'

'He owes you money.'

Grand nodded. 'Precisely.'

If the silences before were painful, this one was positively agonizing. Again, it was Tanner who broke it. He stood and picked up Grand's papers, passing them to him. Then, as Grand stood, he picked up the gun, twirled it with lightning speed around his finger and handed it butt-first to its owner. 'Don't leave London, Mr Grand,' he said, 'and if I hear that you carry this again, I will take it from you personally, and what I do with it then will bring tears to your eyes, that I guarantee.'

Grand nodded and slid the Colt into his holster.

'And Mr Batchelor?' The inspector turned from the door. 'Next time you go to the Haymarket, I'd be careful of the friends you take with you.'

Once they were well away from the Vine Street Police Station, Matthew Grand thought he would have a quiet, confidential word with James Batchelor. Before that, however, the American picked up the Englishman by the lapels and bounced him against the wall.

'What part of "you must not tell a living soul" did you not understand, Batchelor?'

'You told me it was "the story" – and I quote – "of a lifetime".'

Grand relaxed his grip a little. 'Only when I'm darned good and ready for you to publish it.' And he dropped the man and marched away.

'When will that be?' Batchelor pulled his jacket back into place and followed him. It was barely light yet, and the streets were nearly deserted in this part of London.

Grand stopped and spun round. 'When I've found this son of a bitch,' he said.

'I'm looking for a son of a bitch too.' Somehow the phrase didn't sound quite right coming from Batchelor.

'So what are you suggesting?' Grand asked. He was walking already.

'We work together.' Batchelor ran and skipped alongside him. 'Two heads are better than one, eh? I know this city like the back of my hand, and you know the man you're looking for.'

'That's not going to help you with the Haymarket killings,' Grand said.

'No, that's true. But one thing at a time. Have you tried the street directories?'

'The what?' Grand had never heard of them.

'Street directories. Kelly's is the best. They contain lists of every ratepayer, house by house, since 1851. What if Dundreary's there?'

'I think we can assume that's not the feller's real name,' Grand muttered. 'And now we've got that detective in there thinking I'm up to my neck in murder.'

'Thanks for the swindling card-cheat story, by the way,' Batchelor said. 'I wasn't quite ready for that one.'

Grand stopped walking and looked at the man. 'Look, the only other detectives I know, apart from Tanner back there, are a couple of cousins named Baker back home. Either of them would slit a man's throat if the fancy took them, and I don't suppose your police are any different.'

Batchelor found himself defending the man. 'I think Tanner's straight as a die.'

'Yeah, and I'm Stonewall Jackson's left tit,' Grand rumbled. 'Godammit, Batchelor, I'm working undercover for the American government, for God's sake. I can't go broadcasting that to every flatfoot I meet. Or every hack, come to that.'

'I'm sorry.' Batchelor spread his arms. 'Look, it'll be daylight soon. There's a chop house around the corner that does devilled kidneys which you simply won't believe. My treat, for a change. What do you say?'

Grand had walked on again but now he stopped. It had been a rough few hours one way or another, and perhaps it was time to take stock for a while. He looked at Batchelor. The man was clearly a loose-mouthed idiot, but he meant well. And he *did* know this city like the back of his hand.

'Devilled kidneys, huh?' the American said. 'All right. You

talked me into it. And tell me about these Haymarket killings – one way or another, they've sort of landed in my lap too.'

The next night, as the candles guttered in Mrs Biggs' upstairs room, James Batchelor came to a decision. He had promised to report daily to George Sala at the *Telegraph*, and he hadn't done it. Neither could he walk openly into the offices of Thornton Leigh Hunt for fear of being sued for trespass. So there had to be a middle way, and he dashed off a message in time to catch the last telegraph. 'I have news. Re our American cousin. Batchelor.'

St James's Park was bathed in sunshine the next morning, and George Sala was sitting on a bench throwing crumbs to the ducks. He'd never felt at one with nature but occasionally his feathered friends were a lot more companionable than those in suits. They squawked and squabbled at his feet, threatening to nip his fingers with their lightning bills – very like Fleet Street, really.

'You're late.' He didn't look up as James Batchelor sat down beside him. The younger man opened up a box of sandwiches and started munching as though he and Sala had never met and were not about to have a conversation.

'Sorry.' Batchelor was talking out of the side of his mouth.

'Are you going to do that all the time?' Sala asked, leaning away from the man. 'Because if you are, this conversation is at an end. People will stare.'

'Sorry.'

'And don't keep saying sorry. What have you got for me?' Sala was already wondering if this truly was a good idea.

'Well, not a lot, George, actually.'

'I happen to know you've been to Vine Street,' Sala said, still throwing crumbs, 'and that friend Grand was taken into custody.'

'All a misunderstanding,' Batchelor explained. 'He was in the wrong place at the wrong time.'

'Yes.' Sala sighed. 'Rather like he was at Ford's Theatre. Look, I'm not remotely interested in some harlots going the way of all flesh. I'm interested in what happened in Washington on Good Friday.'

'You can't believe Matthew was involved in the Lincoln assassination,' Batchelor said. 'He's working for the government.'

'Oh, Matthew, is it?' Sala sneered. 'Take my advice, Batchelor, and don't get too close to this man. And I know he's working for the government. What I don't know is what else he's up to.'

'There was a murder on the *SS Orient*. She sailed into Liverpool two days before Grand arrived. He thinks that murder is connected somehow with the Lincoln conspiracy.'

'Does he?' Sala had stopped throwing his bread now, and the ducks were becoming rebellious, pecking his shoes and socks. 'That's interesting. Did he say why?'

Batchelor was torn. Here was a journalist he respected enormously, and the man was paying his wages at the moment. On the other hand he'd developed a liking for Grand and he had betrayed him once already, to Tanner. He wasn't about to do it again. 'No,' he said, straight-faced.

'Well, get on to it.' Sala slipped a plain, buff envelope into Batchelor's pocket. 'I want to know about the *Orient*. And for God's sake, Batchelor, will you stop this ludicrous hole in a corner meeting nonsense? We're not spies, dammit. Only spies meet in St James's Park.'

At the telegraph office that afternoon, George Sala was at his terse best. Usually a verbose and flowing wordsmith, telegrams cost money, and he could hardly put it down to the *Telegraph*'s expense account.

'Nothing yet,' he wrote. 'Will keep you posted.' And he sent it to Lafayette Baker, Washington.

Matthew Grand had sat in the Reading Room of the British Museum for what seemed like days. Bearded old men covered in cobwebs sat with him, their noses buried in tomes as dry and dusty as they were. The clerk was helpfulness itself, except that he was no help at all. Various maps and deeds appeared before Grand, brought up from the bowels of the building on a little hand-drawn cart. They all contained the same thing:

umpteen depictions of the red cross and sword badge on the cufflink Peanut John had found in the alleyway next to Ford's Theatre. And Grand learned for the umpteenth time that it was the coat of arms of the Corporation of the City of London. Their motto read *'Domine dirige nos'* – Lord, direct us. And how fervently Matthew Grand repeated that in the days ahead.

The clerk could be of no further use – but if sir wanted to know more, perhaps he could try the College of Arms in Queen Victoria Street? He couldn't miss it.

Actually, Matthew Grand did miss it, twice. The entrance and west wing were undergoing a rebuilding, and Irishmen with loud voices and unintelligible shouts swarmed all over it, up ladders and along planking, carrying bricks on their shoulders. When he was at last inside, Grand explained the purpose of his visit. A friend of his in America had had a pair of cufflinks made, and he was anxious to track down the craftsman concerned.

A bald man with a permanent stoop did his best to help and cradled the cufflink lovingly. 'Ah, the Corporation,' he said, beaming. 'Argent a cross gules, in the first quarter a sword in pale point upwards of the last.' He caught the look of disbelief on Grand's face. 'Oh, sorry,' he said. 'It's how we heralds speak. I'm Thomas Leslie, by the way, Rouge Croix Pursuivant in Ordinary to give you my full moniker. I don't suppose you have people like me at home.'

'Er . . . not exactly, no.'

'Asprey's,' the herald said.

'I beg your pardon.'

'Asprey's, jewellers for gentlefolk of discernment and pots of money. If anyone makes those things, it'll be Asprey's. New Bond Street. You can't miss it.'

'It's more the man I'm after,' Grand said, 'rather than the cufflink.'

'I don't follow.' Leslie frowned.

'Well, it's ridiculous, really. I met this Englishman in Washington recently and we got on famously. He left this behind inadvertently, and I wanted to return it to him.'

'An extraordinarily generous gesture, sir, if I may say so, to travel three thousand miles to return a gewgaw.'

'Well, I had business in London anyhow, but the silly thing is, I can't remember the feller's name. I was hoping the crest might be a club or a fraternity or something.'

'Well, I suppose the City of London *is* a club of sorts, from the Lord Mayor down. But anyone can purchase cufflinks like these, sir. You don't actually have to be a member of the Corporation. It is made up of the City Livery Companies, and each of them has their own coat of arms, of course. Did your friend not leave you with a forwarding address?'

Grand laughed, bitter, hollow, empty. 'No,' he said. 'Our last meeting was rather rushed. It must have slipped his mind.' He thanked the herald and strode for the door. 'By the way,' he said. 'The College of Arms' motto.' He pointed to the gorgeous carving on the wall. 'What does it mean?'

'Oh, that?' Leslie smiled. 'Diligent and secret.'

James Batchelor thought he had drawn the longer straw when he ended up with the task of visiting Auntie Bettie. He had had his moments with women, or so he liked to claim, but if he were to be scrupulously honest he would have to say that those moments had been very short and very few and far between – and had never featured any of Auntie Bettie's girls, who were in the middle echelons of ladies of uncertain virtue, if only by the parameter of price. The one good thing about this was that she was easily found. Her premises in the strangely apt Charles II Street were palatial by anyone's standards, although possibly a little rococo for some tastes. He was let in by a maid in black bombazine and a flirty little cap low on her brow. He asked, rather diffidently, to speak to Auntie Bettie and was shown into a plush drawing room to the right of the hall. He was looking at the portraits around the walls when he heard a soft step behind him.

'Hello, young man,' a deep voice drawled, almost in his ear. 'Now, how can I help you, I wonder?'

He spun round, his heart in his mouth. There was something about the voice that had made his private places turn to water and ice all at once. The woman standing there was a beauty, there was no denying it. Her hair was blonde and lustrous, her skin like milk. If she was now the wrong side of forty, it didn't seem to matter. She laid a gentle hand on his arm, and he felt it through the fabric as though it were a red-hot iron.

'Oh, I see,' she said and smiled kindly. 'This is your first time and you thought you'd come to Auntie Bettie. You won't regret it, my boy, not for a minute.' She appraised him by holding him at arm's-length. 'You're not tall, so Sophia is out. She would overwhelm a little tiddler like you. Anna, now she might be the answer; she is very good with the inexperienced among my clientele. I would give you Bertha, but . . . well, she rides her gentlemen hard and I'm not sure you'd—'

'I'm not here for a girl,' Batchelor blurted out and blushed immediately.

Auntie Bettie didn't miss a beat. 'I can't help you myself, but if you turn left out of here and then right at—'

'No, no, no.' Batchelor had an idea that things were not going as he had planned. 'I'm not looking for a girl or . . . well, that's not why I'm here. I wanted to see you specifically.'

She patted his arm and laughed musically. 'Sweet boy,' she said. 'I don't actually take gentlemen myself these days, although for a dear little thing like you I might make an exception.' She narrowed her eyes at him. 'You might have to take it slowly. I'm older than I look.'

'No!' Batchelor all but stamped his foot. 'I want to talk to you about these murders in the Haymarket. I work for the *Telegraph.*'

'*Press?*' Auntie Bettie hissed. 'You're *Press?* You little weasel, coming in here, pretending you wanted to lose your cherry in my establishment. I'll call the police! False representation! Fraud!'

Batchelor was on firmer ground now. Threats, he could handle. 'I don't think you will call the police, will you?' he said, reasonably. 'Why wouldn't you want to talk about your girls? They did nothing wrong.'

'The last I heard prostitution was against the law of the land. But I'm not here to talk morality with you. They picked a wrong 'un,' she said, sourly. 'All three of them. They had been trained. *Trained*, I tell you, by the best in the business.

Me! I tell them not to go anywhere dark unless they know who they're with. First-time customers, stay in the light.'

'Really?' Batchelor was intrigued despite himself. 'In the light? Don't your . . . gentlemen . . . mind?'

'In the light needn't mean in the open.' Auntie Bettie had moved away and was lounging on a chaise longue by the window with the light falling just so on her hair and profile. She had had long years to perfect her best side. 'I just encourage them to take their gentlemen somewhere a little secluded but not a dark alley – so common, I always think, don't you? I'm not naive enough, Mr . . .'

'Batchelor,' the journalist told her.

'Your real name?'

'Of course.'

She smiled indulgently. 'So sweet,' she murmured. 'I am not so naive, Mr Batchelor, to have failed to notice that my girls do a little work off the cuff, as it were. Making a few extra pennies for their retirement. For heaven's sake,' she said, chuckling, 'that's how I got started, after all. But even so, I tell them until I am blue in the face, stay away from dark places. And now, look, Effie, Marie and Francine, all gone.'

'None of Lady Eleanor's girls have been involved,' Batchelor said. 'Is that just bad luck for you?'

She tossed her head. 'Even a maniac can see that my girls are superior, Mr Batchelor. And I'll forgive you your foe par of a moment ago.'

'My . . . er . . .?'

'You mentioned the name of a certain "lady" – and I use the word loosely, as you may expect. Her name is never to be mentioned under my roof.'

'This maniac – do you have any idea who it might be?' He decided on the direct approach.

'No, and that's the truth,' she said, gazing at him. 'My boys would soon deal with the madman if I knew who he was. I just don't have a single idea. I've told my girls to work in pairs for a while. Some of the gentlemen like it that way, and if they don't, one can keep watch. I'm letting them keep an extra shilling, so they don't lose money.'

Batchelor found himself telling her, 'That's very generous of you.'

She nodded. 'I love my girls, Mr Batchelor. You may find it hard to believe, but I do. If you find out who's doing this, let me know. The boys will soon sort him out. You can't trust the peelers to get it right. They're idiots to a man. Especially that fool upstairs right now; he's the worst of the lot.'

'Upstairs?' Batchelor looked up as though the ceiling might be glass. 'Who is it?'

'Wouldn't you like to know?' Auntie Bettie chuckled. 'And him so highly placed at the Yard, too. But discretion is my middle name, lad.' She got up suddenly and, in a few sinuous strides, was at his side. 'Now, about that cherry of yours . . .'

FOURTEEN

'Tell me about your co-workers.' Grand blew smoke rings to the ceiling of the Cavendish.

'My . . .?'

'Oh, really, James. We've had this conversation. The men you work with . . . at the *Telegraph*.'

'Past tense, dear boy, I'm afraid,' Batchelor said. 'Well, there's Joe Buckley . . .'

'No, not him. Tell me about Dyer.'

'Edwin? Why?'

'Humour me,' Grand said.

'Well, he's my age, I suppose. A year older, perhaps. Got an eye for the ladies.'

'Has he now?'

'According to him he hasn't paid any rent for the last three years. Moves every other month, however, so that his various landladies don't get all proprietorial over him.'

'Is there an American connection?'

'If you mean, was he a conspirator along with John Wilkes Booth, I don't think that's possible. Anyway, you saw the man in the alley by Ford's. Dundreary or whatever his name really is. You said you'd know him immediately you clapped eyes on him.'

'Yes, I would.' Grand nodded solemnly. 'But isn't that the whole point about a conspiracy? It's not down to one man. What about Horner?'

'Old Gabriel?' Batchelor chuckled. 'Come on, Matthew. The man's in his dotage . . . Oh, my God.'

'What?' Grand sat upright.

'Oh, it's probably nothing, but, well, he's been around has old Gabriel. Don't ask me which paper he was working on at the time, but he once went to Washington.'

'Washington?' Grand repeated.

'This must have been in the late 'forties. He was doing a

follow-up piece to the burning of the place by the British. I don't think it went very well.'

'But he knows the capital?' Grand was thinking aloud.

'Yes, I suppose he does. Look, Matthew, what's all this about?'

'The cufflink,' Grand explained. 'The one I wrenched off in my tussle with Dundreary in Baptist Alley.'

'What about it?'

'The arms of the City of London Corporation.'

'Yes, I know. So what?'

'So, when you have spent as long in the library of the British Museum as I have, your mind wanders. The clerk there told me the Corporation was made up of what he called livery companies.'

'So?'

Grand leaned closer, looking his man in the eyes. 'So, two of those Worshipful Companies are the Dyers and the Horners. Had a good look at the cuffs of these gentlemen lately?'

'Nobody actually lives at the Alhambra,' the clerk at Inman's had told Matthew Grand. So why then had the *Orient*'s passenger Charles Dundreary given that as his address? Could he not have chosen an anonymous suburban villa somewhere, even if actually a cowshed stood on the spot?

Grand had never seen a building quite like it. Even the theatres of New York could not rival it for opulence and space. It occupied nearly the whole of the eastern side of Leicester Square and loomed over the surrounding buildings with its huge dome and imposing towers. Grand had never been to Spain, so the elegant copies of the Moorish facade were lost on him. And he had never been to Constantinople either, so he saw no resemblance to the great mosque of Hagia Sophia.

James Batchelor, on the other hand, had seen it all before and swept past all its glories, clattering up the broad steps to the front door and into the lushly carpeted vestibule. From somewhere beyond the ticket office a band was belting out a Parisian tune, fast and furious, but every now and then it broke off to the tap of a bandmaster's baton and would start again.

There were whoops and shrills from what sounded like an army of girls and the thud of dancing feet.

The pair made their way through a velvet curtain into a darkened auditorium. On the stage ahead, a line of chorus girls sashayed backwards and forwards, with a swish of skirts over silk-stocking clad thighs. They all had hourglass figures and impossible waists, strutting and pirouetting as the band put them through their paces.

'No,' a voice called out from a corner near the stage. 'Again, Anton. Sally and Fiona, will you *please* come in with the others? There are no prima donnas here except me . . .' There was a pause, and the voice turned on the new arrivals. 'What do you want?' it asked. 'The show doesn't start until eight.'

Matthew Grand was standing stock still, his mouth slightly open, his eyes wide.

'Careful, Matthew,' Batchelor muttered. 'I nearly tripped over your tongue there. Mr Strange?' The journalist marched off, hand outstretched, to find the voice in the corner.

A huge man rose to his feet. 'I'm Frederick Strange,' he said. 'Who are you?'

'James Batchelor, sir,' the newsman told him. '*Telegraph.*'

'Ah.' Strange took the man's outstretched hand. 'Gabriel Horner usually writes our reviews.'

'I'm sure he does,' Batchelor improvised, 'but I'm afraid old Gabriel's a little indisposed. He sent me.'

Strange waved his hands, and the band stopped playing in a clatter and squawk of instruments. 'As you were, ladies,' the impresario said, and the grateful girls flopped in various positions on the stage, nattering nineteen to the dozen.

'The cancan, eh?' Batchelor winked and nodded at them. 'I don't think old Gabriel's seen that. Or, perhaps he has and that's why he's indisposed.' He nudged the theatre man in the ribs. Batchelor then became confidential. 'Tell me, is it true that they . . . well, that the girls actually . . .?'

Strange smiled, his teeth flashing gold in the limelight. 'In the last line-up,' he said, 'the *piece de resistance* as it were, all twenty of the luscious lovelies you see on stage now will lift their gowns and reveal their all. There will be no stays, no kecksies, only stockings gartered above the knee.'

Batchelor gulped.

'After that, these ladies will be only too delighted to explain the finer points of *theatre de danse* to any gentlemen of . . . shall we say, an inquisitive nature.' Strange's smile faded, and he looked in Grand's direction. 'Is he all right?' he asked.

'Ah, our American cousin,' Batchelor said. 'Matthew is recently arrived from America.'

'Ah,' Strange said. 'You must find our frivolities somewhat boring after a civil war, Mr . . . er . . .?'

'Grand.' The ex-captain moved at last as the girls giggled. 'Matthew Grand. Tell me, sir, does the name Charles Dundreary mean anything to you?'

Strange blinked. 'As a matter of fact, it does,' he said. 'Well, I'm not sure about the Charles, but Lord Dundreary is a character in a play. *Our American Cousin*, funnily enough, Mr Batchelor . . . or was that a mere coincidence? Gentlemen, would you like to tell me what is going on?'

'Would you do something for me, Mr Strange?' Grand asked. 'Would you say the words, "You didn't think Johnnie would come alone, did you, soldier boy?"'

Strange's mouth opened but no sound came out. He half turned and clapped his hands. In an instant, four large men were making their way through the tables and chairs of the auditorium, and the girls on stage huddled a little closer. 'If you're journalists, I'll eat my hat,' said Strange. 'You've come to gawp at my girls. Well, that's perfectly understandable; we're all men of the world. But there is a time and a place, and the cost is ninepence, drinks and supper extra. Now, I'm a busy man. Get out.'

'Mr Strange!' Batchelor tried to protest, but he suddenly felt large hands on his coat collar and he was being propelled towards the door. About now he expected Grand to employ his thumb-breaker, courtesy of Colonel Colt, but Grand was moving just as rapidly as he was, half lifted by the other two roughs. The pair landed hard on the pavement outside the Alhambra, where a befurred lady started, tutted and whisked away her sickly-looking child.

Batchelor reached for his hat and brushed off the pavement detritus. 'Matthew,' he said. 'That went well.'

Matthew Grand and James Batchelor sat in the smoking room at the Cavendish, enjoying – in Grand's case – a large and well-earned cigar. Batchelor had never really taken to smoking but was quite happy to sit there too, a large port in his hand, all on Grand's tab, and watch the world go by. For a journalist, he was very little versed in the ways of the rich, and everywhere he looked he saw something new, much of which would make a damn fine story under an anonymous byline. Grand was quiet, but he had been knocked unconscious and been thrown ignominiously – and painfully – on to a pavement in the last day or so, and Batchelor left him alone with his aches and pains. Although they had yet to get to know each other well, there was nevertheless an air of friendly contentment in their little leather-clad corner of the world.

Grand suddenly leaned forward, tapping off his ash into the huge cut-glass ashtray on the low table in front of him. 'James . . . do people call you Jim, by the way?'

'They do, but I prefer James. Do people call you Matt?'

Grand smiled. 'Touché, James. I prefer Matthew.'

Batchelor raised his glass a touch. This room was so soporific that he hoped that when it became time for him to go home, someone would just throw a blanket over him and turn out the lights. The chair was certainly far more comfortable than the lumpy bed at Mrs Biggs'.

'You were going to say something?' Batchelor murmured.

'Yes. I was going to suggest that we went back to the Alhambra.'

Batchelor twitched a shoulder, the one that had hit the pavement first. 'Is that wise?'

'Incognito,' Grand said, blowing out a stream of smoke.

Batchelor looked across the table at Grand and wondered if he realized how he stuck out like a sore thumb. At six feet tall with shoulders like a dray horse, he was not the norm in London, where the population tended towards the undernourished and weaselly. His complexion, too, was not burnished like that by any English sky, and his accent – pleasant enough in its way, no doubt – was very noticeable, to be generous. He said none of this, but something *had* to be said. 'They might recognize you,' he said, tentatively.

Grand was taken aback. 'You reckon?' he said. 'I was thinking a disguise. Some eyeglasses. Or some whiskers.' He sketched a set of dundrearies along each side of his face with a wave of his hand.

Batchelor narrowed his eyes, as if trying to decide. 'I'm not sure that would work, you know,' he said eventually, a diplomat to the last. 'Why don't we go to a performance? That way, we can blend in with the crowd.'

'But,' Grand pointed out, 'we can't snoop around during a performance.'

'Not *during*, perhaps,' Batchelor said. 'But afterwards we could. We just need to stay when everyone else has gone, and there you are, the world's your oyster.'

'The what now?'

'Shakespeare.'

'It's very strange, James,' Grand said, 'how you Englishmen manage to bring Shakespeare into every conversation, more or less.'

'That wasn't my point. I was saying that we will have the whole theatre at our fingertips, once everyone has gone.'

'Right. That does sound like a good plan. Do we know what show is on at the Alhambra?'

'I have seen posters, but . . .'

'Hold on. These waiters know everything.' Grand extended an arm and clicked his fingers. On silent feet, a flunkey appeared.

'Sir?'

Grand screwed round in his chair until he was looking up into the man's face. He managed to hide the fact that the position was hideously uncomfortable. 'Tell me, what's on at the Alhambra?'

'Maskelyne, sir,' the flunkey said. 'The Magician.'

'I've heard of him,' Grand said. 'Will we be able to get tickets, do you think?'

The flunkey pursed his lips. 'I doubt it, sir,' he said. 'Not through the box office, I shouldn't have thought. But if sir—' he bowed slightly to Batchelor – 'and sir would like to approach the queue before the show begins, I feel sure that someone will be willing to part with their *carte d'entrée*, should the right amount of remuneration be forthcoming.'

Grand looked puzzled, and the flunkey leaned in closer.

'If you give the person enough money, sir, you can have his ticket.'

'I see.' Grand leaned forward and carefully ran his cigar end around the edge of the ashtray, extinguishing it but leaving it smokeable. The flunkey smiled; such a thoughtful gentleman. 'Do you know what time the shows are?'

The waiter pulled out a pocket watch and consulted it solemnly. 'If sirs would like to hurry,' he said, 'you may just catch the end of the queue as it goes in. They won't be the best seats, mind.'

'We *don't* mind,' Batchelor said. 'Anything to see the Great Maskelyne.'

He and Grand jumped up and were gone, dodging and weaving around the high backed leather chairs in the smoking room. If the waiter was surprised that they should be so keen to see someone who, just a few minutes ago, they seemed unaware of, he didn't show it. Cavendish employees received careful training so that they never showed surprise, no matter what the guests might do – and running off to the theatre was nothing, in the scheme of things. He picked up the cigar and pocketed it for later.

Grand and Batchelor emerged on to Jermyn Street and stopped. Both of them realized at once that they weren't really dressed for the theatre, not even the less good seats. Maskelyne was certainly the talk of the town, and Batchelor had an idea that even the cheaper seats would be filled with some rather wealthy people, and he thought he should mention it to Grand. He hadn't seen him slow to put his hand in his pocket yet, but he didn't really know how much he had behind him.

'This might cost quite a lot,' he said, beginning the conversation in such a way as not to cause offence.

Grand shrugged. 'How much is a lot?' he asked. 'I'm not quite as experienced as I might be with your money. For example, what's a bob? A tanner?'

'Don't worry about that,' Batchelor said. 'These tickets could cost you as much as five pounds.'

Grand did a quick sum in his head. 'Twenty dollars!' he said. 'That's enough for two theatre tickets, I must say.'

Batchelor gave him the news gently. 'I think that might be each.'

'I'm not sure I have that much on me,' Grand said. 'Let me look.' He took out his pocketbook and looked inside. 'Nope. I only have—' he flicked the notes in his fingers – 'four pounds. Hold on a minute.' He opened a small purse on the other side. 'Two sovereigns, that's all. Not enough.'

Batchelor felt somehow warmer towards the man. So his pockets weren't bottomless after all. 'How are you going to pay your hotel bill?' he asked, kindly.

Grand gave him an old-fashioned look. 'My father's man of business is looking after all that. I just need to go and see him tomorrow for some more money. It's just that, for tonight, we would be wasting our time dashing off to the theatre. I don't know whether they would let us in, in any event, dressed like this.' Grand's clothes were, as always, immaculate but perhaps a little too casual for the theatre. In the good old days he would simply have put on his dress uniform. Batchelor tried to stand so the darns didn't show.

'We'll leave it until tomorrow night, then,' Batchelor said. At least he now knew how rich Grand was. Very.

Grand put his hand on the journalist's arm. 'Come back inside with me,' he said. 'We need to plan tomorrow with a lot of care.'

Batchelor turned and suddenly was aware of a growing noise, the clash of hoofs on stone, the rumble of wheels and the flick of a whip in the air. All familiar enough, but should they be just over his shoulder and getting nearer by the second? He looked up and was almost eyeball to eyeball with a terrified horse, which reared up and away to avoid him if it could. The little gig it was pulling was rocking from side to side, now on one wheel, now on another, and Batchelor felt the breeze as it ripped past his waistcoat buttons. He knew he should cry out, but there simply wasn't the time. He pushed Grand, but Grand was already leaping for safety. Within what could only have been seconds, they were picking themselves up from the pavement, shaken but unhurt.

From nowhere, a crowd gathered, brushing the two men down and twittering their excitement. It wasn't a new thing on the streets of London to see someone knocked for six by a runaway horse, but everyone was agreed – this horse was being aimed deliberately, should anyone ask them.

Someone did. 'Was the driver aiming at me?' Batchelor asked.

'Nah,' said a cab driver, who had been forced off the road by the careering gig. 'No offence, mate,' he said to Grand, 'but it was you the bloke was after. He lashed out at you with his whip when he missed you. Never seen nothing like it.'

There were murmurs of agreement from the crowd.

'You're bleeding,' said a girl standing by with a basket of violets on one arm. 'Your ear, look.'

Grand put his hand up and, sure enough, blood was trickling down his neck from a clean nick in his ear.

'That's from the whip,' said the cabbie, by default the expert in the crowd. 'I should get inside, if I was you. He might come back.'

All heads turned anxiously in the direction in which the gig had gone.

Again, the cabbie had the knowledge. 'Don't think he'll come that way,' he said. 'He could come back round the same way, or he could come out of any of these turnings. A little light gig like that, it can be round a corner and on yer before yer know it.'

The crowd started to disperse now. Excitement was one thing. Being knocked down by a maniac in a gig was another. Within less than a minute, Grand and Batchelor stood alone on the pavement, the echo of the whip's crack in their ears and a nagging sense of unease in their chests.

Grand cleared his throat. 'Shall we?' he said, gesturing to the hotel's imposing entrance.

Batchelor tried to summon up a smile. 'I don't mind if I do,' he said, and the two men made for the safety of the lobby, trying not to break into a run.

'If I was of a more melodramatic constitution, sir, I'd say it was a murder attempt.'

'Murder?' Richard Tanner looked up from his paperwork. He had to admit the man in front of him looked the part. From the top of his leather cap to the shit-encrusted boots, Constable Bennett was every inch a London cabbie. He even smelt of horse liniment. Tanner put down his pen. 'I won't bore you with the Metropolitan statistics of traffic accidents, Bennett, but let's just say they are legion on account of the chaos on our streets . . . for which, needless to say, we are blamed.'

'Yes, sir, I know.' Bennett wasn't just about the best undercover man Tanner had, he was also the most obstinate. 'But this one was deliberate, I'll swear. The bloke drove directly at the American. It's a miracle he wasn't killed.'

'Ordinary cab?' Tanner twirled the pen between his fingers, spraying fine gobs of ink in all directions.

'Standard rig,' Bennett told him.

'Growler?'

'The cabbie was medium height. Usual schmatte. Three days' beard.'

'In other words, anybody.' Tanner sighed. 'You didn't get a cab number, I suppose.'

'It all happened so fast,' Bennett and Tanner chorused.

The inspector shook his head. 'Well,' he said. 'This is a bit of a turn-up, isn't it? A man who habitually carries a revolver turns up looking for a man who owes him money and becomes – or nearly so – the victim of a hit and run.'

'So . . .' Bennett was doing his best to stay with the Inspector on this one. 'The cabbie is the bloke who owes the money?'

'The mysterious Mr Dundreary,' Tanner said with a nod. 'Although somehow, I don't think it's nearly that simple. Who's on Grand now?'

'Shannon, sir.'

'Disguise?'

'Man about town, sir. He wanted to go as a cleric, but I did point out to him that if Mr Grand were to go to a house of ill repute, he, Shannon, would be something of a sore thumb.'

Tanner winked at him. 'Quite right, Bennett,' he said. 'You're coming on, there's no doubt about that.'

Dick Tanner knew that his current tactics would be frowned on by his superiors at the Yard. Dolly Williamson in particular

hated disguises and expressed his disapproval on every conceiv-
able occasion. Here at Vine Street, however, Tanner's rule was
law, and it sometimes paid off. 'All right, Tom,' he said. 'Get
yourself out of those clothes – and, for God's sake, have a bath!'

The room was quiet, except for the scritch of pen-nibs on
paper and the sighing of inspiration-free men with deadlines
to meet. The editor prowled the lines of desks, looking over
shoulders and tsking or nodding approvingly, with rather more
of the former in evidence. His paper was losing out to the
competition, its circulation was dropping like a dying man's
– and Thornton Leigh Hunt had no intention of letting it die
just yet. There must be something he could do to revive it,
but what was new in the newspaper game these days? It had
all been tried; the number of newspapers had blossomed, but
nothing lasted. Almost all the new papers had gone to the wall
in very short order – scarcely having time for the paint to dry
in their offices in most cases. It was so stuffy in here; perhaps
that was why he couldn't think. A breath of fresh air, yes, that
would be just the thing.

As the door swung to behind the editor, there was a huge
sigh of relief, and the noise in the journalists' room rose to
its normal level, which was that of a parrot house with a cat
loose. He was a good enough editor, as editors went, but
everything ran so much more smoothly when he was out of
the building. Perhaps not smoothly, some of the more reasonable men would agree, but certainly with a little more flair; it
wasn't easy to let the creative juices flow when ones buttocks
were clenched with nerves.

Dyer turned to Buckley and voiced the thoughts of most of
the men there. 'I don't know where he's gone, but I'm glad
he has.'

'I couldn't agree more,' said Gabriel Horner, from Dyer's
other side. 'It was never like this in the old days. In the old
days, editors knew how to behave. Why, when I was on the
old *Register*, we never saw John Walter from one week's end
to the next.'

Dyer and Buckley exchanged glances. Whose turn was it
to ask the question?

Buckley said, 'John Walter, Gabriel?'

The old journalist chuckled phlegmily. 'That's the son, of course. I'm not *that* old, oh dear me, no. He wasn't an easy man, mind, to work for. Had very strong views. I remember he had a screaming row with Pitt – that's the Younger, of course – right in the office. None of us were allowed to write it up, of course, though . . .'

Dyer, Buckley and everyone else within earshot was mouthing the words along with Horner. He had told the same story, word for word apart from the odd preposition or two, for more years than anyone could remember. It had become a kind of race memory at the *Telegraph*, and it would probably outlive him; it might well outlive them all.

Horner was just reaching the punchline, involving the King of Portugal or similar dignitary, when the double doors swung again and Leigh Hunt was back in the room, his hair awry from the spring breeze outside and his cheeks pink. Silence descended again, leaving Horner's voice alone for a few syllables before he realized what was happening.

'. . . sent it back with a note, which said . . . oh!'

Leigh Hunt silenced him with a flap of the hand. 'I've just been out there, and do you know what I saw?'

'Pink elephants?' muttered Dyer out of the corner of his mouth.

Leigh Hunt spun round. 'I'll ignore that, Dyer. But only because I need all of you to listen and then to work as you've never worked before. I repeat, do you know what I saw?'

This time the silence was palpable.

'I saw . . . *women*. Hundreds, if not thousands of them. Working, walking . . . they're everywhere.'

No one quite knew how to answer him. It was Fleet Street's worst kept secret that he had been having an affair with Agnes Lewes, the wife of the editor of the *Ebullient*, for years. In fact, three of her children definitely had his chin. And here he was, claiming to have just noticed there were women in the world. Several people shuffled their feet, and there was an outbreak of nervous coughing.

'And do you know,' Leigh Hunt continued, 'these ornaments of our homes have nothing to read? Oh, yes, there are lending libraries. But do they have something *new* to read, when their husbands are enjoying the news at breakfast? No, they do not.'

A few people grunted in agreement. No one could see quite where this might be going.

'So, the *Telegraph* will fill that yawning chasm. We will produce the first newspaper precisely for women.'

'Er . . .' Horner raised a finger. 'Who will buy it?' he asked. 'I don't know many husbands who would fork out for something so the little woman had her nose in it and neglected her . . . duties.' He left just long enough a gap to make some of the younger journalists splutter and redden.

Leigh Hunt looked at him long and hard but eventually had to turn away from his bland gaze. 'You have a point there, Gabriel. But if it were *free*, free inside the paper, then the husbands would buy it.'

'Yes,' Horner piped up again. He had seen it all in his years in print. 'But they already buy it. All we get is a lot more work.'

'Ah,' Leigh Hunt cried. 'That's where you're wrong. Women will insist that their *Times*-reading husbands change their paper, so they can read what everyone else is reading. Circulation will rocket.' He narrowed his eyes. 'Bonuses will be forthcoming.'

Everyone sat up rather straighter and tried their best to look intelligent.

'I need to speak to the printers, to see how much can be done to make the Little Woman's Supplement look different from the main paper. We don't want them to be accidentally exposed to the world of finance and politics by picking up the wrong part of the paper. But that is just a wrinkle; we need to start working on content straight away. I throw this idea out to see who wants to run with it. Let's get some interviews done with some of the lions of the theatre. The fair sex enjoy a play, or so I'm told. Thrash it out between you – I want copy on my desk by tomorrow deadline at the latest.' He ran a hand through his hair, suddenly aware of how tousled he was, and went back into his office, a new spring in his step, looking for a comb.

When his door had slammed to, the room seemed to hold

its breath. Every brain was whirring; who had they spoken to lately, leaning on a bar or queuing in a bordello, what conversation could they turn into an interview with no effort? After a few minutes of private cogitation, everyone turned back to the task they had been engaged in before Leigh Hunt's impassioned outburst, and his Little Woman's Supplement died almost before it had taken its first breath.

Batchelor would never tell Grand, but he was increasingly impressed by Grand's apparent imperviousness to pain. Not only had he been knocked out, but he had also suffered cuts and bruises being thrown out of the Alhambra, and now there had been a murder attempt, culminating in another collision with a hard London pavement. Yet still he carried on each time, never wincing or complaining. He would simply change his shirt and any other clothes as necessary and soldier on. Perhaps that was it. Did being a soldier actually make you feel pain less? Batchelor, still with his mind on his article about the American in London, asked him.

'Do you mean, do you feel pain less if you have seen people die around you?' Grand asked, in his usual laconic way, giving nothing away as to how he really felt.

'I don't think I mean that, as such,' Batchelor said. 'I mean, if you have been injured, do you feel pain less?'

'I came through Bull Run, Gettysburg and The Wilderness without a mark on me, since you ask,' Grand said. 'I have been injured far more since I left the army than ever I was when I was in it. But I guess my childhood might have been a bit more rough and tumble than yours.'

Batchelor cast his mind back to when he was young. It was true that he had been luckier than many, having never been shoved up a chimney or forced to work down a mine or in the racket and danger of a factory. But his childhood had not been idyllic. His mother had died when he was ten, and his father had immediately left the children in the care of his own mother, a slatternly old body who had not so much taken care of them as ignored them almost to the point of starvation. Batchelor had managed to scrape an education almost in spite of himself, and he had dragged himself up by his bootstraps and by slow degrees until he worked for Leigh Hunt at the *Telegraph*. So, no, there had been no rough and tumble, just plain old boring hardship. He precised it. 'Possibly.'

Grand knew better than to pry. 'I was raised on a farm. I was allowed to run a little wild, by your standards, I guess. Got lots of bumps and grazes. Few broken bones. Boy stuff, you know how it is.'

'Your father is a farmer?' Batchelor was surprised. He hadn't thought farming was quite as lucrative as all that. Grand appeared to be very well off indeed.

'Not as such. Had been, oh yes, before I was born. But then they found some gold.' Grand shrugged. 'The crops were more of a hobby after that. Then he ran for Congress . . .' Another shrug, and Batchelor realized again that he and the American had absolutely nothing in common, except perhaps a strong sense of fairness and justice.

'Gold. That must have been . . . nice.'

'Biggest nugget since the Reed nugget in 1799.' Grand couldn't help some pride creeping in to his voice. He still remembered the day his father had put the lump of dirty rock in his mother's lap, while he was still in rompers, and their lives had changed forever.

'How big was that?' Batchelor was thinking he would say 'thumb-sized' or some such, but the reply was astounding.

'Seventeen pounds, or near enough,' Grand said. 'We'd have been set for life if that was all there was, but of course, there was more. I don't know how much money my father has. We don't speak much. He just gives me a line of credit at his bank.'

So they *did* have something in common. 'Who does he bank with?' Batchelor asked. He knew that Grand needed a cash top-up, and the least he could do was help him find the nearest branch.

Grand looked puzzled, then his brow cleared. 'No. *His* bank. He owns it. But I have to go and see his agent here – he doesn't have his own place of business in London. If you want to wait for me here, I'll go to his office now and then we can plan what we can do tonight, after the show.'

Batchelor looked around him, watching for ears that might

be cocked. He couldn't shake off the feeling that he was being followed, ludicrous though that idea was. Here in the Cavendish foyer, sunk into leather sofas almost as big as his entire room at Mrs Biggs', they were surrounded by people, but everyone seemed to have somewhere else to be. No one was lingering, listening, taking notes. It seemed the best place to be alone really was in a crowd.

'Gentlemen.' Inspector Tanner tapped the blackboard with his cane. Many of the detectives in front of him should have gone home hours ago, and the gas lamps spluttered and flared in the bowels of Vine Street nick. 'I don't have to tell you that three unfortunates have met a sticky end near the Haymarket Theatre over the last fortnight. You've all been out there with the uniformed branch, knocking on doors and asking questions. And it pains me to say it, but you've got absolutely nowhere.'

The detectives shifted uneasily and muttered among themselves. They would all walk through fire for Dick Tanner, but they knew he was right. The Haymarket Strangler, as the Press now called him, was making fools of them. He always struck in the same place, and his targets were all ladies of the night, the flotsam of the streets. Yet luck or the devil hovered at this man's elbow, and he was as elusive as a will-o'-the-wisp.

'I'm doubling the night patrols,' Tanner told them, 'and I'm issuing uniform with rubber strips for their boots. Who knows, we might get lucky and catch the bastard red-handed.'

'With respect, sir,' Will Henry piped up, 'it's those bloody silly helmets. With the old stove-pipes, the lads stood *some* chance of blending in with the crowd. Now they look like bloody soldiers. A killer can see them a mile away.'

There were *hear hear*s and rumblings around the room. Will Henry hadn't long been out of uniform himself, and Tanner knew the lad was bright. He tapped the board again and waited for the noise to die down. 'When the commissioner and the Home Secretary want your advice on the sartorial splendour of the Metropolitan Police, Henry, I'm sure they will beat a collective path to your door. But at the moment, we have more pressing matters.'

'Guv.' Sergeant John Hunter's hand was in the air. This man

had been round the block a few times and had seen it all. 'Our problem is the clientele. The Haymarket's not like the East End.'

Indeed, it wasn't. Hunter had cut his teeth in H Division, which covered Whitechapel and Spitalfields, an area teeming with the Irish. The street women there serviced men of their own class because only men of their own class lived there. The lads who brought their hay to Spitalfields wet their whistles at the Ten Bells and the Britannia before slipping one to their chosen mot up against a wall in the shadow of Itchy Park. But the punters of the Haymarket were swells and toffs, gentlemen out on the razzle with more money in their pocket than Tanner's detectives would see in a month. Such men were devious, suspicious, anxious to cover their backs on their slumming sprees, and they looked down their collective noses at policemen, who were inferior beings in every respect.

'Make 'em sweat,' Tanner insisted. 'If a swell's being diffi-cult, bring him in. "Obstructing the police in pursuance of their enquiries" should do it. I wouldn't say it beyond these four walls, gentlemen, but we're dealing with the gutter here, and we must expect to get our hands dirty. If a man protests that he has a wife and children, is a pillar of the community, a sidesman at his church and regularly gives to charity, I want to know what that man is doing in the Haymarket of an evening. And I want you to let him know that we shall be spreading the word.'

The detectives looked at each other.

'Er . . . isn't that blackmail, sir?' John Hunter was the only one with the nerve to say it.

Tanner looked at him. 'A little harsh, John,' he said. 'But, in essence, right. We've got to break a few eggs if we want to sort this bloody omelette.'

FIFTEEN

When Grand and Batchelor set off for the Alhambra that night, they were dressed for the part. Batchelor's clothes were a little less at the cutting edge of fashion than Grand's, but that was scarcely surprising as he had bought them piecemeal over the years in various second-hand emporia; Grand had had his entire wardrobe made bespoke in Savile Row by Henry Poole himself. His father had all of his clothes made there, and so it had seemed only natural to follow suit, as it were. They made an odd couple, therefore, but they weren't abroad to make a sartorial splash – this might be the night that Grand avenged, if only in part, the death of his President.

As predicted by the Cavendish flunkey, the queue to see the Great Maskelyne snaked round the theatre and almost met itself, like the serpent Ouroboros eating its own tail. Everyone looked rather well-to-do and unlikely to want to part with their tickets for hard cash, but Grand wandered the line regardless, jingling a handful of sovereigns. Eventually, they saw just the opening they needed. It was the sound of the slap that alerted them first, and they had to move aside, doffing their hats, as a young woman flounced past, her nose in the air and her eyes looking suspiciously as though they were full of tears.

'Excuse me, ma'am,' Grand muttered, a Yankee gentleman to the core.

She rounded on him and looked him up and down. Most women became more amenable at this stage of the exchange, but she was far too furious for that. 'Don't you "ma'am" me, you . . . foreigner!' she spat. 'You patronizing foreigner. I'm no man's plaything, and don't you forget it.' She fetched Batchelor a nasty one across the chest with her reticule and stormed off.

The two stood for a moment, startled by the suddenness of the exchange, and then Grand was off, like a greyhound. 'Look for a man with one red cheek,' he said over his shoulder to Batchelor. 'He'll have a couple of tickets to get rid of, if I'm any judge.'

Batchelor set off in the direction from which the irate young woman had come, and it wasn't long before he found her ex-inamorato. He stood, staring resolutely forward and ignoring the sniggers of his fellow queuers. His left cheek bore the unmistakable imprint of a small but determined palm.

'Excuse me,' Batchelor said, 'I wonder if you could oblige my friend and me by selling us your tickets?'

The man spun round. 'What makes you think I should want to sell my tickets to you?' he asked.

'I . . . er . . . I was just asking along the queue, you know,' Batchelor said, rattled.

'No, you weren't. You just asked me. It's because you think I don't have anyone to go with, isn't it? Well, you're wrong, as it just so happens. I am awaiting the arrival of my young lady, who has been held up with a domestic matter at home. She'll be here . . .' He took out a pocket handkerchief and blew his nose loudly. 'Any minute.' As he spoke, the queue started to move, and Batchelor knew they were running out of time. He couldn't think how to get this idiot to part with his ticket, though, and looked round frantically for Grand. He was further down the line, and Batchelor gestured for him to come over.

'Oh, you've found him,' Grand said, with all the callous disregard that only a handsome man could manage without giving offence. 'She threw you over, did she?' he said, clapping the man on the shoulder. 'Happened to me just before I came to London. Hits you here, don't it?' He thumped himself in the chest, in sympathy. 'I know it did me. Look, why don't I buy your tickets—' he dug into his pocket and came out with a handful of gold coins – 'then you can go and drown your sorrows, find a nice girl, whatever it'll take to make you forget . . .' He politely left a space.

'Rose,' the man said, on a sob.

'Nice name. Rose. Well, what do you say?' Somehow, Grand had already insinuated himself into the moving queue, and the spurned lover found himself on the outer edge of the line. 'Go and have a good time, eh? She didn't look like someone who liked a good time. Am I right?' Grand was relentless, and there was no longer any question as to who would be going to see the Great Maskelyne that night.

'She is a very religious person,' the man in the queue said, drawing himself up. 'A very good person. She teaches at Sunday School.'

'Exactly,' Grand said, as if this clinched some kind of deal. 'Have a good time, then, and don't make the same mistake again. Good women are to marry not to go to the theatre with,' he finished, and his elbow deftly flicked the heartsick Lothario out of the line and their lives.

The pace was hotting up now, and the doors of the Alhambra were in sight. The management had brought in extra gate-keepers, and the queue was split at the foot of the steps into four, one for each set of doors, and they were being herded like sheep into the stalls and balcony. They had good tickets. It seemed a shame that the poor chap had spent so much money on a sour-faced madam – Batchelor felt better when he considered that at least he had made a profit in the end.

They took their seats in the second row, centre, in the balcony. They had a superb view of the stage but also into the boxes at either side and across a wide swathe of the front circle. For the most fleeting of moments, Grand saw again the interior of Ford's – the Treasury flags with their Stars and Stripes; he heard again the Derringer's bang and saw the smoke drift.

The tables and chairs were gone in the Alhambra tonight, replaced with lines of seating to pack as many people in as possible. The Great Maskelyne never performed to less than packed houses; securing his services was a licence to print money, and it was almost possible to hear the dry rasp of Frederick Strange's hands rubbing together prior to counting the takings. The orchestra were also visible in the pit, just tops of glossy Macassared heads and the gleam of brass and mellow wood of the instruments. The tuning up was reaching a consensus, and everyone settled back in anticipation of an evening of spectacle and prestidigitation par excellence.

The woman to Batchelor's right nudged him with a sharp

elbow. 'Have you been to see the Great Maskelyne before?'
she hissed.

'Er . . . no, this is my first time,' he told her.

'Only, I noticed you buying a ticket in the queue,' she said.
'There's a lot of that goes on, people who come back night
after night, who even follow him around the country. He is a
marvel. A complete marvel.'

'Looking forward to it,' he said.

'I must say,' she said, leaning forward and tapping Grand
on the knee, 'it's very egalitarian of you to bring your valet
to the theatre. Very much what one would expect of someone
of your country.'

'Oh, no,' Grand said. 'He's not my valet. He's just a . . .
friend.'

'Oh.' The woman visibly recoiled. There had been something
in the hesitation before the final word that had given her a
clue to what was going on. 'I see. Well,' she said, before
settling back in her seat, 'I won't say I condone it, but live
and let live, I say. Yes.' She gave them a final glare and then
addressed herself to the stage, holding up her opera glasses
in a flamboyant gesture.

Batchelor shrugged at Grand who shrugged back. There
wasn't time to do more before the orchestra struck up, the velvet
curtain whispered back behind the side flats and the show began.
Rapturous applause filled the theatre.

A single spotlight picked out a young man in tails and white
waistcoat standing alone centre stage. He held out his hands
with an elegant gesture, and without flashes or kerfuffle, he
suddenly held a pure white dove on each palm. With another
flick, they disappeared, and the audience gasped. He beckoned
into the wings and a beautiful girl appeared, dressed in very
little, or so it seemed to Grand and Batchelor up in the balcony
and without benefit of an opera glass. Batchelor thought that
perhaps the woman to his right might misunderstand any
request of his to borrow hers, so he squinted across the lime-
lights as best he could. The girl, after a flourishing curtsey
which looked somehow very louche without the long skirt – or
indeed any skirt – to go with it, skipped off stage and came
back immediately towing a cabinet which looked not unlike

a coffin standing on end. She spun it round and round so that
all sides were visible, and then opened the door at the front.
The cabinet was empty, and as if to prove it, she got in and
knocked sharply on all four walls and the ceiling. She stamped
with her golden heels on the floor. Maskelyne stood while this
was going on with head bowed and arms crossed over his
chest, in an attitude of meditation. Then, without looking up
or speaking, he stepped into the box, and the girl shut the
door. Two more girls, equally scantily clad, walked on from
the rear of the stage, carrying between them, with every show
of effort, a length of chain which was wrapped around the
casket and locked at the front with an enormous padlock,
the key of which the first girl dropped with a flourish down
the front of her costume. The men in the audience suppressed
a mass groan – how wonderful it would be, they all thought,
if the next part of the trick was for some lucky person to be
chosen to pluck the key from its mysterious location.

But it was not to be. The casket was now attached to a hook
which descended from the ceiling, and it disappeared into the
unknown space above the proscenium arch. The audience
waited with bated breath. Suddenly, there was a scream of
shearing metal and the casket plummeted to the ground and
broke into a dozen pieces on the stage. Someone in the audience shrieked, and the beautiful girl on the stage ran forward.
'Is there a doctor in the house?' she yelled.

A figure detached itself from a seat on the edge of the front
row and bounded up the steps, kneeling at the wreckage of
the box. Then he stood up. 'Is this some kind of joke?' he
cried. 'There is no one here.' Then, as the mutters in the seats
grew like a tidal wave rushing to a defenceless shore, he turned
to the audience and swept off his opera cloak, and there –
amazement dawned on every face – there stood the Great
Maskelyne. As if to prove it, he raised a hand in the air, and
from it streamed doves which settled like snow on the three
girls now curtseying centre stage. The audience went wild,
Grand and Batchelor among them.

'That was amazing,' Batchelor said, leaning over to shout
in Grand's ear above the applause. 'However did he do that?'

'Some trick,' Grand muttered, but he couldn't for the life

of him see how. But there was no time to wonder – Maskelyne was off again, this time projecting a shower of playing cards, apparently without end, from his hands. When the fluttering cards had finished flying he held up his hand for quiet. In seconds, you could hear a pin drop.

'Ladies and gentlemen,' Maskelyne was saying, in a gentle voice which nevertheless carried up into the furthest seat in the gods. 'Those of you who caught a playing card, please hold them up in the air. Those of you who have more than one, pass the extra ones back and the person behind them do likewise until all who have a card has but one.' He waited while the audience did as it was told. 'While you do that,' he said, 'I will ask Hetty to bring on a portrait.' He gestured to the girl, who tippy-toed off on spangled feet. She came back pushing an easel on wheels, with the painting turned away from the audience.

'Using nothing more than the cards, thrown, as you will all agree, at random into the crowd,' Maskelyne said, 'I will reveal the person whose portrait this is. Now, I have never met any of you before tonight, have I?' Again, he waited as everyone shook their heads and checked that their neighbours were doing the same. 'Are you sure?' This time there was a ripple of laughter.

'So, we can begin,' he said and gestured into the wings. The lights went low and a very quiet drum roll began. 'First,' he said, 'I would like everyone with a card to stand up.' There was a rustle and a scrape of chairs as everyone got to their feet. 'Now, will everyone pass their card one to the right. Those with no one to their right, please just drop your card on to the floor. Those on the left, please sit down. Your role in this illusion is over and I thank you.' A disgruntled line of punters sat down, trying to look good-natured.

'Now,' he continued, the audience in the palm of his hand as surely as any dove, 'will everyone with a red court card please sit down.' There was a loud shuffle again as people randomly scattered throughout the crowd took their seats again. 'And now, will everyone with a black seven please exchange cards with the person to their left.' And so it went on, until everyone's brain was thoroughly addled and fewer and fewer people were standing. Finally, just one man at the back of the ground floor was left standing, and he was invited on to the stage, to thunderous applause.

Maskelyne quietened everyone down with a single gesture. 'Do you think that the portrait will be of this gentleman?' he asked.

The audience all called back a unanimous 'yes'.

'Ladies and gentlemen,' the magician said, 'you disappoint me. A trick like this is far too simple for the Great Maskelyne. No, I must carry out one more task to convince you that no cheating has been possible. Sir,' he said to his guest, 'may I ask you to turn your back on the audience? Thank you. Now, take this rose. You will see it has been weighted a little on the end of the stem, but this is just so that you can throw it further, should you have a mind to. Now, throw the flower out into the audience, as far or as near as you please. Take your time.'

The man swung the rose experimentally once or twice then flung it into the audience. A woman caught it to yet more applause.

'Please, madam,' Maskelyne said. 'Come up on to the stage.'

The woman made her way along the row and up on to the boards where Maskelyne kissed her hand with a courtly gesture. He turned to Hetty, who slowly turned the portrait around as he slowly turned the woman to face the audience. There was a gasp – the portrait was of her, there was no doubt. But not only was the face the same, so was the hat, the fur wrap and even an elegant necklace that gleamed around her throat. She clasped her hands to her face in bewilderment, and the audience rose to its feet, clapping and calling out. The magician bowed and gestured to Hetty, who curtseyed and led the woman back to her seat.

Grand turned to Batchelor, whose eyes were shining as only the eyes of the stage-struck do. 'What a good trick,' the American ventured, but knew his words would fall on deaf ears. Batchelor was an adherent of all that was magical, and he would never be the same again.

Trick followed trick, and even the interval didn't break the spell. Batchelor stood in the press of people with an indifferent brandy in his hand and even then didn't lose the sparkle in his eyes. Grand, who had seen much the same tricks performed in carnival shows since he was knee high to a cricket, looked on indulgently. Magic usually went along with the selling of snake oil, the elixir of life and a quick 'hallelujah' along the Potomac. Tonight's work was well done, he couldn't deny it, but he hadn't seen anything yet to make the crowds queue for hours in the uncertain English weather. Perhaps the second half of the show would give him a clue.

When they settled into their seats after the bell, they could almost feel the tension in the air. Although Maskelyne took great pains to vary his show from night to night there were a few set pieces which he was never without, and one of them took up almost all of the second half. He had started his career as an unmasker of fraudulent mediums, and he had turned to the stage only to fund this, his main work. So, to show the naive public just what could be done, he staged a seance there on the stage. Sadly, his plan had come to bite him, because all he had done was make many more people believe in the Great Hereafter. Now he was between the Devil and the deep blue sea; to continue and therefore make money, or to stop performing and have no money to do what he saw as God's work. No one in the audience saw him sigh, but sigh he did.

Batchelor was leaning forward, anxious not to miss a moment. The magician sat, centre stage and under a single, unforgiving spotlight, as Hetty and her helpers shackled him to the chair. They tied bells to his fingers and placed his feet in a heavy box, which they also locked. Then, they put a velvet bag over his head and brought in a table, which they placed in front of him. Muffled by the bag, the front rows were lucky enough to hear him speak, and they could have attested, if asked, that Hetty repeated his words accurately, down to the smallest comma.

'Ladies and gentlemen,' he said. 'You have seen me shackled and confined by Hetty, and I can assure you, I cannot move, nor can I see anything. My hearing, too, is muffled. In a moment, Hetty will spin the chair and will stop it when the drum stops rolling.' As he said that, the drummer started a roll, on a gradual crescendo. 'I will then,' Hetty translated, raising her voice to be heard over the drumming, 'not even know which way I am facing. But—' And here Hetty raised her arm dramatically. 'I will still be able to appear all over the theatre, wherever any poor soul who has lost a loved one might need my comfort. Spin!' And with that Hetty grabbed the back of the chair and spun it round and round on its castors while the drum rolled ever louder and then stopped, with a silence like a crash. Hetty grabbed the chair and brought it to a halt, with Maskelyne facing the back prompt corner. She took up his tale.

'I will now meditate, and the spirits will come to me. If everyone who has lost a loved one would please concentrate on that person, it will help me to find their spirit. The spirits are crowding round . . . wait, wait, don't push or . . .' Suddenly, the magician arched his back and howled. 'The pain,' they all heard him cry. 'The pain. My legs. Not my legs.'

Somewhere in the audience, a woman screamed. 'Is that my Nancy?' she cried. 'My little Nancy!'

The audience all craned round to look at her, and there was a gasp as they saw, standing by her side, Maskelyne, with a pale hand on her shoulder, his head bowed, chin on chest. 'Do not distress yourself, madam,' his deep voice rumbled. 'Nancy is at peace.'

A cry from the stage had everyone turning back – how could this be? The man was on the stage, his black bag still over his head, his hands shackled, his feet enclosed in his box. 'Water. Water is everywhere. Can't breathe. Can't . . .' Hetty rushed over to where the magician was struggling in his bonds. She bent over him, then walked to the front of the stage and spoke to the audience, shielding her eyes to see over the lime-light. 'The Great Maskelyne has a spirit here who met his death through water. Does that mean anything to anyone?' The audience muttered and looked at each other, but no one stood up or spoke. The magician called again. 'Not drowning, the spirit is saying. But water. Water on the lungs. Is that making sense to anyone?'

Behind Batchelor and Grand, up in the back of the balcony, a man stood up and called out. 'My mother,' he said. 'She died of water on the lungs. She couldn't breathe, in the end.' He sat back down and, sure enough, behind him, lit with a graveyard glow, Maskelyne stood, his hands above the man's head in benediction.

Hetty spoke again. 'She says to let her go,' she said, turning every now and again to listen to the man behind her. 'It wasn't your fault. You had to go out sometimes, and it was not your fault she died.'

The man had his face in his hands, and the magician gave his shoulder a pat before melting into the darkness.

Again, the audience was still, all eyes on the dark figure slumped on the stage. Then, the man sat up straight and seemed to grow taller. A deep, sonorous voice rang out, not muffled by the bag. Hetty started and stepped aside, the better to watch what was happening.

'I will be avenged!' the voice said. 'The man who will avenge me is here tonight. I will be avenged. And I should like to see Jerusalem.' The voice rang around, waking up echoes in the Alhambra's furthest corners and making the dust fall like magical snow in the spotlight. Batchelor looked at Grand, with eyes wide, but the American seemed to have missed the significance of the pronouncement. Then, Batchelor's eyes opened even wider, because, at the end of their row, stood Maskelyne, dark shadows under his eyes and a white and quivering finger pointing, pointing at Grand. He nudged his friend, but when he looked again, the magician had gone.

The rest of the show passed in somewhat of a blur for Batchelor. He saw but did not see the spinning tables, the flights of doves, the playing cards flying out from under Hetty's tiny skirt as she was spun like a top by Maskelyne, using just the power of his mind. All he could think about was that ghoulish figure, standing at the end of the row, pointing, pointing at the unsuspecting American by his side. Finally, as the orchestra struck up 'God Save the Queen', Grand turned to the ex-journalist with a smile.

'James,' he said, 'you are so gullible.'

'Gullible?' Batchelor was hurt. He hoped he was no more gullible than the next man – less so, indeed. Maskelyne was a marvel, there was no doubt about it. If he, Batchelor, had ever doubted the afterlife, he didn't do so now; Maskelyne had pierced the veil and knew what men should not.

'It's a trick,' Grand said, kindly. 'It's all a trick. I've seen snake oil salesmen perform the same or better a dozen times.' He looked closer at Batchelor. 'Don't forget that we are only here so we can search the place. Don't lose sight of that.'

Batchelor gave himself a little shake and tried to throw off the Maskelyne glamour. 'Of course,' he said, adjusting his tie. 'But you didn't *see* him, Matthew. He was standing there. Pointing!'

'Yes, yes,' the American said, patting Batchelor on the shoulder. 'Now, we need to go with the crowd and then slip out when we have a chance, through any door that looks as though it might lead backstage. Stay close – we shouldn't get separated.'

There was no fear of that. Batchelor was impressed by what he had seen that night and not a little disconcerted. If Maskelyne could draw aside the veil so simply, could he be sure he had drawn it back again? Were there spirits even now prowling around, looking for a home, looking to live again? Batchelor followed in Grand's footsteps, treading on his heels from time to time in his eagerness not to be left behind.

As they made their way down from the balcony, past the bar and the auditorium, Grand began to wonder if in fact he had miscalculated and that there was no backstage entrance. Then, he suddenly saw it. Just behind the box office, a small and unassuming door, with no signs or labels to say where it went. It also had an ordinary handle, not a lock or bolt or anything to draw attention to it. Sliding effortlessly out of the press of people, all of them still muttering and whispering in their awestruck remembrance of the show, Grand was through the door in seconds, leaving Batchelor to flounder in his wake. The door slammed shut behind them, and both men held their breath but no one came running.

It was dark back there, behind the scenes, but neither of them wanted to risk a light. Reaching out with both hands, Grand found a wall to his left, and he turned over his shoulder and hissed instructions to Batchelor, passing on skills learned in battle and brothel alike; how to move silently and not be found out.

'Slide your feet,' he hissed into Batchelor's ear. 'Walk your fingers along the wall to find your way. Don't hurry; more haste, less speed. Hold on to my coat hem and don't let go. Come on. Easy does it.' He turned and inched his way through the room. There was something about the atmosphere that told him that this was not a big space, and sure enough, after only a few yards, his questing fingers found a door jamb, and in it a door. He turned the handle with infinite slowness and inched the door open, applying his eye to the crack. The dark was less intense on the other side, and he could see a flight of stairs going down and, at the bottom, a corridor which was quite floodlit by comparison. With his finger to his lips he turned to Batchelor and pointed forwards and down, to show what they must do next.

Step by agonizingly slow step they went down the stairs and stopped just short of the first bend in the corridor. For the first time, they could hear voices, and the voices all seemed to be having a good time. There was laughter, the chink of glass on glass and muted music. Grand turned again to Batchelor and raised an eyebrow. He beckoned him closer so that he could whisper in his ear.

'Sounds like a party,' he mouthed. 'Let's see if we can blend in.'

Batchelor drew back and shook his head. 'No,' he whispered back. 'I can't do that. They'll know at once that I'm not theatre folk. You go; I'll stay here and keep watch.'

'Keep watch?' Grand was so frustrated that he almost spoke out loud. 'What for?'

'People,' Batchelor said, then, so quietly no one could have heard it, 'things.'

Grand shrugged, then, tugging his jacket into place, stepped out of the shadows and straight into some kind of nightmare. Standing not two feet away from him, John Nevil Maskelyne, sometimes called the Great, was leaning on Hetty's shoulder, whispering something in her ear. That it was scurrilous was beyond question, because Grand heard a few words and almost blushed, soldier though he was. Hetty flicked him with her boa and walked away laughing, and Maskelyne straightened up. But that was not the nightmare. The nightmare came from the fact that there was not one, not two, not three but many

Maskelynes, dotted in various poses all around the room, most of them with a girl on his arm. Doves sat on every place that offered a perch, quietly adding their own special touches to the decor and, over in the corner, the woman of the portrait was talking to the man who had thrown her the rose. Grand had expected trickery, but not on this scale. Anyone who could arrange a spectacle such as this and yet arouse no suspicion, even in people who watched him night after night, could easily be Grand's man, although the slim youngster who stood watching the room just a few feet from him was not the man of Ford's Theatre. Even so, Grand smelt, along with the grease-paint and faint whiff of sulphur, something that also smelled of conspiracy and corruption. He backed out slowly, turned Batchelor around, and pushed him towards the stairs, the light and sanity.

'Smoke and mirrors, James, my boy,' Grand whispered as their feet padded on the treads. 'The grand deception. If ever you want a story to unmask Maskelyne . . .'

SIXTEEN

It was raining on Kensal Green the next morning, as it always seemed to rain when mourners said their farewells to the dead. No expense had been spared when Auntie Bettie laid her girls to rest. Three black hearses, each pulled by sable horses, the ostrich plumes nodding on their heads, rattled slowly through the cemetery's yawning gates on their way to their resting places. Not even Auntie Bettie's purse could run to the catacombs here, but Effie and Marie and Francine would have to lie side by side for eternity in a small vault to the left of the carriage drive, under the sheltering arms of a yew.

Behind the last hearse, its coachman and pall-bearers with black weepers trailing down their backs, Auntie Bettie led a procession of her girls, all on foot, the sodden grass soaking their black dresses. For once they had abandoned their bright apparel and lowered their hems, as respectable women did. No sense in outraging society in this hallowed place, and Auntie Bettie was conscious of the susceptibilities of the vicar, a kindly old soul who had never got out much.

Weeping angels carved in stone watched the mourners glide by. Broken columns jutted to the leaden sky. The rain bounced off the feathers and hat-brims of the girls, but none of them carried an umbrella, holding their heads high as they passed the tombs of the great and good. Bishops and engineers and poets and soldiers lay here, their names carved in marble under Gothic canopies and crawling gargoyles. Willow trees shed their tears to the ground, and the hearses halted by the little chapel as the pall-bearers hoisted their sad loads and carried them over the sodden turf.

The cold light of the morning flashed on the brass fittings, and the cemetery's bell tolled solemnly for the dead girls' passing. At the side of the path, another group of women stood waiting, dressed in black like Bettie's meandering column, though fewer in number. The tall, hard-faced woman at their head crossed the grass to Bettie.

'Eleanor,' Bettie said, nodding to her.

'Good morning, Bettie,' Lady Eleanor said. 'We've never been friends, you and I, but this . . . I hope you'll allow me and my girls to pay our respects.'

Auntie Bettie had cried so much in her life that she had no tears any more. But an iron lump swelled in her throat as she answered. 'That's kind,' she said.

'Well,' Richard Tanner muttered to John Hunter at the edge of the crowd, half hidden by the yews. 'I never thought I'd live to see the day.'

'No more did I,' Hunter said with a nod. 'Bettie and Eleanor walking arm-in-arm. Makes you wish you had a camera.' Hunter was by way of being a camera enthusiast, and the things he knew about collodion dry plates could make your eyes water.

Tanner didn't really know why he was here. The entire West End, it seemed, had heard the rumour that Auntie Bettie was burying her girls in style. If they had ever had any real family, they stayed away. Only Bettie was their family now; her, and the other girls who sobbed over their graves. But if the West End had heard the rumour, why not the man who had put these girls into the ground? It was the longest shot in a detective's handbook, that the murderer might just turn up to gloat over the sorrow caused by his handiwork.

'Well, now.' Tanner's eyes narrowed as he peered under the rim of the umbrella he and Hunter shared. 'There's a pair I didn't expect to see. Or did I?'

Beyond the group who huddled around the grave as Kensal's ingenious little machine lowered the coffins to the dark earth one by one, two men stood bareheaded in the downpour, watching the solemnities.

'I didn't think I'd be at another funeral so soon,' Matthew Grand said. All this was a far cry from the military spectacle along Pennsylvania Avenue with its Negro mourners and gun carriages and white horses. The vicar and the undertakers' mutes, their faces white with greasepaint, were the only men here.

'Sorry to drag you to this one,' Batchelor murmured. 'I just wondered . . .'

'Whether the killer might be here?' Grand finished the sentence for him.

'Just imagine,' Batchelor said, 'if John Wilkes Booth had carried out his act in secret; if no one knew who killed Lincoln. Wouldn't he have been there, in the crowd? The great actor as tragedian, weeping tears of pure joy as the President passed?'

Grand nodded. 'I'm sure of it,' he said. 'Say—' he was staring into the distance – 'isn't that . . .?'

'Good God!' Batchelor scurried over the grass as far as the solemnity of the place and the time would let him, and he heard his boots crunch on gravel. Under the rim of another umbrella was a face he and Grand knew.

'Joe Buckley.' Batchelor shook the man by the hand.

'Hello, Batchelor,' the journalist said, smiling. 'If I'd known you would be here I wouldn't have bothered.'

'You're covering this for the *Telegraph*?'

Buckley nodded. The rain had trickled down his neck inside his collar, and he felt his head muzzy with an incipient cold. 'Leigh Hunt's got an attack of the sentimentals. I'm supposed to talk to these women and get their insights. He's suddenly realized there are females in the world.'

'Can't you do that at the Haymarket?' Batchelor asked. 'Any night of the week?'

'Yes, but I'm not sure that the old hypocrite knows his staff frequent the place. Anyway, this is difficult, isn't it?' He scanned the huddle of girls comforting each other, drying tears and blowing noses. 'Without their paint, they look almost human. You couldn't . . .?'

'No, thank you, Buckley.' Batchelor stepped back from him. 'I don't work for the *Telegraph* any longer, remember? Anyway, I've done your job for you once too often.'

'Ingrate,' Buckley muttered, scribbling on his notepad and juggling it and his umbrella in an attempt to keep the pages dry.

Batchelor and Grand crossed back to where they had been standing only to find two officers from London's finest waiting for them.

'Gentlemen.' Tanner tipped his hat. 'Not, all in all, a good day. May I ask what you are doing here?'

'Come to pay our respects,' Batchelor said. 'You?'

'The same,' Tanner lied. 'But, seeing as how you're here, Mr Batchelor, might I have a word?'

'He wants you to do what?' Edwin Dyer nearly dropped his glass in the Haymarket's bar that night. The rain was still pounding on the glass roof and cascading into the alleyways outside.

'You heard.' Batchelor sat back, his feet crossed on the table. 'I am to write a series of articles exposing the hypocrisy of the swells who hang around this place. Over there, for instance. Isn't that Lord Herbury?'

'The third earl,' Gabriel Horner chipped in. 'Got a fancy for anything under fourteen.'

'And there.' Batchelor pointed to a large man in a silk topper.

Horner recognized him. 'Marquis of Grendlesham. Likes a little light chastisement of an evening.'

Batchelor looked at the old soak. 'Shouldn't you be doing this job, Gabriel?' he asked. 'You seem to know everybody's peccadilloes.'

'Where does Tanner expect you to publish this story, Batchelor?' Buckley wanted to know. 'The *Telegraph* won't touch it.'

'Neither will *The Times*,' Dyer said. 'No respectable paper will.'

'Who said anything about respectable?' Batchelor smiled. 'Gabriel?'

The old man downed a good sized brandy in one go. 'The *Ebullient*'s your best bet. Georgie Lewes is no stranger to libel actions, and if he knows TLH has turned a story down, he'll print it out of spite. It can't be easy, having all those children running about with the TLH chin; a man has to take his revenge where he can.'

'Collaboration then, Gabriel?' Batchelor said. 'My exquisite writing style with your nose for smut?'

'Well . . .'

'There's a drink in it for you. Inspector Tanner's paying.'

'Is he now?' Horner chuckled. 'Make mine a triple, then. Now, to business . . . See him over there?'

The offices of the *Ebullient* stood at the dingy end of Fleet Street where the open sewer that was the Fleet River now bubbled with its noxious odours feet below the pavement. Here, long ago, had stood the Bridewell, the London prison where ghouls on a diet of bread and water had thrust their scrawny arms through the bars, clawing the air as they begged for charity from passers-by.

A locomotive clanked and hissed as it rattled over the viaduct, and the horses at Ludgate whinnied and stamped. All around this end of the street, the new and the old struggled to survive side by side.

Struggling to survive, too, was Georgie Lewes. He had a magnificent set of Piccadilly weepers which offset his long hair, but these days he'd taken to wearing a smoking cap to disguise the baldness on the top of his head. Lewes was between posts, ever the position of a journalist, and he had left the radical *Leader* to disappear without trace. The philosophical *Fortnightly Review* was whirring in his brain that morning, but meanwhile, until he took over the running of it, a man had to eat. And that he could do so was thanks to the *Ebullient*.

It had to be said that Georgie Lewes was no stranger to scandal. If his Agnes had borne children with Leigh Hunt's chin, more than one paramour had done likewise with the Lewes lip, which jutted defiantly at James Batchelor that morning.

'You're joking, of course,' he said, looking the reporter up and down.

'Emphatically not.' Batchelor sat opposite the man.

Lewes adjusted his pince-nez. 'Let me see if I understand you. You are a freelance journalist hoping to make his way in the literary world, and you offer me an exposé of—' his eyes widened – 'several prominent men who have been seen in the company of ladies of low morals.'

'In a nutshell,' Batchelor said, beaming.

'You are doubtless unfamiliar with the laws of libel.' Lewes sat back and folded his arms.

'Leigh Hunt said you'd say that.'

This time Lewes' pince-nez fell off the bridge of his nose. 'You know Leigh Hunt?'

'Intimately,' Batchelor said with a smile. 'I offered him this and he said he, regrettably, had to decline. But that you and the *Ebullient* would lap it up.'

'Did he now?' Lewes' mind was racing. 'To what end, Mr Batchelor?'

'To the end, sir, of catching the Haymarket Strangler.'

'The Strangler?' Lewes was all ears. Philosophical debate among the literati was one thing, but nothing sold papers like horrible murder. The more horrible the better. 'How?'

'Tell me, Mr Lewes,' Batchelor said, crossing one nonchalant leg over another, 'are you a student of nature?'

'Passingly,' Lewes said.

'Consider an ant's nest,' Batchelor suggested. 'Poke it with a stick. What happens?'

'Er . . . they run around, panicking.'

'Precisely. And while they're panicking, for the briefest of moments, their eggs are unguarded, their young defenceless.'

'They are,' Lewes concurred.

'There you have it. Print that in the *Ebullient* and the gentlemen concerned will run around like headless chickens – if I am not confusing nature there – and, with any luck, the murderer will be exposed.'

Lewes was still wrestling silently with the ethics of it all.

'If the Strangler's not one of the names in my article,' Batchelor said, 'these men have at least all walked past him. They have drunk with him. Shared, perhaps, the charms of the very women he went on to slaughter.'

'Is that line in here, Mr Batchelor?' Lewes asked.

'No,' Batchelor said, then leaned forward. 'But it could be.' He looked at the *Ebullient*'s editor and knew that he had him.

'There'll have to be a few asterisks,' Lewes warned. 'The

Ebullient isn't made of money. And, of course, if the Strangler is caught, we get sole editorial.'

'Don't you mean *when* he's caught, Mr Lewes?'

For nights now Richard Tanner had been burning the midnight oil trying to piece together the last moments of the life of William Whicker, also known as Winthrop. He knew perfectly well that the man had been killed by his own ambition. He was streetwise and plausible, but trying his own brand of sleight-of-hand in a foreign country in the middle of a war would have been beyond him. Tanner had written to Allan Pinkerton, the Glasgow ex-copper who had failed to protect Lincoln, as all his people had, but he didn't hope for much information from that source.

Peg Whicker had not known precisely where her husband had been, but the letter on Tanner's desk, the one she had passed to him, was postmarked Washington. Whicker had been staying, already using the name Winthrop, at Room Fifty-Eight of the Kimmel House Hotel, and he wrote that he was annoyed by the behaviour of George. 'The man drinks, Peg, like we all do, but he can't hold his liquor. He knows his way across the Potomac, though, and has never been arrested, so I need him.'

Who, Tanner wondered for the umpteenth time, was George, and what was the reference to the Potomac? It was a river; Tanner knew that much. Then, a thought struck him. There was one man, right here in London, who may be able to shed light on this riddle. The man who had expressed such an interest in the passengers on the *Orient* in the first place. Matthew Grand.

'What say we help each other with our enquiries, Mr Grand?'

Matthew Grand had been summoned peremptorily to Vine Street by a couple of boys in blue quite early that morning. At least this time he hadn't been dragged there. Neither, bearing in mind his first meeting with the Baker boys, had it been at gunpoint. Speaking of which, he had been careful to leave his thumb-breaker back at the Cavendish.

'Does the Kimmel House Hotel, Washington, mean anything to you, Mr Grand?'

'It does,' Grand said, gritting his teeth as he took a sip of Tanner's tea. 'Most folks call it the Pennsylvania House. It's on the south side of C Street, if memory serves, between Fourth and Fifth Streets. Why?'

'Mr Winthrop stayed there,' Tanner told him. 'Prior to boarding the *Orient*.'

'How did you find that out?' Grand asked.

The inspector waved Winthrop's letter in front of him. 'Why would a man not be arrested,' he asked, 'for knowing his way across the Potomac?'

Grand frowned. 'The Potomac is the river that divides the North from the South,' he said. 'The Blue from the Grey. Can I see that?'

Tanner passed the paper across.

'The only kind of man who would have been crossing the Potomac over the last few years would be a Confederate or a Yankee spy, Inspector, depending on the direction.'

'Would such a man have carried money? Gold, for instance?'

'Sure. Who had you in mind?'

'I think I should tell you, Mr Grand, that the late Mr Winthrop was actually William Whicker. He was a confidence trickster with an arrest sheet as long as your arm. I believe that was why he was in America, and it's probably why he died.'

'Wait a minute.' Grand sat bolt upright. 'This reference here – George not holding his liquor.'

'Does that mean anything to you?'

'It might,' Grand said.

Tanner sat upright too, then leaned towards his man. 'Isn't it about time you came clean with me, Mr Grand?' he said. 'You're no more chasing Charles Dundreary over a card game than I am. What's *really* going on?'

Matthew Grand never knew, to his dying day, why he suddenly changed his mind about Richard Tanner. That morning he had trusted him about as far as he trusted John Wilkes Booth or the Great Maskelyne. But now, suddenly, he saw a converging of the ways, that Tanner's path and his might not be so very different after all.

'I should throw my badge on your desk,' Grand said. 'Except

that I don't have one. I work for Lafayette Baker of the National
Detective Police in Washington.'

'The National . . .?'

'It's a secret police service,' Grand explained. 'Run by
Secretary of War Stanton since 'sixty-two. Baker runs it within
the War Department and reports directly to him.'

'So you're a copper, too?' Tanner was almost smiling.

'Of sorts,' Grand said. 'But it's not that simple. I'm chasing
the son of a bitch who helped Booth get away at Ford's Theatre.
I owe him a bump on the head.'

'Mr Dundreary.' Tanner nodded. 'Does the letter help?'

'If I remember the *New York Tribune* article I got hold of
the other day in Fleet Street, it said that the conspirator detailed
to kill Vice President Johnson was staying at the Pennsylvania
Hotel. His name is George Atzerodt.'

'The George who can't hold his liquor,' Tanner said.

'According to the *Tribune*, Azterodt lost his nerve on Good
Friday and got liquored up at the Kirkwood House. When the
balloon went up at Ford's that evening, he got the Hell out.'

'Did the *Tribune* . . . do *you* know anything about this man?'

'Some of it came out at the conspirators' trial. Atzerodt had
been spying across the Potomac – I guess that's how your
man Whicker knew him – throughout the war. He must have
known Booth and some or all of the others.'

'Including Dundreary,' Tanner chipped in.

'It's my guess your man panicked,' Grand said. 'Got out of
Washington – and the country – as soon as he could.'

'That's my guess too,' the inspector said. 'Bill was never
one for guns and violence. He'd have been terrified.'

'But Dundreary panicked too.' Grand was reasoning it out.
'And he needed to leave just as fast – faster, in case I should
recognize him again.'

'And it was just Will Whicker's bad luck that the two of
them ended up on the same ship.'

'Well.' Grand passed the letter back to Tanner. 'Now we
know the why. All we got to work out now is the who.'

The great lion over the entrance to Northumberland House
looked down on the people of London as they scurried and

swarmed like ants around Nelson's column. Two of the ants that morning were James Batchelor and Matthew Grand, and they were walking east along the Strand.

'Tell me about this place,' the American said.

'It's like everywhere else in London,' Batchelor told him. 'Heaven and Hell cheek by jowl. There used to be a menagerie over there when I was a kid – I saw my first bear there. Mind you, it had seen better days; its fur looked like something out of a mattress. On this side used to be old John of Gaunt's palace, but the peasants burned it down in their Revolt.' Batchelor looked at his companion. 'That was in 1381, by the way, when Gabriel Horner was a cub reporter.' Both men laughed. 'And here is Alsatia.'

'Alsatia?' Grand stood still.

'Named after Alsace, between France and Germany, a kind of no man's land along the Rhine. Technically, the police can't arrest a man here because it belongs to the Duchy of Lancaster.'

'Can't arrest a man, huh?' Grand murmured. 'That could be useful.'

'Useful . . .' Batchelor repeated. 'Why?'

But Grand was already striding towards the river where the ramshackle houses jostled each other in their urban quest for the sky. Batchelor scurried after him and watched the American turn into a blind alley, then climb some steps to a large, brass-studded door. Batchelor had no idea this house was here. It was four storeyed, Georgian and looked out over the Adelphi and the great, brown artery that was the Thames.

'Useful—' Grand slotted a key into a lock and opened the door – 'because I have taken rooms here.'

'Have you?' Batchelor was impressed. Alsatia it may have been, but all London property cost the earth, even Fleet Lane, the home of the redoubtable Mrs Biggs. 'Which floor?'

'All of them,' Grand said, leaving Batchelor open-mouthed in the vestibule.

'What was wrong with the Cavendish?'

'Nothing,' Grand said, sweeping up the staircase. 'Except that it's a hotel, and in my experience, they're too darned wide open. Flunkeys everywhere, listening in barrooms and

hovering at tables. My God—' he stopped on a half-landing
– 'listen to me. I'd never have thought like this before Ford's
Theatre.'

'Yes,' Batchelor said with a nod. 'Murder will do that to
people. Every time I wander west of Temple Bar I find myself
looking at faces, wondering . . .'

'I'm having my things sent over later today,' Grand said,
ushering the journalist into a vast drawing room. A portrait of
Victoria and Albert looked benignly down from above the
fireplace. 'That'll have to go,' he said.

'Wise choice,' Batchelor murmured.

'Well, I just wanted you to see my new place, James,' Grand
said. 'What's your line on servants?'

'They listen in barrooms and hover at tables, Matthew,'
Batchelor reminded him. 'You said it yourself.'

'Good call,' Grand said, nodding. 'I cooked for myself in
the Wilderness. I guess I can do it now. Cup of tea?' He said
the words as though he was chewing a wasp.

'Thank you, no. I have to see S . . . someone. Nice place,
though, nice place. I'm sure you'll be very happy.'

'I'm not very happy, Mr Batchelor.' Mrs Biggs was standing
there on her front porch with a metaphorical rolling pin in her
hand.

'Why ever not, Mrs B?' The eternal lodger tried the familiar
title, if only for old times' sake.

'I had occasion to visit the offices of the *Telegraph* this
morning.'

'You did?' Batchelor could see the way this conversation
was about to go.

'Now old Mr Kitchen has passed away, I needed to advertise
his room. I got talking to a clerk there, a clerk who knows
you well.'

'Clerks, eh!' Batchelor clicked his tongue. 'Can't believe a
word they say, in my experience.'

'And in my experience, Mr Batchelor, you are out of work,
aren't you?'

'What? No, I—'

'The clerk told me you had been given your marching orders.

"Chucked out", that was the phrase he used. Not very journalistic, I don't suppose, but accurate.'

If truth be told, James Batchelor was less fond of his landlady than had once been the case. He was now more aware of her narrow eyes, her ill-fitting dentures and the falsity of her hair colouring.

'I am freelance, Mrs Biggs,' he told her, 'writing not merely for the *Telegraph* but for others.'

'That's as maybe—' she folded her arms – 'but freelance work brings freelance wages – intermittent, shall we say. And the whole point about rent is that it is regular. You see how the two things don't add up?'

Batchelor could.

'So—' Mrs Biggs took a deep breath – 'in the light of my discoveries, I must ask you to leave forthwith.'

'Forth . . .?'

'With. Now.' She looked levelly at him. 'You may clear your room, of course, but if I see you here after three o'clock, I shall be obliged to call a policeman.'

The bottom had suddenly fallen out of James Batchelor's world. He had no job, no roof over his head. And he had a murderer to catch. Never mind – there was still George Sala, and he would see him right.

'Is that it?' Sala asked, blinking in the early evening sun. 'Matthew Grand is chasing a conspirator he ran into outside Ford's Theatre?'

'Well, yes . . .' Batchelor was checking the street, north and south. If Sala refused to meet him in one of London's parks, and the *Telegraph* offices were out of the question, an ordinary street it would have to be. This one was Whitehall, where the government's offices rose grandly to the sky and the smell of horse shit floated like a miasma from the Horse Guards' barracks.

'Dammit, man, I knew all that before I left Washington. What I am looking for is any evidence that Grand is a conspirator himself. Has he met anyone in a low dive? Sent any telegrams you've intercepted? Been anywhere near the American embassy? Is he trying to spend Confederate dollars?

Any careless slips about the good ol' boys or reminiscences of Jeff Davis? Good God, Batchelor, I chose you for this work because I thought you were a journalist. Had a newshound's nose for the truth. Instead, what do I find? An idiot! Well, that's it,' Sala said, adjusting the cane in his hand. 'I'll have to find another way. Here.' He slipped the man an envelope from his inside coat pocket. 'And that's the last. Newshound, indeed. Now, if you'll excuse me, I'm off for a night at the Haymarket.'

James Batchelor trudged east again. He walked across the decaying frontage of Northumberland House, and ragged urchins ran at his heels.

'Spare a copper, guv'nor.'

'Come on, guv'nor, I ain't ate today.'

'Neither have I,' he grunted, but he threw them sixpence if only to avoid tripping over them. Now he had no job, no rooms and no George Sala. And he suddenly found himself, complete with a depressingly small bag in which were his entire possessions, in Alsatia, by the Adelphi, where the steps went down to the river. Near the new rooms of Matthew Grand.

SEVENTEEN

James Batchelor didn't remember going to bed that night. He had a very vague recollection of a cheery fire, of rather good brandy, of chops being sent in from the Cavendish, but the details were hazy. He lay very still, wondering where in the world he might be. He carefully extended a hand to the right, to the left, and didn't encounter the edge of the bed. Not Mrs Biggs' therefore; her beds were as mean and narrow as the landlady's mind itself. Then he investigated the bedclothes covering him; smooth, soft and warm. It was confirmation, if confirmation was needed, that he was not back in his room; his coarse blanket had no connection with this down-filled coverlet. He then became aware of something else, and this was completely incomprehensible. He was wearing a silk bed-gown, but so roomy that it could only belong to . . . and he remembered. He was at Matthew Grand's new rooms in Alsatia. He let his head sink into the feather pillows, and he breathed a sigh of relief as everything suddenly came flooding back. He was not just in Matthew Grand's new rooms. He was in *his* new room – he had been invited to stay and had gratefully accepted.

Batchelor sniffed the air; bacon! Enveloping himself in a robe he found over the back of a chair, he made his way down two flights to the basement kitchen, following his nose, and was soon tucking in to bacon and egg. 'Over easy' was not a phrase he was familiar with, but he wasn't in any position to complain; besides, the eggs – as it turned out – were delicious. He spoke through a mouthful of food. 'Where did you learn to cook?'

'This isn't really cooking, is it?' Grand said. 'But, such as it is, on campaign, I guess. Bacon and beans is as good on the Strand as it is along the Shenandoah.' He looked around the kitchen, which was already looking a little the worse for wear. 'I am going to have to get me some staff, though. The cooking's not so bad – the washing up is beyond me.'

'I don't see how a cook would be too much of a worry when it comes to eavesdropping,' Batchelor agreed. 'Don't they usually spend all day in the kitchen?'

'I guess they do,' Grand said. 'All we need do is stop talking when she brings the food up.' He nodded. 'I'll go out this morning and see about hiring someone. And you? Do you have any plans?'

Batchelor looked up from mopping up his bacon fat with a piece of bread. 'Yes,' he said. 'I have been thinking about that Maskelyne performance, and the more I do, the more doubtful I get about him.'

Grand smiled and slapped him on the shoulder. 'Your eyes were shining like a child at Christmas,' he said.

'I know, I know,' Batchelor said. 'I was taken in. But he's a fraud – you saw all his people at the theatre; nothing was as it seemed. I wondered if he was even more of a fraud than we thought him. I wondered if he might be Mr Dundreary.'

Grand thought for a moment. 'No,' he said. 'Too small. Too slight altogether. Too young as well. I felt that my man was . . . older.'

'How could you tell that?' Batchelor asked. He didn't like his fledgling theory being shot down in a hail of lead this early in the game.

'It was just an impression. His voice. His bearing. Hard to tell – but the Maskelyne we saw on stage was not my man. Not Dundreary.'

'Perhaps one of his entourage then?' Batchelor was like a dog with a bone when he had a theory in his head.

'We didn't see them all, at least not clearly. So you may be right. But what can you do to check on him?'

'I thought I might go to the theatre this morning. See what I can find out there.'

'The Alhambra? Are you crazy? Strange threw us out last time, and he wouldn't hesitate to do it again. My shoulder is still paining me, and you must be worse – you landed far more awkwardly than I did.' Grand flexed his arm and winced.

'That was because I hit the pavement. You just hit me. I may be a bit bony but I'm a softer landing than cobbles.'

'True. Your sidewalks are on the hard side. So, again, what's your plan?'

Batchelor poured another cup of coffee and sipped it thoughtfully. Then, he put it down hard in the saucer, slopping half of it. 'Argyll!' he said. 'I doubt there is any love lost between him and Fred Strange – these impresarios are always trying to outdo each other. If there's anything scurrilous to know about Maskelyne, Argyll will know it.'

'You're a genius!' Grand said. 'Or a journalist.'

'One and the same,' Batchelor said, wiping his mouth. 'I'll get dressed and be off.' He gathered the folds of his dressing gown about him. 'Thank you for the loan of these, by the way.'

'You didn't seem to have anything to wear in bed, so I lent you some of my things.'

'Mrs Biggs didn't agree with night clothes. They just make extra washing, she said.'

'Very possibly,' Grand said, wrinkling a fastidious nose. 'But although there won't be rules as such here, James, a bed gown is mandatory, I'm afraid, as is a fresh shirt daily and underclothes. You only seem to have one pair.'

Batchelor was a little bemused. 'I'm in my summer ones,' he said. 'My winter ones are in my grip.'

'Yes,' Grand said. 'Along with the moths. While I'm out, I will order you some more. No—' He held up his hand as Batchelor opened his mouth to protest. 'This isn't for your benefit, but mine. I spent long enough with men who wore the same clothes for weeks on end. A battlefield is an excuse; Mrs Biggs' standards are not. Please accept, as a favour to me.'

Batchelor grinned and nodded. 'Not too fancy, now,' he said, draining his coffee from the saucer. 'I'm a simple man at heart.'

'And now,' Grand said, 'a fresh one too.' He fished in his waistcoat pocket for his watch. 'It's nearly nine. You will probably have to get Argyll out of bed, but needs must when the devil drives. I'll see you back here later.' He fished in his other pocket and brought out a key. 'Here – this is yours.'

Batchelor took it and grabbed Grand's hand as he did so. 'Matthew, I . . .'

'Tchah!' Grand slapped him on the shoulder again. 'You're a strange one,' he said. 'I'm only doing what any decent man would do.'

Batchelor looked at him, his head on one side. 'I hope London never rubs off on you,' he said. 'We're a hard-hearted lot, you know. We'd tread on anyone to get an advantage. But you . . . you march to a different drum.'

'Yes,' Grand said, his face solemn. 'And the drum is playing "Strike the Tents". Off you go and beard Argyll in his den. I have to face a household servant agent – if tales my mother told me are true, I will be lucky to be the winner.'

'A cook can't be that hard to hire,' Batchelor said. 'We don't need anything fancy.'

'No,' Grand agreed. 'But speaking for myself, I would rather have one who won't steal the spoons.' He got up and made for the door. 'See you later. Good luck.'

Dressed in his own clothes again, Batchelor strolled along the Strand towards the Haymarket Theatre. He was a little early to be visiting anyone in the theatre – he imagined that no one in that business was awake much before midday – but his time on the *Telegraph* had shown him that it was always better to have the element of surprise. There was a spring in his step as he made his way west and dived into the little maze of roads that would take him to the Haymarket. It still seemed strange to be setting his back so firmly to Fleet Street and the life he had known there, but there was a freedom too, a feeling that all things were possible.

He had forgotten Lavenham. Not for him the late start, the morning in bed. There he stood, leaning on his mop, barring the way in to the theatre. Batchelor tried the 'hail fellow well met' approach. It hardly ever worked, but it was worth at least one attempt. He stuck on his friendliest smile and approached the man, hand outstretched.

'Lavenham!' he cried, as though the man were his greatest friend. 'How lovely to meet you again. How are you?'

The hall keeper looked him up and down and pointedly ignored the hand. 'Do I know you?' he said, and the absent 'sir' hung in the air like a bad smell.

'You must remember me,' Batchelor said, still pitching his voice at a friendly level. 'I found one of the poor girls, do you remember?'

'Effie. Aye, I remember you.'

'So, you know me then.' Batchelor's smile was becoming a little fixed. Perhaps the old man was soft in the head after all.

'I remember you,' the man said. 'That don't mean I know you.'

The journalist in Batchelor doffed his cap to the fine distinction. 'My name is James Batchelor,' he said. 'You let me in to see Mr Argyll before, do you remember?'

'I do.'

'So,' Batchelor said, getting desperate, 'can I go up?' He tried to sidestep around the man but got nowhere. As if by magic, the mop bucket and mop barred his way.

'I don't think so,' Lavenham said. 'He near chewed my ear off last time, as I remember. He didn't give me my usual tip, not after that.'

The light dawned. Batchelor fished in his pocket and came up with his last half-guinea. He proffered it to Lavenham, and it disappeared into the man's clothing as quick as a wink.

'I have to mop over there,' Lavenham said. 'Watch that door and make sure no one don't go through, there's a good gentleman.'

Batchelor needed no second bidding and was in the theatre even quicker than a wink and was knocking on the door of the inner sanctum seconds later.

Straining his ears, he heard soft footfalls approaching the door and a bolt being drawn back. An eye applied itself to the crack in the door that was opened and a voice whispered, 'Yes?'

'Mr Argyll?' Batchelor said. 'I'm—'

'No,' the voice said, still in a whisper. 'I am Mr Argyll's private secretary. Mr Argyll is asleep. What may I do for you? We're not auditioning today, you know.'

'No,' Batchelor said. 'I—'

'Sssshhh!'

'Sorry.' He dropped his voice so he was whispering too. 'My name is Batchelor. I'm here to see Mr Argyll. I wondered if he might have some details on Maskelyne. The magician, you know.'

If it were possible to whisper, 'Ha!' the man behind the door did it now. 'He'll have plenty to say about Maskelyne, but, as I think I said, Mr Argyll is asleep at present. Come back . . . come back in a day or two.'

'Surely he will be out of bed in less than a day or two,' Batchelor breathed.

The secretary allowed himself a small chuckle, quickly suppressed. 'It depends,' he said. 'I have not as yet checked on Mr Argyll's sleeping companion, but it has been known . . . Let's leave it there, shall we?'

'I see.' Batchelor was a little nonplussed. This had not featured in his plans for the morning. 'It is rather important. Could you . . . could you perhaps just peep round the door?'

The secretary sighed. 'I shouldn't . . . Oh, come in. We can't keep up this stupid whispering through a crack.' He opened the door fully and ushered Batchelor in. The secretary was a dapper little man, around the journalist's height but better groomed in every department. Batchelor couldn't imagine that he wore the same combinations a whole season long; indeed, he looked as though he probably changed for different times of the day. The secretary was also appraising Batchelor. 'Press?' he asked.

Batchelor was impressed. 'Yes and no,' he said. 'I am a freelance journalist, but that is not why I am here this morning. I am here for a more personal reason.'

'Oh, so you *are* here to audition!'

'No,' Batchelor said, 'I am *not* here to audition. I want to see . . .'

Behind the secretary a door opened, and Roderick Argyll stood there, in a dressing gown that made Matthew Grand's look like sackcloth. 'Is there a problem, Pearson? No, but wait, it's Caliban!'

'Pardon?' Pearson was confused. 'No, sir, I think the gentleman's name is Batchelor.'

'Yes, yes.' Argyll flapped the air in an imperious gesture. 'Just my little joke. How may I help you, Mr Batchelor, now I am awake?'

A voice floated through the half open door. 'Roddy? What's going on?'

Pearson and Batchelor froze, but Argyll took it in his stride. 'Pearson, please take Mrs . . . Er . . . home for me, could you? Oh, wait, I did say we'd pop in to Asprey's on the way. My wallet is on the nightstand, so if you could do the honours?'

'Certainly.' Pearson didn't appear fazed by the request. 'The amount?'

'Oooh, let me see . . .' Argyll tapped his chin with a long forefinger. 'I think a hundred, don't you?'

'Guineas?' Pearson checked.

'Hmm. No, pounds, I think, on this occasion. Thank you, Pearson. Back stairs, if you please. Now, Mr Batchelor, what has brought you here so early?'

'I went to the theatre with a friend to see the Great Maskelyne,' Batchelor began.

There was a discreet cough from the doorway. 'The lady would like to say goodbye, Mr Argyll.'

'Really?' Argyll turned to his secretary. 'Can't you . . .? Well, perhaps not. Do excuse me, Mr Batchelor. I will be but a minute.'

Pearson stepped aside and the door closed, leaving the secretary and the journalist looking at each other in an awkward silence.

Batchelor rummaged in his pockets and came up empty.

'A problem?' Pearson asked, for something to say rather than from any concern.

'I appear to have left my notepad at home. All I have is a pencil.'

Pearson indicated the desk, in front of a window on the far side of the room. 'There is waste paper on there,' he said. 'Do help yourself to a piece.'

'Thank you.' Batchelor chose a piece from the top of a pile and folded it in four, to give himself a surface to lean on. Not the same as his trusty notebook, but it would serve.

The door swung open, and Argyll was back, smoothing down his hair and rebuttoning his dressing gown. 'Ladies, eh!' he remarked to the room in general, and then, to Batchelor, 'Sorry, I can't remember what you said.'

'I went to see the Great Maskelyne at the Alhambra.'
Pearson discreetly withdrew.

'What fun for you.' Argyll threw himself down in a wing
chair and picked up a cigarette case, which he proffered to
Batchelor.

'No, thank you, sir,' Batchelor said. 'Yes, we went to the
show, and afterwards we went backstage.'

'My word.' Argyll was impressed. 'Dear John doesn't
encourage too much of that, oh, dear me, no.'

'Well, we didn't exactly get invited,' Batchelor said.

'And, now, don't tell me, you saw something you shouldn't.
His little cabal, his coterie, his . . . what's the word I'm
searching for? His *co-conspirators* who engage with him in
fooling the paying public.'

'I didn't see them, my friend did, but that sounds about
right. *Is* he a fraud, Mr Argyll?'

'You saw him,' Argyll said, lighting his cigarette with a
flourish. 'What do you think?'

'I was mesmerized,' Batchelor admitted. 'I was totally taken
in by everything he did. My friend, Mr Grand, was not –
apparently, in America, they have travelling shows that do
much the same. But I had never seen anything like it, and I
was . . . well, I was totally taken in.'

'Grand. Where have I seen that name?'

'You may have read it in the paper – he was guest of honour
at George Sala's dinner.'

'Of *course*. I was particularly interested in Mr Sala's articles
from America, as I have friends there. They have gone through
so much, and now they have peace at last.'

'Their President has been shot, though. Not so peaceful, I
wouldn't have said.'

Argyll made one of his dismissive gestures. 'There is always
another President,' he said, then, seeing Batchelor's face,
added, 'not that it wasn't tragic, of course. But when one deals
with drama on stage day in and day out, it is hard to come
down to earth sometimes. Anyway, I digress. Maskelyne is,
as you have deduced, a fraud. He has travelled the world – or,
perhaps, one should more accurately say Europe and America
– exposing mediums and also, sadly, picking up their cunning

tricks. He *claims* he only puts on his shows to fund his researches, but one wonders. He preys on the gullible just as the mediums do, so how is he any better than they? His people are everywhere – he has spies in the queue, he finds out all about everyone before their backsides, if you'll excuse my bluntness, touch a seat. He knows about the human heart. He knows about the human soul. He has a following that is only just short of discipleship – people follow him everywhere he goes, believing every word he says. I believe they would do anything he asked of them.'

Batchelor was scribbling furiously. 'Do you believe he should be stopped, Mr Argyll?' he asked.

Argyll convulsed with laughter. 'Indeed I don't, Mr Batchelor,' he said. 'I believe he should move his show to the Haymarket and make *me* a fortune instead of that charlatan Strange. Now, if there is nothing more, I should get myself dressed. I have other people to see before the show this afternoon, and I don't expect to see Pearson again today.'

'Will it take him that long to see . . . the lady home?' Batchelor asked, innocently.

'Taking her home won't take long,' Argyll assured him. 'Escaping once there will be more difficult. Oh, don't worry about Pearson—' he had seen Batchelor's aghast expression – 'he isn't as frail as he looks.' The impresario leapt to his feet. 'It has been a pleasure, Mr Batchelor. Don't hesitate to visit me again. I enjoy our chats, indeed I do. Please see yourself out.' He whirled back through his bedroom door, and soon the room was ringing to the strains of an operatic aria that Batchelor didn't even try to identify. He looked over his notes once more, folded the paper again and stuffed it in his pocket. With a last glance around the opulent room, which reflected its owner down to the last gesture, he let himself out.

Old Lavenham was waiting for him in the alley.

'Find him, did yer?'

'I did, thank you.' Batchelor tried to squeeze past.

'I saw 'em leave, that secertery and her, no better than she should be.'

'I didn't meet the lady,' Batchelor said.

'Don't have to,' Lavenham said. 'They're none of them no better than they should be. It's a lot calmer round here when he's away. None of them trollops up and down the stairs, day and night.'

Batchelor managed to get past the old man into the alley. 'Is he away much?' he asked, to be polite.

'Nah. He just goes now and again, away for a month or two, then he's back with his trollops . . .'

Batchelor, making deprecatory tuts, made for the main road at the end of the alleyway and turned his feet back towards the tall house in Alsatia that he already thought of as home.

Using his key gave him a thrill – Mrs Biggs didn't hold with keys; only made people secretive, or so she said – and he was soon bounding up the stairs, calling for Grand.

He heard Grand shout, 'In here,' from the drawing room, and he opened the door and went in. A stout, bombazined little person was standing in front of Grand, who wore a slightly hunted expression. 'Just planning the menus for the week, James, if you could just excuse us,' he said, and Batchelor subsided into a chair.

'H'is this gentleman the one of h'whom you spoke?' the woman said.

'Oh, yes, pardon my manners,' Grand said. 'Cook, this is Mr Batchelor. He lives here with me and will be at all meals unless we let you know otherwise.'

'I shall need to know, sir,' she said, 'h'otherwise there can be terrible waste.'

'Yes, I do understand,' Grand said. Batchelor could see that he was making a huge effort not to aspirate every word. 'But if there should be waste at any time, please don't worry. I'm sure you have family, friends, that sort of—'

The bombazine seemed to grow too small as the little woman expanded with indignation. 'H'I'm sure that my references was h'all quite clear on the matter, Mr Grand,' she said, quivering. 'H'I have never taken so much as a h'egg from a h'employer!'

'No, no, Cook, I didn't mean . . .'

Batchelor stood up and went across to the woman. He was

used to her kind. His *mother* was this kind, for heaven's sake. 'Now, now, Cook,' he placated, 'Mr Grand didn't mean anything by it.' He dropped his voice. 'He's *foreign*; we mustn't forget that, must we?'

She subsided and looked into Batchelor's eyes. Such a nice boy. A credit to his mother. Not like that . . . *foreigner*. Accusing her of all sorts! With a huff, she left them to it.

When the door had closed just a touch too loudly behind her, Batchelor turned to Grand, who was lying prone in a chair with a hand over his eyes. 'So, what's for luncheon, Matthew?'

The answer was faint, but not without humour. 'I have simply no idea.'

'But I have lots of ideas about Maskelyne,' Batchelor said, waving his piece of paper. 'Just listen to what I have found out!'

'So, you've had an interesting morning, have you?' The look in Grand's eye was almost manic. 'You haven't been cross-examined by a deranged woman who seemed to think I wanted not a cook but a woman . . . Well, you're young, James, and innocent to a degree. Apparently, they have been having some trouble with an Arthur Munby and they've had to change their rules. That is why we have Mrs Manciple as our cook. She wasn't too worried about what I had in mind, although I think it's safe to say we will be sticking to cooking. But, I apologize.' Grand hauled himself upright and looked more alert. 'What did you discover?'

Batchelor unfolded his paper and put it down on the arm of the chair, in case he needed to refer to it, but everything was quite clear in his mind. 'Argyll was . . . Remind me to tell you later. He had some woman in his room, he—'

'Once you start, James, try to stick to the story. You meander off, has anyone ever told you that?'

'Sorry. Yes, they have. Well, Argyll said—'

There was a thunderous knocking on the door.

'Will Mrs Manciple get that?' Batchelor asked.

'No. As I understand it, opening doors is not one of the extra duties she is willing to perform.' Grand shuddered.

Batchelor jumped to his feet. 'I'll get it,' he said. 'It's the least I can do, Matthew, after all your kindness to me. Are you expecting anyone?'

'No,' Grand said. 'Don't be long – I'm dying to find out what you know about Maskelyne.'

On his way down the stairs, Batchelor hoped that Grand wouldn't be too disappointed. After all, he only knew a little more than he knew before; the smoke still hung in front of the mirror. Before he was halfway down, the knocking came again.

'All right, all right,' he shouted. 'I'm on my way.' He hauled open the door and recoiled. The smell emanating from the man on the step was almost visible. 'Who in Hell are you?'

'No need to talk like that, guv'nor,' the man said, affronted. 'The name's Cockling, Arthur Cockling and I'm the cats' meat man for your area. I come because I heard you just moved in and I didn't want your little pussies to go hungry.'

Batchelor started to shut the door, but the cats' meat man was quicker and stuck his foot in the gap. 'We don't have cats,' Batchelor muttered, leaning on the door.

Cockling was aghast. 'No cats?' he said. 'No cats, and you nearly in the river? What's to be done about the rats?'

'We don't have rats,' Batchelor said, giving up the unequal struggle and opening the door again.

The man laughed, showing blackened teeth. 'No rats! Don't make me laugh, guv'nor. Course you got rats. But this is your lucky day.' He reached into his coat and pulled out a squirming bag. 'Look in 'ere,' he said, holding it out for inspection. 'Best ratter in London, that is. Won prizes, she has.'

Batchelor was not a journalist for nothing and came back with a question. 'If she's such a good ratter, why are you selling her?'

The cats' meat man narrowed his eyes. He loved a challenge – it made the day pass quicker. 'Run aht o' rats, ain't they? No point in having London's best ratter when there's no rats. So, movin' her on. Somewhere where she might do some good.'

Batchelor looked in the bag. 'She's rather mangy,' he said.

'Sign of a good ratter.'

'There seem to be rather a lot of teeth missing,' Batchelor pointed out, having caught the cat mid-yawn.

The cats' meat man decided to change his tack. 'Look, do you want this cat or not?' he said. 'Because I've got other calls to make. I can't stand here all morning jawing with you.'

Batchelor opened his mouth to give a clever riposte, but there didn't seem to be one. While he mulled over how to best get rid of the man, who was stowing the cat grumpily back into his coat, but who looked anything but beaten, there was a thundering of feet on the stairs.

'Oh, look out,' said the cats' meat man. 'Here's the master to see why you won't buy this 'ere cat.' He raised his voice as Grand came into view, struggling into his coat. 'Here, sir, your man here—'

'I'm not his man!' Batchelor knew he would have to improve his sartorial level if this mistake was not to go on and on happening.

'He won't buy my cat.'

'Buy the man's cat, James,' Grand said as he hurtled past. 'Then follow me.'

'There you are!' The cats' meat man was triumphant. 'The master says buy the cat.'

'Oh, for heaven's sake,' Batchelor said. There was something in Grand's eye which worried him, and he was already almost out of sight. He shoved the man into the hall and closed the door behind him. 'Go and ask Cook,' he yelled through the letterbox. 'Say the master says she has to buy the cat.' And he took off up the road, in hot pursuit, knocking over the cats' meat cart in his haste, to the joy of every animal in the neighbourhood.

EIGHTEEN

Batchelor hurtled around the corner, using a passing nurse-maid as a pivot. With her scream dying away behind him, he pounded along the pavement, in time to see Grand jumping into a cab. Despite the blood already pounding in his ears, Batchelor heard him yell, 'Haymarket Theatre,' as the cab pulled out into the melee of the Strand.

He ran up to the next cab on the rank and yelled the same. But the growler wasn't born yesterday. Anyone who smelled like this man was not likely to have a fare on him; otherwise he would have surely spent the money on a bath. 'Fare first,' he said. Batchelor jumped back on to the pavement and rummaged through his pockets.

'I don't . . . I don't seem to have any money on me,' he said. 'But that man, the one who just got that cab, look, that one, there.' He pointed to where Grand's cab was disappearing down the street. 'He'll pay my fare. When we get to the Haymarket. Please!'

But the growler had his whip already raised, and Batchelor knew a lost argument when he saw one. There was nothing for it; he took to his heels and ran as fast as his legs would carry him. It wasn't much above a mile, perhaps less, but he wasn't a man who courted exercise, and it wasn't long before his lungs were screaming for air and his muscles felt as though they were being stabbed by red hot pokers. He put his head down and ran through the pain – he didn't know why Grand had run out like that; it could only be something he had missed. But Grand would need him, that much he knew.

'Now then,' a voice said, and a hand like a vice grabbed his arm, making him spin round. 'What's the hurry?'

Batchelor dashed the sweat from his eyes and looked up into the face of a policeman, Roman helmet and all. He would rather not be stopped but, if he had to be, this was the boy he needed. He grabbed for the man's rattle. 'Call reinforcements,' he gasped. 'Haymarket Theatre. Inspector Tanner. Batchelor.

That's me. Tell Tanner.' And he wrenched his arm free and ran on, almost stumbling but saving himself before he fell.

The policeman looked after him as he went. He hated having to make decisions. That was why he had joined the police, after all. He thought over the consequences. If he called out his colleagues and it turned out to be a hoax, he would look an idiot. If he *didn't* call them out, and it turned out to be a real emergency . . . he would look an idiot *and* people might be hurt. Might die, even. He dithered and then made up his mind, turning and walking off down the Strand, in the direction from which he had come.

'Buy a flower, guv,' the girl said, holding up a sprig in front of the big American. 'Lucky white heather.'

Grand swept past her. The noise of the Haymarket was rushing in his ears – the street cries, the rattle of the wagons. It was not yet midday, and the march past had not begun. This afternoon was the last performance of *The Tempest*, the bills said. But culture lovers need not worry – it was to be replaced the next day with *Little Susan's Garter*, a play in three acts.

He flung himself against the big double doors at the front of the building, but they were locked and bolted fast. They didn't even give as he pounded his fists against them. He dashed round to the alleyway at the side. Here he had stumbled in the darkness over the boot of a murdered girl, and he was surprised to find the place so peaceful now, still in the shadow of the day, but giving no sign at all that blood had recently run in these gutters. There was a door ahead of him, and it was locked. He pounded on it briefly. The show was not due to start until two o'clock, and the whole place looked like a morgue. He hammered on the second door, the smaller one to the right, and it swung open under his fist.

He took the stairs that snaked upwards to the right. Somewhere in this theatre lay the answer he had been looking for so long, the answer to a question that had changed his life. At the top of the stairs a plush carpet led along a corridor with various doors off it, and the pale sun streamed through the open one, gilding the theatrical portraits on the far wall. Grand turned into that sunlight and found himself facing a huge desk. The sun hurt the American's eyes momentarily, so he could only see the figure behind the desk in silhouette. He saw the figure rise and heard the unmistakable click of a revolver's hammer. Instinctively, he reached inside his coat. Damn. So anxious had he been to conform to Inspector Tanner's polite request, and in such a hurry to get here, he had left his Colt back in Alsatia.

'You never seem to be carrying a gun at these crucial little moments, do you, Captain?'

Grand froze. He knew that voice. Knew it like his own. Knew it because it had roared and rumbled through his dreams for weeks. The last time he had heard it, it had said, 'You didn't think it would be that easy, did you, soldier boy? You didn't think Johnny would come alone? The Devil's with him.' And Matthew Grand was alone with the Devil now, staring at the man beyond the muzzle of his pistol.

'Tell me,' the voice said. 'The gun you hoped you had in your pocket. A Navy Colt?'

'Point thirty-two,' Grand said. 'The Navy bulges a tad.'

'Yes,' the voice said. 'Spoils the line of the coat, doesn't it? That's why I prefer a Tranter. So neat. So powerful. So *British*.'

'I thought you'd have preferred a Derringer,' Grand said.

The voice chuckled. 'I did have my doubts about that, I must admit,' it said. 'But Johnny was determined. Said he'd carry the knife for self-defence, but one shot would do the trick.'

'Who are you?' Grand asked. He had not moved, rooted to the spot by the realization that his journey was over. The hopeless task was hopeless no more. Here, in front of him, was the needle in the haystack.

'I am Charles Dundreary,' the answer came, 'or any one of a dozen other aliases I had reason to use. My real name, for the record, is Roderick Argyll. I own this place.'

'What's your link with John Wilkes Booth?' Grand asked.

Argyll had moved now, crossing to the front of his desk. The revolver was steady in his hand.

'A great actor,' Argyll said. 'I saw him several times on the stage, both here and in America. His Richmond in *Richard III* in Baltimore wasn't marvellous, but he got better. Such a handsome fellow.'

'What did you have against Lincoln?' Grand asked.

'Lincoln? My dear boy, this had nothing to do with Lincoln. No, it was all about Johnny. He had those eyes, hypnotic in a way that makes Maskelyne look like a conjuror. He cast a spell over us all – Atzerodt, the Surratts, Powell – we were all under it. If Johnny had planned to fly to the moon, we'd have followed him. As it happened, he chose to kill the President. Well, what does it matter? They've got another one now, haven't they? And the world's still turning. *My* problem is what to do with you. The cab idea was a shambles.'

'The cab? It was you?'

Argyll laughed and croaked out an oath. 'I'm the man of a thousand voices, Grand, and my wardrobe here is stuffed with a thousand costumes. It's easy enough to grime up the face and hands, and you can hire a gig for a trifle.'

'But how did you know I was in London?' Grand asked him.

'*You, keep back!*' Argyll snarled in a Cockney rasp that was not his own. '*This is police business.*'

'*You* were the copper in the alleyway on the night that girl was killed?'

'Not exactly.' Argyll smiled. 'I happened to be outside the theatre, and I was carrying a bullseye lantern. As soon as I saw your face I recognized you. I had to think fast and get rid of you – "*Get back. There's a woman butchered!*" It worked. And when the real coppers and the girl laid you out, well, I knew I was safe, at least for a while. Your coming here like this has saved me a lot of work, and I'm grateful. But before I end this, satisfy my curiosity. How did *you* know where to find *me*?'

'I didn't,' Grand said. 'My friend Batchelor scribbled down some information at his last meeting with you. He's a journalist – he always needs something to scribble on; he doesn't trust his memory. It was the back of a shipping-line ticket. The Inman company's *Orient*. In the name of Charles Dundreary.'

Argyll tutted and shook his head. 'Lavenham,' he said.

'Who?'

'The old boy who cleans up around here. He was supposed to have burnt all my American papers as part of his duties. Obviously, he overlooked that. You really can't get the staff these days.'

'Why did you kill Winthrop?' Grand asked.

'That was unfortunate. He was lodging with George Atzerodt in a hotel in Washington—'

'The Kimmel House,' Grand said.

'That's right,' Argyll said, chuckling. 'You're very good at this, Captain. You've lost your vocation somewhere along the line. I met Atzerodt and the others there several times. Couldn't stay there myself, of course. I mean, the Kimmel House . . . how perfectly ghastly. I was at the Kirkwood, *much* more salubrious. As soon as I saw Winthrop on board ship I recognized him. And he me. It occurred to me the frightened idiot might panic and blurt out what he knew, or thought he knew, to the captain. I couldn't take the chance. Now, it's been fun, Captain Grand, but I do have a show to start shortly, so perhaps you'd be so good . . .' He waved the revolver towards the door.

'Where are we going?' Grand asked. Somehow he had to get that gun from Argyll.

'You'll see. Turn slowly and walk along the passage to your right. I shall be behind you all the way, and you won't know by exactly how many paces. As a military man, however, I'm sure you know the range of one of these things. And I'm sure you will have realized, too, that I know every inch of this theatre, every nook and cranny. Why don't we go up to the royal box? You can relive the moment you should have caught Johnny.'

Grand walked out of Argyll's study, out of the sunshine, into the dark.

'Right,' the impresario barked as they reached a door. 'Open it.'

Grand was following orders now as he had followed orders for the last four years. Other than the click of the lock and a slight squeal from the hinge, the theatre was silent. The silence hung there like a cloak, and the wafts of lavender and beer and lime all hit Grand at once. He was standing now in the Upper Circle of the Haymarket, with rows of plush seats laid out in readiness for the afternoon's show.

'Be so kind as to walk down the steps, Captain,' Argyll said, his gun arm extended, his nerve steady.

Grand began the descent, hearing his boots pad on the carpet. The only light came dimly from the stage, where the sun filtered in through an undrawn blind in the wings. He saw the orchestra pit and the rows of seats that fronted it. Instinctively, he glanced to his right, to the fashionable boxes of the well-to-do. For a moment he saw Henry Rathbone there, smiling and waving on the arm of Clara Harris; Henry Rathbone, before he had gone mad. He saw Mrs Lincoln holding the gloved hand of her husband, old Abe, the lines of sorrow and exhaustion etched on his face.

'You can turn round now,' Argyll said.

Grand twirled slowly, realizing that his back was against the balustrade. To his surprise, he saw that Argyll was wearing his astrakhan coat and launching into a new role already. 'I've no idea how it happened, Officer,' he was saying. 'I'd just come in to open the theatre for the afternoon's performance, and I was making my way to the stage when I stumbled on this man's body. He must have fallen from the balcony up there, I suppose. But who he was and what he was doing here, I have no idea.'

In a split-second Grand realized his true situation. If that was the scheme that Argyll had planned, that Grand's death was to look like suicide or an accident, there would be no place in that for a bullet. How could the impresario square that with the authorities? And if Argyll did not intend to use the gun, then . . . But the man who had killed Winthrop and helped kill a president was faster. He brought the barrel of the Tranter down with crushing force on Grand's head, and the man sank to one knee. He was vaguely aware of Argyll's arms encircling his body and lifting him on to the balcony's rim. His vision swam, and his head reverberated with noise he could not explain. He reached up and caught Argyll's left arm, but blood was trickling into his eyes and the man was hugely strong. He brought his head forward to crack against the impresario's nose, and Argyll roared. A weaker man, one with less commitment perhaps, would have fallen back at that, his nose broken, his eyes brimming with tears. Instead, Argyll used his free hand to slap Grand across the face, and he rammed his jaw upwards so that Grand's head was dangling over the parapet and his upper body was perpendicular to the balcony. One more shove and he would be tumbling downwards thirty, forty feet to the rows of chairs below, any one of them hard and solid enough to break his back as he fell.

Suddenly, there was a grunt and a growl.

'You bastard!' were the only words Grand heard, and then there was a scream as a body hurtled past the American's blurred vision to land with a sickening thud on the ground below. Grand swerved to get himself off the parapet and looked down. There, his legs and neck twisted to an impossible degree, his face like a devil's leering up at him, lay the mortal remains of Roderick Argyll.

Grand's breath left his lungs with a sharp, painful burst. At his elbow, a distraught-looking James Batchelor was leaning over the parapet with him, staring down at the ghastly sight below. 'My God,' the journalist whispered. 'What have I done?'

'You've saved my life, James,' Grand murmured, his head still ringing from the gun-barrel blow.

'I just saw this lunatic trying to kill you,' Batchelor said. He felt Grand's hand on his shoulder.

'You have my gratitude,' the American said, 'and, for what it's worth, Abraham Lincoln's.'

'Put the bloody lights on!'

Both men recognized Dick Tanner's voice in the auditorium below. There was the thud of running policemen and the green gas lights, courtesy of old Lavenham, glowed into life one by one.

Inspector Tanner looked up at the two faces looking down at him. 'Mr Batchelor, Mr Grand,' he said, crouching beside Argyll's body. 'You two do keep turning up in the oddest places, don't you?'

'There'll have to be an inquest, of course.' Tanner slid a mug of tea across the desk to Grand, followed by another for Tanner. It was difficult to say which of the two looked the worse for wear – Grand with his own blood matted in his hair and a nicely developing pair of black eyes, or Batchelor, pale and shaken to the core. 'It's just a formality,' the inspector assured them. 'From what you've told me, it's a good result. Argyll's secretary, a Mr—' he checked the papers on the desk in front of him – 'Pearson, is filling in the details at the Yard as we speak. He has the dates of Argyll's visits to America, both this latest one and earlier ones. Who can I check this with, Mr Grand?'

'I'm sure Lafayette Baker would make sense of it,' Grand told him. 'He doesn't know it yet, but he has a photograph of Roderick Argyll taken at Lincoln's inauguration. Argyll would probably have said it wasn't his best side.'

'All in all,' Tanner said with a smile, 'a very good day. You have your man, and I have mine.'

'Yours?' Batchelor queried.

'Well, it might strain credulity, gentlemen, but the conspirator of Ford's Theatre, Washington, is also the Strangler of the Haymarket Theatre, London.'

'What?' Grand and Batchelor chorused.

Tanner smiled. 'Yes,' he said. 'I'm glad it's not just me who finds that a bit pat. But, you see, how else do we explain this?' He pulled something out of his pocket and laid it down on the desk.

'What's that?' Grand asked.

Tanner raised an eyebrow. 'Mr Batchelor?'

'It's wire,' the journalist said, grimly. 'And it's my guess it's the wire used on the throats of the Haymarket victims.'

'It's the right thickness,' Tanner said, nodding, 'and, as you see, it's formed into a loop. Our murderer has, of course, washed the blood off.'

Batchelor frowned. 'But I thought no weapon was found.'

'At the scene of the crime, no,' Tanner said. 'But I found this in the pocket of the late Roderick Argyll, not two hours ago. Curious, isn't it?'

Number Four, Whitehall Place was under siege by lunchtime. A crowd of disgruntled gentlemen, in silk toppers and tail coats, had formed a disorderly queue up the front steps, pushing and shoving to get in. There must have been fifty of them crammed into the little vestibule where the oil of Commissioner Rowan looked nobly down at them. No one was paying much attention to that gentleman in his scarlet coat. Instead, everyone had fixed their gaze on Sergeant Steers, the hapless desk man at the Yard that morning.

'I can assure you, gentlemen,' he shouted above the chaos, 'the fact that some of you have had your name written up in a newspaper has nothing to do with Scotland Yard.'

'Nothing to do with Scotland Yard?' The nearest top-hatted gent slammed his fist down on Steers' counter. 'My name is Jarvis, of Jarvis, Jarvis and Jarvis, and I represent his Grace the Marquis of Grendlesham. The *Ebullient* is guilty of libel, impugning His Lordship's character by implying that he frequents places of low repute, viz and to wit the Haymarket Theatre.'

'Then you must take that up with the *Ebullient*, sir,' Steers explained, feeling that he had well and truly earned the stripes on his sleeve, and it was not even one o'clock yet.

'We have, you oaf.' Another gent shoved his head through Steers' window. 'Thomas Russell, representing Lord Herbury. That snivelling cur of an editor, Lewes, declined to accept any responsibility at all and told us flatly who had given him the story – total falsehood as it is. His name is Batchelor. He is a freelance journalist. And we want him arrested.'

'We'll handle the civil side later,' Jarvis said. 'For now, we'll settle for this Batchelor to be dragged through the streets.'

'Er . . . we don't do that any more, sir. Dragging people through the streets. Went out with Good Queen Bess, I understand. Now, if you'd care to get along to Vine Street; the name to conjure with is Inspector Richard Tanner.'

It wasn't until they were safely back in Alsatia, in front of a comforting fire, enjoying Mrs Manciple's crumpets with gentlemen's relish and some tea with – as the cook had told them – 'a little something in it for the nerves' that either man allowed any sign of what they had gone through to show. Grand, who had gone through so much already in his life, surprisingly showed it most, curling up in the biggest chair, with the cat on his lap. He ran his fingers through its somewhat mangy coat and derived great pleasure from the creature's purr, which sounded like the distant drilling of Mr Bazalgette's latest project. Batchelor took refuge in chat about this, that, and the other, but none of it very relevant or consequential. A nervous laugh was beginning to show at the end of every sentence or so.

How long this could have gone on was anybody's guess, but Mrs Manciple turned out to be made of sterner stuff than her bombazined exterior suggested. Once her young gentlemen had eaten and drunk enough to please her, she took them by the elbow and marched them upstairs and put them to bed. In vain did they protest that they felt perfectly well and had things to do. She began by removing coats and waistcoats until they realized that the only way to get rid of her would be to go along with her ludicrous plan. Sleep, indeed. It was hardly half past two in the afternoon – it was no time to sleep. They had caught a murderer. A conspirator in the worst crime of the century. They had places to be. Articles to write. Telegrams to send. But her implacable calm invaded their limbs and, despite themselves, soon they slept like children.

Mrs Manciple stumped down the stairs to the kitchen and booted the cat off her chair. She had planned a simple supper so that she could have some time to herself. She hadn't been sure about taking on a post with a foreigner – you heard such things – but so far he and the other gentleman had turned out to be pleasant enough. But bless their hearts! Just like children in some ways, rushing about and coming in as nervous as kittens, all because they had been telling each other some taradiddle about murders and people falling from balconies. Perhaps she ought to give them a less invigorating diet – they were both a little touched, perhaps, poor gentlemen. She congratulated herself again for taking this post – although, of course, since that last time, she didn't have the choice she once had. But still – she shook herself and levered herself out of her chair to start preparations for supper – beggars can't be choosers. Now – chops or turbot? Turbot was brain food, but did her gentlemen need their brains exciting? Perhaps something bland . . .? And so she wittered the afternoon away, while above her Grand and Batchelor slept the sleep of the just.

Dick Tanner sat at his desk, a coil of wire on the blotter in front of him. As a clue, it couldn't have been clearer. Here, it seemed to say, is the murder weapon from the Haymarket killings. Ergo, the killer is the man in whose pocket it was found. But it simply wasn't that easy, tempting though it might be. Previous investigations had shown Argyll to be away for the first murder at least, and he had alibis, although from some rather dubious ladies, for the other two. The ladies, Tanner felt, could be discounted as no better than they should be. But being out of London, en route from Liverpool, was a different thing altogether. He would have to interview Grand at some point to get more detail about the conspirator nonsense – and Tanner was as yet unconvinced that an Englishman could do something so quintessentially un-English as to conspire to kill a president – but Argyll as the Haymarket Strangler just didn't hold water. He pressed the bell behind him and waited, but as usual no one came. He tried another method of calling his sergeant, the more successful in his experience. Opening the door, he just yelled the man's name. 'Hunter!'

This time, Hunter appeared so quickly that he made Tanner jump.

'Sir?'

'Oh, Hunter, there you are. Could you step into my office for a minute? I have something I need to talk over, and your ears are as good a pair of receptacles as any other.'

'Thank you, sir.' Hunter tried to pick the compliment out of that and failed. 'What seems to be the trouble?'

'It isn't trouble, as such,' Tanner said, sitting down and pushing the coil of wire closer to his sergeant, perched on a hard chair on the other side of the desk. 'It's this.'

Hunter looked alert and said, 'That's right, sir. The wire from the Haymarket Stranglings. Found in Mr Argyll's pocket, sir, at the Haymarket this morning.'

'Correct on both counts, Hunter. What do you deduce from that?'

Hunter was floored by this. Had the Inspector gone a bit simple? Was it a trick question? 'Er . . . that Roderick Argyll is the Haymarket Strangler?' he suggested.

'No, Hunter. That's exactly wrong. It means that someone else is the Haymarket Strangler and they were hoping to put the blame on Roderick Argyll.'

Hunter opened his mouth to speak, but Tanner forestalled him. 'No, hear me out. I think that the Haymarket Strangler feels – wrongly, unfortunately – that we may be getting close to an arrest, so he has planted this wire on Argyll. He couldn't have known that Argyll would die like this, so he must have planted it and just bided his time.'

'But he *might* have known,' Hunter said. 'Known that Argyll would die, I mean. Batchelor found the first victim and Grand the third. Batchelor killed Argyll, and Grand . . . well, Grand may have set up the murder. What if *they* are the Haymarket Strangler? Er . . . Stranglers?'

Tanner gave it a few seconds thought and then shook his head. 'They didn't meet until after the first two murders,' he said, 'and these aren't the kind of murders men do in pairs. No, we're looking for someone else. Someone who had access to Argyll's coat is the first thing we need to bear in mind. Someone who may be a little . . . unusual, if I can leave it as broad as that.'

'Does it have to be someone who fits the description, sir?' Hunter asked, sitting up alertly.

'You sound as though you have someone in mind,' Tanner said, lighting a cigarette and leaning back.

'Well, if you agree with me that the eyewitness accounts aren't worth a tinker's cuss, sir, then yes, I believe I do.'

'Who?' The inspector blew a cloud of smoke in the sergeant's direction.

'Pearson.'

'Pearson?' Tanner had expected to recognize the name, but didn't. 'Remind me.'

'He's Argyll's secretary, general factotum,' Hunter said. 'A weird little bugger if you ask me. I'd say he was Argyll's pimp, if saying things like that about giants of the theatre was allowed.'

'You can say things like that about conspirators to kill the President of the United States,' Tanner said, 'so don't hold back.'

'Thank you, sir. Pearson was definitely Argyll's pimp. Oh, strictly high class, of course. Not always working girls either – from what I got from old Lavenham . . .'

'Again,' Tanner said, 'remind me.'

'Hall keeper. Bloke with the mop.'

Tanner held up a finger. He remembered him. Funny old codger, but straight as a die.

'Lavenham reckons there was all sorts of shenanigans going on.'

'So why would Pearson want to finger Argyll?'

Hunter shrugged. 'Threatened with the sack? Could see the writing on the wall? I dunno. I just think we should talk to him.'

Tanner stood up sharply and reached for his coat. 'You're quite right, Hunter,' he said. 'Shall we go and ask the gentleman to accompany us to the station?'

'I think that is a very good plan, sir,' Hunter said, with a smile. 'It's time the Haymarket Strangler – the *real* Haymarket Strangler – got his comeuppance.' And he opened the door for his boss as they went to solve the case, once and for all.

Mrs Manciple was waiting at the foot of the stairs when Grand and Batchelor made a rather shamefaced reappearance just in time for supper. Although they would never admit it, they both felt better for the sleep, and the smells from the kitchen were making their stomachs grumble. This wasn't quite the behind the scenes servant situation that Grand had envisaged, but somehow it felt good to hand over the reins to someone else once in a while.

'Supper is in the kitchen,' the woman said. 'If you don't mind, sirs. I haven't quite got everything organized yet, and—'

'The kitchen is perfectly acceptable, Mrs Manciple,' Grand said. 'But before we come down, may I ask you something?'

'Of course.' The cook folded her hands in front of her and looked helpful.

'Do you have a cat?'

The woman was confused. 'No, sir,' she said.

'I remember a cat. It was on my lap.'

'Yes, sir,' she said, still helpful. 'That's your cat. Mr Batchelor told the cats' meat man to tell me that I should buy it.'

Grand looked at Batchelor, one eyebrow raised. 'James?'

'It's a long story,' Batchelor said. 'Can we discuss it later?'

'Yes. But we *will* discuss it, James. A cat, indeed. Anyway, lead on, Mrs Manciple. Whatever it is you've made for us, it smells delicious.'

Lavenham stood, as he always stood, mop akimbo, in the doorway in the approach to Argyll's private entrance. 'Yes?' he said. 'Can I help you gentlemen?'

'Come on, Lavenham,' Hunter said. 'You know who we are. We're the police.'

'Bit late, arntchya?' the old man asked. 'He's dead, y'know.'

'Yes, Lavenham,' Tanner chimed in. 'We do know that. We're here to see Mr Pearson.'

'Better 'urry up, then,' the hall keeper told them. 'Packin' up, he is. No job for him, y'see. Not now.'

Hunter gave Tanner a triumphant look. Nothing pointed to guilt like a man running. He had said it before and he would say it again – show me a man leaving the scene, I'll show you a murdering bastard.

'We just want a word,' Tanner said. 'So, if you'd let us through . . .'

Lavenham stood aside and followed the policemen with his eyes. He had no worries about his job. The Haymarket was bigger than any owner, and there would always be a job for a man and his mop.

Tanner led the way up the stairs, led by the sound of drawers being slammed home and a muffled sobbing. Eventually, the policemen reached the innermost sanctum of Argyll's rooms, where Pearson was ripping clothes out of presses and into a large, leather suitcase. To their surprise, he was also the one who was sobbing.

'Mr Pearson?' Tanner asked, for confirmation.

The man dashed the tears from his eyes and sniffed. 'Yes. Who are you? Oh, wait – I know *you*.' He pointed to Hunter. 'Police.'

'That's right, sir,' Tanner said. 'We just want to ask you a few questions.'

'I don't have time,' Pearson said, pouting. 'I'm packing, can't you see?'

'Well, I can see that you may have to find other employment, sir,' Tanner said, 'but surely not tonight. Might the new owners not wish to keep you on in your . . . post?'

Pearson laughed, a dry, quick bark of a laugh. 'Likely to want a pimp, are they?' he said, bitterly. 'Somebody to finish off their women if they are a bit lacking any night? Somebody who knows where the bodies are buried but has the sense to keep quiet? If they want that person, then, yes—' he spread his arms wide – 'here I am.' He bent to his packing again. 'Otherwise, I must be on my way.' Another sob racked him, and he sank down on the bed, a linen shirt held to his eyes.

Tanner was not an unkind man, but he had a string of murders to solve. He nodded to Hunter, who stepped forward and hauled Pearson to his feet. 'I don't care what you need to do or not do,' he said. 'Inspector Tanner needs to speak to you on a matter of some urgency. Is there a room here where we can speak?'

Pearson sniffed and pointed to a door standing half open and led them through it. The room was opulent in the extreme but still felt as though its soul had been ripped from it by force. The logs lay half-burned in the grate, and already there seemed to be a thin film of dust over everything, as though it had begun to settle the second that Argyll's last breath was driven from his body as it hit the ground in the auditorium below.

'Here,' Pearson said. 'We can talk in here. But . . .' He bit his lip for a moment. 'Can we not sit at the desk? It's a little too soon for me, as yet.'

Tanner nodded and pulled up a hard chair for himself, while Pearson, with Hunter in close attendance, sat on the chaise longue. Tanner put his hand in his pocket and came out with the coil of wire, which he held out to the secretary. 'Do you recognize this?' he asked.

'It's wire,' the man replied, with a shrug.

'Yes,' Tanner said, patiently. 'But have you seen this specific wire before?'

'May I hold it?'

'Of course.' Tanner passed it across. 'We believe it is the coil of wire used by the Haymarket Strangler.' He watched the man's expression and was not helped at all by the spasm of distaste that crossed his face. Either he was disgusted or he was a very good actor, and with these theatre types, who could tell?

Pearson passed it hurriedly back. 'Where did you find it?' he asked, in a shocked whisper.

'In Roderick Argyll's pocket,' Hunter told him.

'Mr Argyll?' Pearson said. Then, with a chuckle, 'No, it couldn't be him. He wasn't even here for the first murder.'

'Where was he?' Tanner asked.

'Oooh.' Pearson pursed his lips. 'I'm not sure . . .'

'Come now, Mr Pearson,' Tanner said. 'That grave is well and truly turned over. You don't have to lie for him any more. Where was he?'

Mrs Manciple sat her gentlemen down at the table and removed the lid of the tureen with a flourish. Grand and Batchelor leaned forward in anticipation and recoiled almost at once.

'What in the name of Hell is that?' Grand said in a low voice.

'Tripe,' Mrs Manciple said proudly. 'Tripe and onions.'

The men were silent.

'With just a hint of parsley,' she said, disappointed. Mr Manciple had always loved a bit of tripe when he was feeling nervy.

'Is it food?' Grand asked. He had been asked to eat some weird and wonderful things on campaign, but never anything like this.

'Of course it is,' she said. 'It's *tripe*. Lovely. Very savoury, but bland on the stomach. You've both had a shock. You need something bland on the stomach.'

Grand and Batchelor looked at each other through the steam, then Grand turned to his cook. 'I think we'll eat out tonight, Mrs Manciple,' he said. 'Thank you for going to so much trouble. Please feel free to eat it up yourself. Perhaps you could share it with the cat.'

It said a lot for the good upbringing of both of them that they didn't express their real opinions until they had set their feet in the direction of the Haymarket Theatre for the second time that day. Even if they couldn't catch the other killer who haunted their dreams, they could at least get something to eat that didn't look like a stewed tablecloth.

'You know anyway, don't you?' Pearson said. 'He was in America. Always going over there, been doing it for years. I had to hold the fort, plan all the plays, pay the actors, see to his women . . .' The tears were welling up again. 'And now . . . he's gone . . .'

'Pull yourself together, Mr Pearson.' Tanner had had enough. 'I doubt Mr Argyll deserves your tears. If he couldn't have murdered these women, who had the chance to put this wire in his pocket? Or could it be that he put it there himself, having confiscated it from the murderer, or found it just lying about?'

'As for who put it there,' said Pearson, wiping his eyes on his sleeve, 'it could be one of dozens of people. This room was where he hung his coat.' He gestured to a row of hooks on the wall, some of them full, some empty. 'He interviewed in here, he paid staff in here, he . . . well, he just ran his life from here, you might say. So, for your list: everyone who worked for the theatre; newspapermen—'

'Newspapermen?' Tanner interrupted. 'Do you have names?'

Pearson reached across and took a large book off the desk. 'It might be in here,' he said.

'A diary?' Tanner said, his eyes lighting up.

'Not as such,' Pearson said, thumbing through it. 'It's more an aide-memoire. He just jotted things down, then crossed them through when they had happened, were finished with. If there was anything important, he would ring it round in red.' He flicked to the last few pages. 'Here we are. Look.' He turned the book and pointed. 'There, where it says "int newsp".'

'Int newsp?' Hunter was confused.

'Interview newspaper,' Tanner said, filling in the gaps for him. 'Is that it?' he asked Pearson. 'No name?'

'No.' Pearson took the book back and searched a few more pages. 'No, no detail. I'm very sorry.'

'Does it show anyone else as a visitor? Take your time.'

NINETEEN

'Is this too soon to be going back?' Grand asked Batchelor. 'Too soon for what?' Batchelor asked, not making eye contact.

'To try to catch the Strangler,' Grand said. 'Let's face up to things, James. Argyll was definitely not the Strangler, but the Strangler is panicking. If he hid that wire in Argyll's pocket, it's because he fears capture. He was hiding the evidence.'

'But who would do that?' Batchelor asked. 'Anyone who works at the Haymarket would know that he had not been there for the first murder. A case against Argyll wouldn't hold up for a moment. But who apart from the household would have the opportunity?'

'You,' Grand said with a smile.

'True,' Batchelor said, solemnly. 'And I am the only person who was here for all three murders. I quite like me as a suspect, and I know I didn't do it! Tanner will get there eventually.' His shoulders slumped as he foresaw the trouble certain to come.

Grand slapped him on the shoulder. 'Chin up, James,' he said. 'And step out. Your little short legs are a real drawback when you want to get somewhere quickly. Come on, let's go.' And, setting a cracking pace, Grand strode out to the Haymarket Theatre, coat flapping and snapping in the breeze.

The inevitable table of half-drunk journalists greeted them enthusiastically as they walked into the dim auditorium. Some girls were dancing in a lacklustre way on the stage to the thump and rattle of the orchestra, and bottles were circling in advance of the girls who would follow the champagne as night the day.

'Jim!' Edwin Dyer saw them first and beckoned them over. 'What's the story on the excitement this morning? Tanner isn't talking, and that isn't like him.'

'It's a bit sensitive, Edwin, if you don't mind,' Batchelor

told him, pulling up a chair. 'International politics, that sort of thing.'

'Really?' Horner said, honing in. 'I heard it was just Argyll falling over the balcony, pissed.'

'No,' Buckley said. 'It was one of his women, *I* heard. As ye sow, so shall ye reap.'

'I bet it was something boring like that,' Batchelor said. 'It's hard to get to the bottom of things, isn't it?' He looked around the table. 'Everyone got a drink?'

Before the words were out of his mouth, three glasses were raised in the air and Grand, with a sigh, stuck his hand up to call the waiter over. 'Same again?' he asked.

Heads shook. It seemed to be the time in the evening when everyone changed to brandy.

Pearson looked carefully over every page then looked up at Tanner, shaking his head. 'Apart from "int newsp",' he said, 'I can account for everyone, and none of them, believe me, is the Haymarket Strangler.'

'We're left with you, then,' Hunter said, gruffly. He had come out with the clear intention of arresting the Haymarket Strangler, and so, if everyone else was impossible, Pearson it would have to be.

'I have alibis,' Pearson said.

'I wish you'd said,' Tanner said mildly. 'What might they be?'

'Um . . . on the night of the first murder, I was visiting my mother. Godalming. I try to go and see her . . . I *tried* to go and see her when Mr Argyll was away. The others, I would have been looking after Mr Argyll's needs.'

Tanner looked at him for a full minute. 'That's it? Your alibis?'

'Yes.'

Tanner sighed. 'Make a note, Hunter. No alibi.' He clapped his hands on his knees and blew through his moustache. 'Mr Pearson,' he said, 'I think that everything you say has another layer, another lie, another subterfuge hidden within it. Sergeant Hunter here wants to take you back to the police station and give you a very thorough beating until you Confess All.'

Pearson flinched and drew away from the sergeant, as if he would bite. The sergeant, for his part, nodded enthusiastically.

'But I can't help having the feeling that if you do – confess, that is – we would be looking at another dead girl within the week, whether you were in a cell or not. So—' he got up suddenly, and Pearson flinched again – 'I am going to go back to Vine Street now and look through yet more depositions, which surely must have the clue to the killer in there somewhere. And, Mr Pearson, no matter how much you want to get away, no matter how much the new owners of this theatre want you gone, I must insist that you stay here until I tell you otherwise. I may have to let Sergeant Hunter beat you half to death after all, before all this is done.'

With that, the two policemen wheeled right and clattered down the stairs, leaving Pearson a damp and quivering heap on the chaise longue.

Down in the auditorium, things were getting rowdy. The second half of the Music Hall would be starting up soon, with more and more bawdy songs being belted out by audience and performers alike. The band was warming up for the Swell Coves' Alphabet – 'M stands for Maidenhead, I often have drove through'.

At the journalists' table, everyone had become a little intro-spective, in that tiny window that exists between being sober and roaringly drunk. Dyer was lounging back in his chair muttering to himself. Had anyone bothered to listen, it was a whispered diatribe against womankind in general, with specific reference to landladies. Horner was alert, looking around him bright eyed. It would take a very sharp eyed observer to notice the thin trail of drool from one corner of his mouth and the soft clenching and unclenching of his fists. Gabriel Horner was not always himself, these days. Buckley was scribbling on a pad held hidden in the palm of his hand. Every now and again, he would glance up and scribble some more. Batchelor was leaning back in his seat, his eyes quartering the room, there and back again.

Only Grand sat at ease, but he was hiding the busiest brain of all. He had found his man. Now what? Would he return to

Washington? Take up where he left off with Arlette and try
to find his ring under her furniture? Or find a nicer girl, one
who didn't have the temper of a bobcat with a firecracker tied
to its tail? Follow his pa into the bank, or Congress? The army
had no appeal, not any more. He'd ducked too many shells
and earned too many saddle-sores for that. Or would he stay
here in London, crowded, filthy, smelly London, where your
cook gave you boiled tablecloth to eat and bought you cats
you didn't ask for? It was not a decision that he needed to
think over twice. It was clear he would—

Batchelor prodded him in the ribs.

'Hmm?' Grand came back to the here and now. 'What?'

'Have I been asleep?'

'Good God, James, how in Hell should I know? Why?'

'Because . . .' Batchelor waved to the table, which now was
noticeably empty. 'Where are they all?'

'That's easy,' Grand said. 'I haven't known them very long,
but I would say that Gabriel is out back, trying to pass water.
It takes him one or two visits, I've noticed. The other two . . .
I have no idea. Why? It's a saving for my pocketbook every
time they leave, so I'm not arguing. I think we should be
making tracks too, James. It has been one helluva day.'

'But . . . it's ringing a bell, Matthew.'

'Being drunk? Surely not.' The American got to his feet
and staggered slightly. 'I could do with some fresh air.'

'No . . . it's . . .'

'Come on. Let's go outside. If they come back and find the
golden goose has gone, what do we care? If we sober up on
the way home, it doesn't matter – we've got plenty of all kinds
of drink in the cellar. Come on.' Grand tugged on Batchelor's
sleeve, and they wove their way to the door.

The cool evening air hit them like a wet towel across the
face. Grand shuddered and squared his shoulders. Batchelor
winced and hunched over. He clutched his head.

'You see,' Grand said, breathing deeply through his nose.
'I said you would feel better for some fresh air. Now, what's
ringing a bell? Is it the ringing in your ears?'

'No. It's something about when the girl was murdered. We
were all together . . .'

'What girl?'

'The one I found. Effie.'

'I can't help you there. I wasn't even in London then.'

'We were all together then. Dyer. Horner. Buckley. Just like tonight.'

'But nothing has happened tonight.'

'As far as we are aware,' Batchelor said, pulling his coat collar closer around his throat. 'It could be someone we know, Matthew.'

'It could be you,' the American said, reasonably.

'It could,' the ex-journalist said. 'It could.'

'It could be him,' Grand said, pointing ahead to where a girl walked ahead of them, leaning on a man's arm. She was smiling up into his face, her free hand twirling a curl coquettishly. He turned to face her and looked down at her with a look that froze Batchelor's blood.

'Look at him,' he hissed to Grand. 'Look at his face. He *hates* her. You can see it from here. He *hates* her. And . . .' He looked frantically right and left. 'Where's her friend?'

'What friend?' Grand asked.

'Auntie Bettie said they would be working in pairs. And even if she's one of Lady Eleanor's, they'll be doing the same. She *knows* him, or her friend would be near by. And yet, he hates her. Quick, Matthew, it's him.'

Grand tried to pull him back, but Batchelor was off, down the road in hot pursuit. It was Lily, of that much he was certain. And he knew who the man was too. He couldn't believe it, but deep in his guts he knew he had found the killer. But he needed to catch him red-handed – sooner than red-handed, for Lily's sake. The pair ahead of them had turned into a dark alley, and he could hear them whispering. He could hear that other whisper, of silk petticoats being flung up, ready for whatever might come.

He stood at the mouth of the alley and shouted. He knew he couldn't get there in time to stop the wire cutting through that slender neck, making the blood arc and fly. All he could do was shout and hope that the shock of discovery would stop him.

'Buckley!' he yelled, at the top of his voice. 'Buckley! Stop! Lily – run! Run to me, now!'

The light was bad down the alley, and it was a moment before Batchelor knew whether he was in time or just too late. Grand was just behind him and came to a skidding stop at his side. Lily hurtled past them with barely a glance in their direction, her skirts up over her knees and a terrified look on her face. They turned as one to face the shadows in the alley.

'What's the idea, Batchelor?'

'You tell us, Buckley.' Batchelor and Grand moved apart, forcing Buckley to choose which one he would take on, if take them on he dared.

'Just a bit of fun,' Buckley said. 'Lily and I—'

'Have never gone into an alley before, I'll wager,' Batchelor said, finishing the sentence for him.

'Empty your pockets,' Grand said. 'Do it now.'

'My pockets?' Buckley bridled. 'Why?'

'It's over, Joe,' Batchelor said. 'Nowhere to run now.'

For a moment Buckley looked as though he might make a fight of it, smash his way past them both with fist and boot. Batchelor he could handle, but Grand as well? And there was a rumour the man carried a gun. Buckley's right hand came out of his pocket, a coil of wire gleaming in it.

'You don't know what it's like,' he said, his voice a hoarse whisper. 'Night after night with these vermin. I thought you, at least, Jim, would understand. Old Gabriel's too gaga to remember. And Dyer is filth personified, bragging of his conquests among the landlady class. But you, Jim, you must be as appalled by them as I am.'

'They're just offering a service, Joe,' Batchelor said. 'It may not be right. It may not be respectable . . .'

'Respect?' Buckley spat. 'What do you know of respect? I was destined for a career in the church, you know.'

Batchelor knew.

'And one day I went for a stroll with a girl. She was beautiful, lovely as the dawn, with hair like gold. We held hands and talked. I read her poetry. You know what she did?'

'No,' Grand said. 'What did she do?'

'She laughed at me. She lifted her skirts and said, "This is what you're after. Why don't you get on with it?" I was appalled. I couldn't believe it. Then she laughed again and told me I was a mummy's boy and that I'd never be a real man . . . So I killed her. It seemed so right. So natural. Her lying there in the cornfield with my tie around her neck. Such a pretty neck.' He shuddered at the memory of it. 'My mother got to hear of it; that I'd gone with the girl, I mean. Oh, they never found her body, of course. I dumped that in the river, and the current did the rest. No, I'd gone with a girl, my mother said; how could I do that and even *think* of a career in the church? We rowed. I left and came to London. And I saw them, the Haymarket march past, every day like cattle in the market . . .'

'Lambs to the slaughter,' Grand said.

'Whatever analogy you care to use, Yankee,' Buckley spat. 'They were parading themselves. Just like her. Just like the girl in the cornfield. Laughing at me. And pointing. "Mummy's boy. Mummy's boy."' He pulled himself up to his full height. 'So they had to die. Well, you do see that, don't you? Grand? Jim? Surely, you understand?'

Batchelor had reached his colleague by now, and the man slumped against him, sobbing uncontrollably on his shoulder.

'I'm trying, Joe,' Batchelor said, easing the wire out of his grasp. 'I'm trying. Matthew, can you hail us a cab? We need to go to Vine Street.'

If the mob had been angry at Scotland Yard, it was literally furious by the time it reached Vine Street. It had taken a while to reform, as many of its members had had to pop off to their clubs for a light luncheon while yet others had had to return to the House where a division was expected. Eventually, though, they reconvened at Vine Street Police Station, more vociferous than before.

Tanner, forewarned by a patrolling bobby before he reached the front entrance, had sneaked in through a back way and was lurking in his office, trying to drown out the distant hum and quack of very upper-crust voices losing their tempers. That he was the cause of the furore didn't make it any easier to bear, and the accusing looks of Hunter and similar underlings were not improving his temper. Coming close to wrapping up two cases in one day was not something with which he was very familiar, and his desk was beginning to look very tidy as he methodically worked his way through the paperwork on the Haymarket stranglings. Hunter was still affronted that Tanner had not arrested Pearson or at least given him a light beating, but Tanner had not got his reputation through blurring facts, and Pearson was just not a contender in the race for first past the gallows as the Strangler. Hunter would just have to grin and bear it. But Tanner was close; he knew he was very close.

Down in the hallway, things were getting ugly. There was nothing nastier than an angry nob. Gentlemen who had not even been named by Batchelor in his article were there, brandishing sticks and shouting oaths. One never knew when a sequel might be on the cards, and peccadillos had the habit of rearing up and biting one on some very unfortunate body parts. The desk sergeant had stuffed some bread in his ears in lieu of anything more suitable and was calmly filling his pipe to while away the time. There was certainly little risk of anyone else coming into the station with the mob of nobs there; he could safely put away his lost dog ledger for the time being.

Buckley was silent in the cab, apart from the occasional wracking sob. There seemed nothing more to be said either to or about him, and Grand and Batchelor sat silently through the short journey, though each held on to a sleeve, just to be sure. The growler had not been keen to take the fare, until he saw the colour of Grand's money, and the scent of anti-climax was in the air.

At Vine Street Police Station, the first thing that was apparent was that there was definitely something very strange going on. There was a mass of people out on the pavement, lit by the spectral light of the blue lamp over the door. It was hard to see quite what they were so exercised about – surely, news about Buckley had not spread this fast – and Batchelor jumped out of the cab without a thought.

The crowd were chanting something, but he couldn't quite make out what it was, and so, waving a hand to keep Grand and Buckley in the cab, he stepped closer. The man he stood beside looked vaguely familiar.

'Bring out Batchelor!' the crowd chanted. 'Bring out Batchelor!'

James Batchelor was no more of a coward than the next man, but he also knew the value of valour. He got back into the cab.

'Look here, Matthew,' he said. 'I don't think this needs both of us, do you? I'll go back to the Haymarket in this cab – we may need eyewitnesses. Can you manage Buckley alone? He seems quite docile. Aren't you, old chap?' he said encouragingly to the journalist, who was now simply staring into space.

'Really?' Grand was dubious. 'How can we even get in?'

The growler leaned down from his box. 'There's a side door,' he said. 'I'll take you round – this mob look dangerous to me.' With a click of his tongue, he urged his horse down the road and into a side street where, sure enough, a smaller door led into the police station. 'Just knock on there,' he said. 'It's where the peelers come when they knock off. There's always someone there to open up.'

Batchelor helped Grand manhandle the almost comatose Buckley out of the cab and knocked on the door, before hopping back into the vehicle and urging the cabbie to be on his way.

Grand had to knock several times before the door opened a crack, and a red-cheeked face peered out.

'Yes?'

'Ah, yes,' Grand said. This was not a greeting he had often had to make. 'I have the Haymarket Strangler here. Is Inspector Tanner in?'

Led up a winding stair, Grand and his captive were taken into Tanner's office with very little ceremony. Once Buckley was sitting in a chair, bent over like a discarded doll, Tanner leaned back in his seat and looked at him, long and hard. He had seen this man from time to time, scribbling in a pad at the scenes of other peoples' distress and disaster. 'Mr Grand,' he said at last, 'am I right in thinking that this gentleman is a colleague of Mr Batchelor?'

'That's right,' Grand said, impressed. 'He is.'

Tanner's sweet smile crept across his face. 'Tell me his name in a minute,' he said. 'For now, we will refer to him as "Int Newsp" – I think it will serve, Hunter, don't you?'

TWENTY

Lafayette Baker felt the sweat trickle from under his dress hat that morning and cursed the heat. It was not eight o'clock yet, and the temperature was already in the nineties, the sun burning fiercely down on the gallows with its four nooses hanging in the morning's stillness. Flies droned around the freshly dug graves, and armed guards lolled on the walkway at the top of the wall.

Boats were chugging, with their black smoke stacks, from Alexandria and Georgetown, and hopeful crowds clustered on their decks, parasols already bright in the morning. Luther Baker fastened his full dress-sword belt and joined his cousin on the ramparts of the penitentiary. 'Great day for a hanging, Laff.' The pair watched Christopher Rath, the executioner, test his equipment one last time. Sacks were tied on to the nooses, and one by one the traps were sprung. One little adjustment, one tweak of the twenty-strand rope, and all was well.

'Mother of God,' Lafayette muttered. 'Will I ever get used to that?' He nodded across the yellow grass below the wall to where Mary Walker rode her horse to the main gate. She was the only female doctor in the Union Army, and not only did she wear trousers under her short skirt, but today she also rode astride, like a man.

Luther shook his head. 'Not natural,' he murmured.

'This is the end of an era, Luther,' Lafayette said. 'In more ways than one. I got a telegram late last night from our friend Sala. Grand got the son of a bitch.'

'The man in the alley? Who was he?'

'Name of Argyll. Ran a theatre in London. Took up with Booth a while back. Confessed it all before he died.'

'And what about Grand? He'll be coming home, I guess.'

'Maybe yes, maybe no,' Lafayette said. 'But whichever way, I'll be watching him.'

Luther Baker smiled. That was so typically Lafayette. End

of an era it might be, but for men like his cousin Laff, the
only real end would be a hole in the ground.

By mid-morning the military had all assembled, as had the
one hundred ticket holders who had paid a high price to see
their President's killers turned off. The talking was a mutter,
muted strangely by the thick walls of the penitentiary and the
dumb press of the heat. The sun flashed on the fixed bayonets
and cap badges of the guards on the walls. Sightseers hoping
for a free show were to be disappointed. They could not even
sit astride the parked cannon for the fierceness of the sun on
the gunmetal.

Suddenly, screaming started from somewhere in the bowels
of the gaol. The Bakers looked at each other and knew who
it was. It was Annie Surratt, daughter of the conspirator Mary.
Hours earlier, she had thrown herself at the foot of the White
House stairs, weeping inconsolably and begging President
Johnson to spare her mother. President Johnson had been
unavailable.

One by one, the prisoners emerged, blinking, into the
sunlight. Mary Surratt, veiled and wearing black from head
to foot, hung limply between two guards. A priest walked
ahead of her, pausing every few steps to press his crucifix
against the woman's lips. After her came George Atzerodt, his
eyes wild and red from crying, then John Herold, trembling
alongside his escort, and finally Lewis Powell, tall, unbowed,
unrepentant. The others might scream and cry and faint, but
he would face the executioner like a man and look him in the
eye.

One by one they were helped up the ominous thirteen steps
to the gallows' platform; one by one they were seated on their
chairs. Somebody held a parasol over the bowed head of Mary
Surratt. Lewis Powell grabbed a straw hat from a bystander
and tilted it on his own head, defying anybody to knock it off.

'Will you look at that arrogant son of a bitch,' Luther Baker
growled, ready, even now, to do the executioner's job for him
with his revolver.

A mustachioed officer stepped forward and read out in a
loud voice the order for the execution.

'Get on with it, Hartranft.' Lafayette Baker had been

standing in the sun for nearly four hours now. He'd had enough.
Rath's men passed along the row on the platform, binding
arms, pinioning legs. Then the four were hauled upright and
white hoods, gleaming in their innocence, were pulled over
their heads. The Bakers could not hear the muted sounds from
the gallows, Mary Surratt mumbling, 'Don't let me fall,' and
John Herold crying, the hood working backwards and forwards
as he sobbed. But they heard, everyone heard, the thick German
accent of George Atzerodt under the canvas. 'Goodbye,
gentlemen. May we all meet in the other world.'

General Hancock clapped his hands twice, and at the second
clap, the posts were kicked away and the traps crashed down.
There was a gasp from the crowd, and one of the soldiers
dropped his rifle with a clatter. Powell, with his thick neck,
refused to die outright, and he jerked and writhed on the end
of the rope. His neck and wrists turned purple, and Rath estim-
ated it took him all of five minutes to pass. Herold's body
struggled against the rope as he desperately tried to take the
weight off the noose and the appalling pain in his throat and
chest. Atzerodt's stomach heaved once and was still. As for
Mary Surratt, she had shot straight down, to bob and bounce
five feet below the platform, and then she did not move at all.

The crowd were ordered away as Christopher Rath's men
let the dead hang for the required half an hour. Solemnly, and
with every care to shield his plates from the sun, Alexander
Gardner set up his camera on his tripod and recorded the
hanging corpses for posterity. The executioner himself was
busy writing out affidavits to acknowledge that the pieces of
rope and timber he was about to chunk up and sell off had
indeed been taken from the execution of the murderers of
Abraham Lincoln.

Lafayette Baker swept off his hat, not as any token of
sympathy but because the heat demanded it. 'I don't know
about you, Cousin Lu, but I'm ready for cakes and lemonade.'

The first little gabble of journalists let themselves in to the
Telegraph offices that morning and flung coats at the rack.
Gabriel Horner, whose eyesight was almost inevitably less
acute than everyone else's, lit the gas and turned to take his

seat in the row of elevated desks down the centre of the room.
He stopped with a suppressed scream. It was that dream again.
He glanced down; he was fully dressed, though slightly awry
in the button department. He was awake then. But there, at
his desk, sat Thornton Leigh Hunt, his face a basilisk's, his
arms folded against his editorial chest.

As the journalists and other hangers-on came to an ungainly
stop in the office's foyer, on the public side of the gate that
kept the hoi polloi and the Fourth Estate separate, Leigh Hunt
slid down from Horner's high stool and approached them, stiff
legged with anger that was barely hidden by his expressionless
face.

'Gentlemen,' he murmured, nodding at them curtly.

Their greetings varied from a muttered, 'Sir,' to Horner's
cheery, 'Morning, TLH,' which he somehow got past his brick-
dry lips.

Leigh Hunt looked, from left to right, along the ragged line
of the motley crew that made up the beating heart of his
newspaper. There were several faces missing. Sala's, of course,
it being before ten in the morning. Sala was taking liberties
as always, but even he could go too far. Batchelor, also, of
course. Leigh Hunt had regretted sacking him almost as soon
as the words were out of his mouth, but there are certain things
that editors don't do, and recanting was one of them. Buckley
– ah, Joseph Buckley, now known, for as long as his notoriety
lasted, as the Haymarket Strangler. Thornton Leigh Hunt
sighed. God, he loved the newspaper business. A lot more than
he loved his wife; he even loved it more than he loved his
mistress, though he prayed she never found out. He loved the
hum of the presses, the smell of the ink. He loved the scritch
of the pens, the smell of the sweat of a journalist with a big
story to tell. He loved the money to be made, the cut and
thrust of the circulation wars . . . in a perverse way, he loved
what he was about to do as well, although it had kept him
awake all night.

He now looked along the line again, from right to left, and
smiled a rueful smile. 'Staff of the *Telegraph*,' he said, in
sonorous tones. 'I have been thinking of you, of every one of
you, all night long. In the end, I got out of bed—' he paused

to make sure there were no ribald asides, but all the staff were too dumbstruck to speak – 'and came down here to await your arrival. I was thinking how you all worked with a murderer in your midst and didn't seem to notice.'

He leaned forward and tapped his nose. 'Do you know what this is? Well, do you?' He waited, but the staff, apart from some nervously shuffling feet, were silent. 'It's a journalist's nose. It has let me down. But not half as much as all of *you* have let me down. What has happened to instinct? Hunches? Gut feelings? Hmm?'

Gabriel Horner cleared his throat. 'TLH . . .'

'Don't TLH me, Gabriel. You and Dyer are most at fault. You were *drinking* with the man on all three nights when he went out and horribly murdered those girls. And yet you *still* didn't notice. And, worse – you were drinking with Matthew Grand, who is the toast of Washington for having hunted down the last of the Lincoln conspirators. And did you write that up? No, you did not.' He wiped a strand of drool from his chin and took a deep breath. 'In view of all this, I have come to a decision. It pains me more than it pains you, but I have to tell you now. It's no good dragging it out.' He paused to wipe his brow with a silk handkerchief.

'He's resigning,' Dyer whispered to the inky devil by his side.

Leigh Hunt composed himself and faced them squarely. 'So,' he said, 'you are all sacked. Miss Witherspoon will make up your wages until the end of the month. She also has made out a testimonial for you all – rather generic, I fear, but the poor woman couldn't be expected to write something different for each one of you, especially as she will be clearing her desk by the end of the week. Does anyone have anything to say?'

The silence was like a velvet pall over the room. It was even hard to tell whether some of the suddenly ex-staff of the *Telegraph* were still breathing. Gabriel Horner in particular had gone a worrying shade of mauve.

'I'll just leave you to clear your desks, then,' Leigh Hunt said, 'not forgetting, of course, that all pens, pencils, penknives, paper, ink and sundries are the property of the *Telegraph*. Miss

Witherspoon has asked me to request that you form an orderly queue in her office. Pushing and shoving will result in a fine up to but not exceeding any monies due. Thank you, gentlemen. Good day.'

The silence was broken by the clack clack of the big doors swinging open and shut. George Sala pushed his way to the front of the crowd, a puzzled frown on his face. A team of journalists standing 'listening' to their editor; that couldn't be right. He waved some sheets of paper in the general direction of Leigh Hunt.

'Thornton, old chap,' he said, breezily. 'Here's my piece on the Argyll scandal. And, of course, on the Haymarket Strangler, it all being wound up in one package, as one might say.' As he spoke, Sala was shooting furtive glances at his colleagues. No doubt they would tell him what was going on in their own good time.

Leigh Hunt stepped forward and took the sheets from the journalist's hand. He glanced at them and tore them in half down their length. 'Too little,' he said, and then tore them across. 'Too late. Miss Witherspoon will explain. Good day, George.'

Sala stood there, speechless, and it was, as Gabriel Horner said later on that day as he broached his second bottle of brandy in the Printer's Devil, the best moment of the whole debacle.

Miss Witherspoon did her best, and not an hour after Leigh Hunt's bombshell, the double doors closed behind the last member of staff, Edwin Dyer. He had cunningly managed to stay at the end of the queue throughout, having worked out that by the time he got to Miss Witherspoon's desk, Leigh Hunt would have seen sense and would rehire anyone still on the premises. Sadly, like so many of Edwin Dyer's best ideas, this one proved to be false.

He stood on the top step, leaning disconsolately on the door, listening to the distant sound of the bolts being rammed home behind him. Life was not looking good for Edwin Dyer. He had never met a drink he didn't like. Money was for spending, and if not for spending, for borrowing and then spending. Rent was for other people. But this couldn't have come at a worse time. His landlady had been hinting darkly about being made an honest woman of, and although Dyer liked her money and her house, the moustache was rather off-putting, and he had been thinking of making a move. In fact, he had already packed, ready for a moonlight flit that very evening. And now here he was. Unemployed, and probably homeless. Or married. He couldn't think which choice filled him with the most dread.

'Hello, Edwin.'

A familiar voice made him look up. 'Jim!' he said. This might be a fortuitous meeting. He had heard of Batchelor's new circumstances, sitting pretty in rooms in Alsatia, all found and no heavy lifting. Perhaps . . .

'What's going on?' Batchelor asked. 'Why are the doors shut? I have a piece here that TLH will give his eye teeth for. "I Caught The Haymarket Strangler." He'll love it – page two stuff if ever I saw it.'

Dyer raised a hand and let it fall, limply. 'He's sacked us all,' he said and was horrified to hear how croaky his voice was. 'Every man jack. And Miss Witherspoon.'

'What?' Batchelor was aghast. 'Is the *Telegraph* gone, then?'

'Who knows?' Dyer said. 'I doubt it. He'll just start again. When he comes down off his high horse, he might even employ us again. But for now, the doors are closed, the paper is resting and I don't have a bean.'

'But, *you'll* be all right, Edwin,' Batchelor said, clapping him on the arm. 'You don't have to find the rent, at least.'

One look at Dyer's face told him the full story.

'Oh. Well . . . but wait. My rooms should still be vacant and with two weeks to run on the rent. You know where I was living, don't you? Of course you do, you've been there. Take this—' and Batchelor hurriedly scribbled a note to Mrs Biggs – 'and see how you get on. I'm sure Mrs Biggs will *love* you.' Batchelor had a small qualm; Dyer had never done him any harm, after all. But he was cheered by Dyer's smile.

'I don't remember Mrs . . .'

'Biggs.'

'Mrs Biggs very well, but I'm sure she's a very nice woman.'

'Indeed,' Batchelor agreed, 'very nice.' He gave Dyer a small push in the direction of Fleet Lane, murmuring, as he went out of earshot, 'and plenty of her to go around.'

The lights burned blue that night in the house at the Alsatia end of the Strand. Mrs Manciple had retired early, as her gentlemen seemed to be intent on making a night of it. The brandy was excellent, and James Batchelor in particular was feeling mellow. All right, he would never write for the *Telegraph* again; perhaps none of them would. But he had caught a murderer – or rather, he and Grand had. In fact, they had caught two. And it had given him an idea.

'I must say, Matthew,' he said, raising his glass. 'It has been a pleasure to work with you.'

'And you.' Grand clinked his glass with that of the ex-journalist.

'And I was wondering . . .'

'Hmmm?'

'Well, what your plans are just now. I suppose you'll be going home. Your fiancée, the army, the bank, Congress. But it's just that, at the moment, there is this rage for private detectives – you know, enquiry agents. And I was wondering whether . . . well, Batchelor and Grand . . . Can you see it? A shingle on the door? A secretary, perhaps. Files. Cabinets. Cases.'

Grand looked at him. 'I don't think so,' he said.

'Well, no, of course, I understand. With all that must be going on at home for you . . . Out of the question. Silly of me to raise it.'

The silence hung heavy between them. Not even the clock ticked.

'Well . . .' Batchelor could stand the embarrassment no longer. Tomorrow he would trudge back to Fleet Street again and eat humble pie and sign on as office boy in any office that would take him. But tonight? Tonight he was going to get roaring drunk. Perhaps not at the Haymarket, all things considered. He didn't have to go that far. 'I'm off to wet my whistle. Care to join me?'

Grand shook his head. 'Not tonight,' he said.

'Right.' Batchelor crossed to the hall and found his coat. 'I'll say goodnight, then.'

Grand said nothing, his mind and his expression far away.

James Batchelor reached the street. It was a fine night, and he could see and hear the swells rolling drunkenly at the end of the Strand in search of their dreams. He heard a window open, and he looked up. Matthew Grand had stuck his head out of the second floor sash.

'But Grand and Batchelor might work.'